For Jeff,
who creates his own worlds

Contents

Chapter 1

KING OF THE CASTLE

OR

SUMMONED

The shiny, candy-apple red limousine turned the corner, and no one even noticed. No one walking his dog or on her way to work saw the slick, spinning rims or heard the laughter spilling out of the open sunroof. They didn't catch the figure in the blinding white suit rise out of it, his curly brown hair reflecting the sunlight. And no one saw him pull a sparkling golden arrow out of a bejeweled quiver and fire it.

The long, glittering arrow shot forward unseen. It cut into the steam rising from the street sewers and barreled down on its target: an innocent, hapless blonde obliviously striding to work and about to have her whole world turned upside down. The targets *never* saw the arrow. And they never would. But the effects were undeniable. Potent. Lasting in a way that mere *affection* never could. The arrow struck true.

"Ha, haaaa! Buuuuuuuulls-eye! Yet another loooooove connection!" crowed the archer before lowering his upper body through the sunroof of that magnificent ride and bouncing down onto the seat where he'd been standing. His slight pooch of a belly jiggled. "And whatcha

think about that, ladies?"

"Ooh, Cupid," cooed a curvy hanger-on accompanying him on this latest mission. The straight-haired Asian angel in the plunging white dress walked two fingers up his suit coat, cuddled up, and sighed. "You're soooo good." Four other groupies, tickled pink to be there, fluttered their eyelashes and giggled along. Cupid straightened his long, diamond-studded necklace in mock humility, that admired, adored, jet-setting love master.

The ladies, all five of them, leaned in to gush over their idol. Cupid's fan club of the day was diverse: a short blonde, a curvy brunette, a fair redhead, the jet-black-haired Asian, and a dark-skinned beauty with a spectacular afro.

Cupid's long, white face was flush with adrenaline. His eyes, beady and blue, scanned them, judging. His uncomfortably bushy eyebrows matched his brown hair and reflected nearly as much sunlight as his dazzling white suit.

He and the angelettes turned on their heals as the limo rolled past to watch the arrow-stricken woman. She was still walking. Hadn't flinched. Was unaware of the total chaos about to enter her life the moment she turned the corner to bump into her Mr. Right.

Cupid cleared his throat to regain their attention and teased his lovely assistants with a crooked grin. "Watch this," he said and stood back up through the sunroof.

He withdrew three more life-altering arrows from his overflowing quiver and fired them off in quick succession: one at a plump and balding middle-aged man; another at a morose, pierced teenager who was sitting on a stoop with his head in his hands; and the third seemingly at no one. Cupid's eager escorts watched in amazement as the final arrow ricocheted off a metal billboard, off a green Volkswagen Beetle, zipped within inches of a thin, severe looking woman, and hit an up-and-coming young business exec walking past her. The freshly stamped MBA graduate halted in his tracks, turned, and watched the severe woman – the new love of his life – continue on her way.

"Er," started Cupid, but he was interrupted by applause.

"Wowwee!" shouted the blonde, pulling Cupid down by his belt. "You don't even take aim" – her eyes widened – "yet you bank the shot, clear the lady, and still hit the mark! Sooooo impressive!"

Cupid raised a brow and glanced over his shoulder at the young man now jogging to catch His Catch. "Hmmm," Cupid said and turned back to the ladies. Seeing their adoration, he shrugged impassively and plopped onto his seat. He threw one arm behind the blonde and another around the afroed in platform heels. Both kissed his pudgy cheeks and placed possessive hands on his shapeless pecs.

"More champagne!" he ordered, and Ms. Brunette was on it, pouring with one hand and handing out filled

glasses with the other. Cupid pushed a silver button on the black leather interior of the door, lowering the partition separating driver from riders. "Tyrone, my work's done for now. Back to Cupid Castle."

"Yes, sir," mumbled Tyrone. The sleepy-eyed driver tipped his hat, which matched his off-white suit. His formal wear was yellowing, duller than Cupid's, but still contrasted nicely with his dark-chocolate colored skin. The limo veered into a billow of steam issuing from a street grate and disappeared. Not that anyone would have noticed.

Moments later, the jazzy red limo pulled up to a gated property. Guarding its tall, elaborately gilded gate was a live cherub hovering at the very top. Tyrone slowed to a stop and lowered his window. The cheeky cherub fluttered down.

"Your business?" asked the little, pink protector.

"Love," answered Tyrone with such boredom that one had to wonder whether the word held any meaning for him. His jet-black eyes had grown dull, his smooth face expressionless, and he rarely flashed his spectacular smile anymore.

"Oooh, you must be escorting Coooopid," cheeped

the little dumpling. "I'm so excited to finally meet him. I've got a message!"

"You can tell me," Tyrone said dully.

"I'm to relay the message to Mr. Cupid only," replied the mite importantly, trying but failing to puff out his featherweight chest.

Tyrone sighed. "Whatever you say, small fry." He ignored the little imp's indignation and held down two buttons on his side console: one to lower the back window nearest Cupid and the other to raise his own. "Try not to sprinkle any fairy dust in the vehicle."

"I am *not* a fa-,"

The closing window cut off his words.

Cupid stuck his head out of his now open window. "What's the holdup?" he called.

"Oh, Mr. Cupid," answered the flustered, celestial messenger, trying to regain his composure. "Mr. Cupid, you're wanted by Mr. Habandash up at Jupiter Heights." The cherub turned toward Cupid Castle, but all eyes swept past the comparatively modest building at the base of Mount Olympus, beyond, to the giant one at the peak of it. That towering, glowing palace belonged to Jupiter, god of the sky, god of thunder, and indeed king of the gods.

Jupiter's home was so big that most heavenly peoples could only see the bottom of it. The upper part, the bulk of the colossus, was veiled by impenetrable clouds. What the people *could* see, however, was imposing enou

The white marble towers and turrets lent it nobility and strength, while the gentle, white glow all around lent it an air of purity that only the god of gods could command.

Cupid had a feeling, though, that *purity* wasn't what Mr. Habandash wanted to talk about. Jupiter's assistant was usually too busy to prattle.

Cupid grabbed the limo's door handle, pulled it, and stepped out, against the ladies' chorus of complaints. "Now, now, my lovely angels. I'll be back soon, after I take care of my business with Jupiter."

"No one sees Jupiter but Mr. Habandash," piped up the pesky pipsqueak.

Cupid threw him a sour look before turning his face back to the window. "Tyrone will take you up to the palace. Feel free to call up a few more of your girlfriends. The more, the merrier, I always say. For me, at least. Oh, and don't touch my stuff."

He slammed the door on their continued complaints and followed the cherub up Heaven's Way, the main thoroughfare winding around the floating mountain paradise. Along the way, every lesser celestial being greeted Cupid, waving in his direction. Some stopped him for an autograph or got up on tiptoes to plant a kiss. Some matronly angels tried in vain to drag him into the house for family tea. Cupid smiled smugly and took this all in stride. It was good to be king.

Or near king. The real king was just behind that

20-foot-tall pearl door. Cupid raised a bejeweled hand to the knocker, but the door swung open to reveal a hurried immortal. Mr. Habandash was short, portly, and scruffy-looking, the kind of celestial who was probably debonair in his youth but now, past his prime, had more frown lines and jowls than he'd care to acknowledge. He still had a great head of deep brown hair, although he made the unfortunate decision to grease it and comb the mop over the top, like the mortal actors of the 1930s. His tan robes had blue ink splotches on them. Cupid wondered if he ever looked in a mirror.

"Well? What are you waiting for?!" barked Habandash. "An invitation? You were summoned. Get in here!" He turned and scuttled into the palace, taking tiny but fast steps. Habandash kept a brisk pace; Cupid hustled to keep up. They stepped into a huge room emitting deafening noise.

"Do you know what happens in this room?" the assistant demanded, flipping both hands onto his hips.

Cupid, who wasn't accustomed to being treated with anything less than veneration, lifted his chin and slowly – very slowly – swept it from left to right to survey his surroundings. Habandash's office was obviously a hub of communication. Electronic maps hung on the walls, each blinking with dozens of lights depicting angels on errands. So many emergency radio scanners squawked that Cupid wondered how anyone could penetrate the

din to hear anything. "I suppose you're going to tell me."

Habandash frowned and stormed to a map, where he pointed at a single brown dot, which Cupid hadn't noticed next to all the bright angel dots. "In this room, I keep track of all of the activities by gods, angels, assistants, and any other beings who are under Jupiter's command." Habandash stormed back toward the door and gestured with both hands down the gaping hall. "You know, the boss?!"

Cupid sauntered to him and gazed down the hall. He was immediately captured by the beauty of the grand, opal-iridescent, double stairway leading into clouds. That staircase had mesmerized him more than once. The music it exhaled was deeply entrancing. Enticing. Suddenly irresistible. Cupid just *had* to get up those stairs. Like the last time. And the time before that. It was imperative that he find out where those stairs would take him. To see Jupiter, he was sure. Cupid took a step forward, but suddenly a pudgy hand slapped hard across his chest, barring his path. Again.

"No one sees Jupiter but me," Habandash reminded him coldly.

Crestfallen and somewhat embarrassed by his own idolatry – *Aren't I a god, too? Why am I acting like a stalking fan?* – Cupid stepped back into Habandash's office.

"Then why am I here?" Cupid touched the side of his mouth with his forefinger and inquired in a tone

sweet enough to rile even the most patient kindergarten teacher. "Please, do tell."

"You are *here*," Habandash continued with derision, "because *you* are screwing up. That brown dot is the young man you hit with your final, ill-aimed arrow who is now in love with your intended target who should have fallen in love with her landscaper."

"Ooooh, wellllllll." Cupid cleared his throat and pulled on a particularly long, brown curl. "It's all right. Now *he's* in love, too. It's my job to share love. No harm done."

"YES, HARM DONE!" roared Habandash. "There is someone for everyone, and your carelessness, had I not caught it, might have taken away that someone from someone else, namely the four involved."

"What four?" asked Cupid, confused.

"The young man, his future wife, the target, and her landscaper!" Habandash threw his hands up in exasperation. "This is the twentieth time this month that I'm having to send out a lesser angel to fix your mistakes. You. Are. Slipping. Up! And I will remind you that there are a hundred lesser angels who would love to have the job of Lead Love Angel and hold the title of *Cupid.* So you've had the position for ages – so what?! The position is *earned* – and can be lost."

Cupid chuckled. Then, seeing Habandash's nostrils flare, he put a hand to his mouth and closed his eyes. He'd

hold his breath. Until ... until he couldn't. Then a spray of spit and air burst out of him as he erupted into laughter.

Habandash yawped in disgust and pulled a filthy handkerchief out of his sleeve to blot the spittle off his face. "And just what's so funny?" he hissed.

"Another *Cupid?*" asked Cupid between howls of laughter. "C'mon, Habbi!" – he used the nickname that Habandash most detested – "You and I both know why I'm the only Cupid. I'm the son of Venus, goddess of love, remember? My arrows are more potent and spark true love better than anyone else's. It would *take* a hundred angels to equal one of me."

Habandash's eyes sparked.

"Oh, all right, all right," soothed Cupid, hands raised in mock defeat. "I'll be more careful. I'll actually take aim," he acceded, adding under his breath, "even though it's so much more impressive with the ladies when I don't."

Cupid turned on his heels and walked out of the room, not having been dismissed and ignoring the calls to come back. He stepped out into sunny Olympus only to learn that his cherubin escort had left him. *Humph*, he thought. *The little brat.*

Turning onto Heaven's Way, Cupid particularly enjoyed, after that ridiculous scolding, the attention and stares he got from adoring and swooning fans. *They* knew who the real Cupid would always be. The female angels

up ahead shivered as usual – but – it was odd how they shivered *before* he'd gotten there.

Cupid heard a crowd approaching and saw the little munchkin who should have been escorting him coming his way, escorting someone else. Another angel. A stranger. Or at least no one that Cupid had ever taken the time to notice. And it was this new angel who was drawing the crowd and inducing shivers.

Cupid watched as if in slow motion as the newbie sauntered by. The stranger wore a glittering, diamond-speckled, silver tuxedo and had the sort of rugged good looks that made everyone stare. Tall and dark haired. A square jaw that not only held when he smiled, but also revealed deep dimples. Mocha brown eyes, full lips, and an undeniably sexy glow that allowed him his confident swagger.

"And you'll be seeing Mr. Habandash," explained the cherub in a servile tone. "He has a speci-..."

But Cupid couldn't hear the rest as the gaggle of female angels pursuing the pair twittered shamelessly about how handsome he was.

And Cupid realized the "he" to whom they referred wasn't him.

Chapter 2

TAKING AIM
OR
FLUSHING

Cupid continued on his way back to Cupid Castle, and, the farther he distanced himself from the stranger, the more regular became the attention lavished upon *him* again. The waves and hellos he got en route restored Cupid's aplomb. To each who doted upon him, and rightly so, he thought, he generously nodded. This unescorted walk, in his mind, became a gift, a promenade of unfiltered celebrity for the lesser celestials to enjoy, and it further served to swell his hugely inflated ego. It was good to be back with those who loved him.

"Tyrone, we're going back out!" shouted Cupid, jogging through the pillared portico of his domain and into the master lounge. "Ladies, back into the limo! I feel like showing off a bit."

Cupid expected to see the angelettes leap up from the many plush sofas dotted with soft pillows, excited to go out, to be seen with him again – or maybe they'd be near tears for not scoring an evening alone with him. But he saw none of that. Instead, he saw greenish-blue light spilling out of his side rec room, the room in which he kept his ERP, or Earthly Reflecting Pool.

All the gods had one. The sink-sized pool held a greenish-blue liquid, which was a mixture of water and ambrosia, the food of the immortals. It was this liquid that allowed the gods to see earthly activities. The viscous goo swirled languidly in ornate bowls supported by tall bases, and each ERP was decorated in the style of the god who owned it. Cupid's pink marble bowl looked like a giant, hollowed candy heart supported by a bouquet of bronzed, long-stem roses.

Tyrone had permission to use the ERP, but not when Cupid was entertaining guests.

"Tell me you did not send the ladies away just so you could watch gods' cable," warned Cupid, startling Tyrone out of a deep daze.

"Sir," gasped Tyrone, gripping the rim of the ERP as if it were threatening to sprout legs and run away. Tyrone was almost unrecognizable; Cupid was used to seeing him looking bored out of his skull.

"Sir, thank goodness you're here. I'm sitting in the kitchen when I hear the ladies scrambling out of here, clicking their heels on the marble, and I ask what's going on, and one says the ERP says it all. Sir, see for yourself."

Cupid sighed and stepped forward reluctantly. "All this fuss better not be for another hurricane or giant whirlpool. Neptune's always whipping those up for attention." Cupid remembered the time he and Tyrone drove across the ocean on a transatlantic short-cut and the sea

god chased them down with a giant wave. Cupid guessed that Neptune was insulted by not being asked permission to pass over his domain. Or maybe the sea god was just grouchy.

"No, sir. Please look," urged Tyrone.

Cupid bent over the ERP and saw Earth as usual, so he concentrated to zoom in. It was then that he saw a trail of glitter across half of Paris with golden arrows soaring out of it. He lowered his nose to within an inch of the water and looked closer. Closer.

Just ahead of that streak of gold and silver glitter – and shining even brighter – was … the stranger. The glitter was flowing off his giant, muscled wings, which were in much better shape than Cupid's as the latter had taken to not exercising them much, instead stuffing them into his suit and traveling by limo. The stranger's silvery suit had custom-made wing-slits, and Cupid noticed that the cut of the stranger's suit was more tailored and refined than his own.

Cupid might have thought, *No big deal; he's just taking in the sights*, had it not been for the rapid fire of golden arrows striking people.

"Sir, what's happ–"

"Saddle up!" Cupid insisted. "We leave NOW!"

The limo slammed down onto the Avenue des Champs-Élysées, Paris' most famous street, and nearly collided into a chestnut tree before Tyrone managed to swerve and hit the brakes. The limo screeched to a halt next to a café, and, as usual, not a soul saw or heard it.

Except the immortals.

There were a dozen of them: Mr. Who-Do-You-Think-You-Are New Guy; the flighty little cherub for whom Cupid was developing a severe dislike; and ten – count 'em – ten angelic assistants, five of whom were the same ladies who'd escorted Cupid this morning and another five whom he didn't know but looked just as tempting.

Tyrone scrambled out of the limo and rushed to open Cupid's door. It was the fastest the Olympic chauffeur had moved since entering the afterlife.

Cupid leapt out and took one angry step onto the grand avenue before remembering who he was: a *god*, as in, *powerful. Dignified. Unique.* He slowed his stride and straightened the lapels of his magnificently white suit. Thus reassured, he crossed the street slowly, deliberately. Cars zipped right through him, their drivers unaware that they were committing hit-and-run on a god, although they'd feel curiously wonderful the rest of the day for the divine contact.

When Cupid reached Mr. Gorgeous, he casually plucked the newbie's bow from his hands and turned it

over in his own. Then he ran his beringed finger along every inch of it: from the nock to the sight arrow to the grip to the other nock and all along the bowstring, testing its feel. It was a move meant to show the newcomer that Cupid could take and handle any bow he wished. He could break it if he wanted. Cupid handed it back with a slight sneer to show his distaste for what he deemed an inferior product. Mr. Gorgeous took it without a sound or gesture, but the cherub dropped down to flutter right between the two of them.

"Would you like something, Mr. Cupid?" it asked, using the proper words but hinting at frustration in its tone.

"Tsk, tsk," clucked Cupid, waving a hand as if to shoo a fly. "I think you've led this lesser love angel astray, and here your job is to see that that doesn't happen. Pity, that slip-up."

Cupid turned to the stranger, who he only guessed was a new love angel by the fact that he was in possession of love arrows. "You're in the wrong place," Cupid pooh-poohed. "You may not know this, being so greeeeen and inexpeeeerienced, but lesser love angels never do Paris. They work Afghanistan or North Korea or, in your case, I'd recommend Antarctica as a start. Paris, however, is *my* territory. No one works the City of Love but me, Cupid, because *I'm* the one who *makes* it the City of Love. My *érotisme* and I are what make this place what it is, and you, Mr.-Whoever-You-Are, are not up to it. I suggest

you leeeeave," he said pointedly, sweeping his arm toward the sky in invitation.

The new angel, who hadn't said a word during the public rubbing, merely cocked an eyebrow at Cupid and asked him in a smooth, deep voice, "I am not up to … what? Pricking Paris? I believe I am."

"And that's exactly what he's been sent to do, Mr. Cupid," the little varmint pitched provocatively. "Mr. Habandash asked that I try him out here and see if his aim is more accur-," the little imp stopped himself, cleared his throat, and continued simply, "see if his aim is accurate."

"Thank you, Pip," said the newbie to the cherub.

The little fart has a name? thought Cupid, who instantly imagined himself popping Pip.

"You're welcome, Mr. Mandre," was the answer. The angelettes shivered.

What kind of a name is Mandre? thought Cupid. *Manly Mandre, ooooh.* He bristled, angry. Now Cupid didn't have just *one* person questioning his skills, but three: Mr. Habandash, the cherub (*who should be falling on his face in servitude*, Cupid thought), and this lesser angel.

"And to prove that I'm up to the challenge," continued Mandre in his cool manner, as if the whole conversation were no great insult, "I propose a test of skills." He pulled from his suit pocket a sheet of glittering golden paper which Cupid recognized as the daily Hit List, the index of names of those to be lovified. "Six names remain. We

each get three. He with the most spectacular hits wins."

Cupid suffered three shades of rage before raising his voice. "Listen, Mongrel," as he'd decided to call him.

"It's Mandre."

Cupid went on raging, "A god does not prove his position to anyone! I'll–"

"But," Pip interjected. "Mr. Habandash – Jupiter's executive assistant, mind you – gave the order that this angel be tried." Pip rubbed his chin and looked as if he were struggling for the right words. "If you forbid Mr. Mandre from obeying his orders, you flout Jupiter. However, if you wish to show *ho-o-o-ow* superior you are," Pip said delicately, "you could accept the challenge and prove that any questioning of your skills was folly."

Cupid bared his teeth, and Pip soared upward out of reach.

Mandre tore the Hit List, separating the bottom three names from the rest. He then pulled a silver dagger out of his front inside pocket, held the torn strip of paper up to the nearest chestnut tree, and stabbed it into place.

No mortal saw the glint of the swift blade striking nor the note left hanging nor Mandre spreading his wings and taking off, but all the immortals did. They gave chase, and Cupid realized he had to, too. He thrust his wings outward, tearing his suit in the process, and cursed the Titans for this brazen interloper.

The new angel was furiously fast, and his glittering

trail was like a wall of dust that Cupid struggled to penetrate. Cupid couldn't see much more than brilliance until he caught a glimpse – and heard the familiar zing – of a flying arrow.

It's way off course! thought Cupid gleefully. The arrow soared toward a rooftop, nowhere near people. It hit a rain gutter with a thwack. "Ha, ha!" Cupid started laughing, but his laughter soon died out. He watched in horror as the arrow ricocheted, sailed through an elaborately engraved metal wind chime – setting off the most beautiful music any nearby mortal had ever heard – hit the base of the chime, ricocheted horizontally, and finally sailed directly into the heart of a sad, middle-aged woman wearing a sweater of crocheted hearts. The arrow centrally sliced both the yarned heart and her yearning one.

"Yay!" shouted the lady angels. "Bravo!"

"A solid hit," said Pip, "featuring two controlled ricochets with such musical accompaniment that shall cheer the nearby humans the lasting day. Well done."

Cupid stamped a foot and hissed, "I never agreed to any challen–", but Mandre took flight again, and the swoosh of the ladies and Pip following triggered a gust of wind that muffled Cupid's protests.

Cupid growled and again shot forward to catch up. He sprinted past the angelettes and almost had that malignant Mandre in his grip when the underhanded sneak plummeted toward the ground.

Mandre dived downward face-first and flipped at the last possible moment to slide skateboarder-style down one edge of the Louvre Pyramid in front of the famous Louvre Museum. Just before reaching the ground, he reached over his shoulder for his quiver and shot an arrow toward the towering statue of King Louis XIV, a monarch who Cupid supposed came as close to godly power as any mortal could.

The arrow skidded along the bronze flank of the king's reared horse and traced the bend in its front leg. Losing speed, the shaft finally gave in to gravity and fell to the ground in a graceful arc, gently pricking the chest of a 20-something tourist with red hair who was admiring the piece. The young man turned to the girl next to him and earnestly declared his love in broken French distorted by his strong Irish accent.

Pip and the ladies landed at the base of the pyramid next to the flustered Cupid.

"Target number two! A fantastic action shot tinged with art and a gentle landing," declared Pip, marking a check on his clipboard.

Cupid was not going to let this showboating continue. He turned with a raised finger to berate the malevolent Mongrel, but the show-off took flight again. This time, Cupid was ready and gave chase. He was again within arm's reach when that meddler – that trespasser, as Cupid saw him – dived toward the Eiffel Tower and shot

his third arrow mid-descent.

Mongrel spiraled to slow himself and grabbed hold of the tower about half-way down. Cupid threw out an arm and snagged the Tower – well, crashed into it – just a bit lower down. Cupid peered above him and found Mongrel resting there, looking like a bright King Kong, except that King Kong wasn't such a hotshot.

A spark of light drew Cupid's attention to his right. It was Mongrel's arrow, bouncing again and again in the tower's lattices, pinging off one iron strip after another, spraying each with a tiny circle of light. It looked like a game of celestial pinball.

No humans looked up at the bouncing "firefly." None of them saw the light. But one human was struck by the arrow, sure and true, after the final ping: a beautiful, muscled, athletic brunette wearing a fitted white dress and red hat. The arrow jetted right through her and stuck in the side of another human, a famed Olympic soccer coach who was gazing upward at the tower. He was the only man in the area not watching her at the moment, but the pinprick that he never felt nonetheless drew his eyes down to his true love. He determinedly held out an arm to escort her wherever she wished. She stutter-stopped, put a hand to her heart, and accepted the gallant offer. Of course she did; she'd accept his gallantry forevermore, for the entirety of their happy lives together.

"Oh, nicely done!" lauded Pip. "A show of lights

to a 2-in-1 hit. Beautiful *and* economical. You've done marvelously, Mr. Mandre. And now, Mr. Cupid," said the peckish speck, "would you do us the honor?"

"I will not!" declared Cupid. He stalked a slow circle around Pip, forcing himself to contain his rage. "Listen, Pimple," as he'd decided to call him.

Pip bristled. "It's Pip."

"Right. Pup." Cupid ignored Pip's gasping mouth. "I will not perform on demand like a caged animal. I discharge my *duties* out of honor." He stopped and folded his arms, holding his ground for his final statement. "And I hold my *title* through divine right!"

"Then I will have to report to Habandash that the challenge is won by Mr. Man–"

"You'll do no such thing!" stormed Cupid, stomping his feet like a petulant child.

"I have no choice, Mr. Cupid, but to report my findings."

Cupid was enraged at the idea of doing anything at the commands of a lesser angel or a cherub, but Jupiter's will, even if it were through Habandash, could not be flouted. The challenge was already too far along, and there were too many witnesses for Cupid to back down. Besides, he reminded himself perhaps too smugly but trying to soothe his jangling nerves, he could outdo a *hundred* angels.

"If you must report, then report my victory!" Cupid thrust out his hand, and the three-name Hit List which

had been daggered to a tree on the Avenue des Champs-Élysées ripped itself free and jetted his way.

As soon as it touched the tips of his fingers, Cupid sensed the names inscribed. He shot into the sky to find his first hit: a young teen, probably 16 years old, about to be one of the lucky ones who finds his future wife in high school. Too bad he was currently in a bathroom stall in one of the city's dingiest educational institutions.

Cupid dived through the bathroom window, which remained fully intact but, in the eyes of immortals, shattered spectacularly. Enchanted shards of glass flew all around him as Cupid twisted in mid air and shot a bullet-fast arrow. It pinged off the dingy mirror, banked upward to the hanging lampshade, and plunged back downward to hit the boy squarely on the top of his red head. It might have been impressive, perhaps, had the boy not hit the flush button a half-second earlier. The gurgle of the quickly emptying toilet echoed around the room.

"Hmmm," Pip muttered, fluttering through the dingy windowpane. "Two banks, but unfortunate timing. The watery swoosh is *less* than musical."

Cupid wasted no time arguing. How could he? He took off again, this time in pursuit of Hit List Person Number Two: a reserved brunette in her late 30s who'd just gone through a divorce – *because she didn't wait for me to strike,* Cupid thought, pumping himself up.

The woman was about to enter a library. Wanting

to catch her outside, Cupid recklessly fired without so much as aiming. Well, the haughty, highfalutin' Herald of Love should have set his sights straight. The arrow swept right past the woman and struck the metal door for which she was reaching. There was no ricochet; the arrow stopped dead at the door and dropped like a bird shot mid-air. It did manage to scratch the target before plopping to the ground and being trampled underfoot.

"Welllllll," mumbled Pimple, even more reluctantly this time around. "You *did* hit the target, but just barely. Um, surely, Mr. Cupid, you can do a bit better tha-"

Cupid ignored the cheeky little zit, expanded his wings for a third time, and again took off.

Finally, the Love Lord would get a target at an interesting location! The Arc de Triomphe. Cupid immediately thought of his dad, Mars, the god of war, who loved all military pomp. The Arc de Triomphe was one of his favorite military monuments. The stone block had a tall arch in its center, which opened it to foot traffic, and highly detailed sculptural reliefs on each face.

Gotcha, thought Cupid, spying the 50-something, greying city worker who was his final target. The man was refreshing the white paint on the fence posts that corral the Arc.

Cupid soared downward and did an opposing arch of his own, swooping through the monument's opening and rising up the other side. He was reminded of the

World War I pilot who flew through the monument in nearly the same way after war's end. The pilot's flight was captured on newsreels; Cupid's could be seen only by immortals.

When he reached the apex of his momentum, high in the sky, Cupid spun on his heels and aimed for the fence post directly *beside* the target. The arrow plunged groundward. It struck the first black link below the fence post and gracefully skimmed the chain, down and up, imitating the flying arc that Cupid himself had just performed so magnificently. When the arrow ran out of chain, it pierced the lucky worker perfectly through the pectoral. Instant change. By tonight, the man would be considering how to propose to that special woman working the grocery store checkout.

"Graceful and perfectly executed," commented Pip, fluttering beside Cupid's head like a pesky mosquito. "But I'm afraid you've been outdone, Mr. Cupid. Mr. Mandre's won the challenge and the day's accolades. I must report my findings."

Pip reached into his armpit and pulled out a handful of glittering dust even while Cupid was telling him to wait just a moment. Pip did not. Instead, he sprinkled the dust onto the paper at his clipboard, tore the paper free, and threw it into the sky. It disappeared almost instantly.

Turning to Mandre, Pip said, "You, sir, will now have the privilege of saying you're the only love angel to

ever defeat Mr. Cupid."

The color washed from Cupid's face. A smirk crossed Mandre's. A flash of light brought a new piece of paper sprinkled in glittering dust, which Pip snatched from the air.

"Ha, ha!" laughed Pip. "And, Mr. Mandre, there's more! We must return to Mt. Olympus at once. Hurry!"

His entire group flew off in an instant. Another bright light brought another note. Cupid snatched this one and found it addressed to him from Mr. Habandash. He was to report immediately, too.

Cupid felt the cold hand of unease grip him, but he was quick to explain it away: just residual anger from the stupid *duel*, he reasoned, which wasn't really a duel because he never agreed to it. No one could claim it was legitimate, least of all Habandash. Still, Habandash had the powers to summon Cupid, report to Jupiter, and who knew what else, so Cupid decided the right hand man might deserve to be shown a bit more respect from here on out.

Cupid plucked a feather from his wing, tossed it into the sky to summon Tyrone, and soon found himself dropping in through the limo's open sunroof.

"Paradise Plaza, Tyrone," he commanded his driver with creeping dread, "and step on it."

Chapter 3

THE FALL

OR

FROSTING

The place was packed. Cupid's options were to order Tyrone to plow the limo through the crowd or to get out himself and walk. Cupid was tempted to suggest the former (Hey, he was the god of passionate love and desire, not of common decency.), but Tyrone would never have allowed it, so Cupid got out and walked. It was the third time today that he'd been forced to do so.

Nearly all of the Olympic population chatted excitedly while waiting in Paradise Plaza, Mt. Olympus' most spacious, open square. The plaza was surrounded by ancient, columned temples, as intact and beautiful as the day they were built. The "ground" of the plaza was made of the puffiest cumulus clouds, and the plaza center was dotted by arrangements of small, circular, marble tables and vine-adorned benches.

Nearly every space was taken. The collective light given off by so many gods and angels would have blinded any human. As it was, the celestial gathering had already changed the terrestrial weather. Mortal forecasters were at a loss to explain why the temperature suddenly jumped 15 degrees; eventually they gave up and blamed solar flares.

Cupid saw Habandash standing on a stage made of straight, wispy cirrus clouds erected center-square. He began making his way over. Normally, pushing through a crowd that size would have taken a long time, what with all his fans stopping him for autographs or to share a somewhat long-lasting and passionate kiss, but this time around, it took no time at all.

"Ah, Cupid," Habandash greeted him as Cupid hopped onstage. The thin mist of the cloud wasn't terribly solid; Cupid sunk in an inch or two and nearly stumbled. Habandash ignored it. "You're here. Good." Habandash raised his arms as if to call for silence, but Cupid pulled one arm back down.

"Before you start, Habandash," whispered Cupid urgently, "I'd like to know what this is all about. What exactly is happening here?"

"The tally, Cupid."

"But the tally's never done this publicly, and here it's drawn this enormous crowd, and you've never nagged me–"

Habandash set his jaw angrily, and Cupid reminded himself that he'd just decided to show Habbi some respect.

"Er, you've never *requested* my presence before."

Habandash unset his jaw and replied, almost apologetically, "You were warned, Cupid."

"What do you–"

Habandash raised his arms again and spoke. "Fellow Mount Olympians, gods, angels, loved ones, and

friends, today we open a new chapter in the long history of Olympus."

Cupid hissed out of the corner of his mouth, "Mr. Habandash, I-"

"Witness the tally!" shouted Habandash to the crowd, whipping the mass to a frenzy and silencing Cupid in the same stroke. He turned to the portable whiteboard beside him and flipped it to reveal the lined side, which heralded the names of love angels and their corresponding, to-date tally.

Dozens of seafoam green pixies, their iridescent wings catching the light, fluttered toward the leader board. Each carried a magnetic gold heart representing a successful love connection. Each heart was a reward for a particular love angel's work, a visual display of competence and accomplishment. The majority of the pixies would rise as always to the top line, Cupid's line, he was convinced.

The crowd silenced, holding its collective breath. Pixie after pixie deposited heart after heart. Cupid held a commanding lead as always.

Ah, all's as it should be, he thought pompously.

That was, until the final few seconds when a slew of fresh pixies flew down out of nowhere and plastered dozens of fresh hearts in the second line – as in, *not* Cupid's line. The crowd gasped. Cupid looked closer and saw – saw –

Wait. What?!

"We have a new champion!" Habandash bellowed,

and the crowd exploded in gasps, boos, and, astonishingly to Cupid, a great many cheers. "New amongst us, Love Angel Mandre has taken the lead in just two short days and far outlovified our perennial leader." Habandash swept an arm toward Cupid, who gaped again and again in shock.

"Today marks history, my fellow Olympians," Habandash boomed. "We crown a new angel as our representative in all things love-related. I know Cupid would join me in welcoming excellence among our ranks–"

No, I wouldn't! Cupid tried to shout, but nothing came out of his mouth.

"–and be glad for his successor–"

You wish! he meant to yell. Again, nothing came out.

"I give you," Habandash swept his other arm toward Mandre, "our newwwww Coooooooopid," his voice swelled as if he were introducing Jupiter himself, "Misterrrrrrrr Mannnnnnnndre!"

There were cheers and shouts and waving of scarves and flapping of wings and a great din, of that Cupid was sure because he *saw* it. But he heard none of it. It was as if someone had suddenly sucked his eardrums clean out of his head, using a very thin straw. He was painfully deaf. And struck lame. He couldn't move.

This has to be a mistake, he thought, trying to writhe and shout without any success whatsoever. He was still as a statue – an outsider looking in. The scene progressed,

and he could only stand there watching – and assessing.

I lost the challenge – sure, perhaps, maybe – Cupid told himself, rather desperately – *but it was just one challenge! One measly challenge over the course of centuries! This can't be happening!*

I'll ... I'll ... I'll go straight to Jupiter! I won't put up with any of that you-can't-see-Jupiter *junk. I'm a god, too! I'll talk to him and clear this all up in no time.*

Cupid looked toward Habandash and found him still gesticulating. The crowd swelled forward, anticipating something. Then Cupid felt a tug at his back and saw Habandash lift his bow and quiver from its harness.

Hold on! thought Cupid. *Don't do that!* He tried to shout, but the only thing that moved for him were his eyes, which were growing wider and wider by the second.

Habandash hoisted the bow and quiver up high and gave them a good shake. That set off a cascade of golden glitter, which turned rainbow-colored in mid-air. As Cupid watched, horror-struck, Habandash swept a different bow and quiver under the glitter cascade, coating it, swaying it back and forth as if he were frosting a huge, imaginary cake. Frosting it with Cupid's *mojo!* The strange *other* bow sparkled and glowed and took on a luminescence all its own, its quiver radiating its brilliance. And then the *pièce de résistance:* Habandash handed the new divine tools to Mongrel, er, Mangy, er, Mandre.

More movement. The crowd jumped up and down.

Mandre bowed.

Habandash hooked Cupid's elbow into his own and steered him down the cloud steps. Cupid stumbled his way down, unable to shuffle his feet. Habbi caught him at the bottom and must have said something because his lips were moving. Cupid felt his hand being lifted and swiveled his eyes to see Habandash plunk his old bow and quiver into it. But the quiver wasn't the beautiful, awe-inspiring, glittering, magnificent thing it once was. Now it looked ... plain. It was just old wood. Unpolished and dried out.

I'm being dethroned, Cupid reasoned thickly, not realizing that he wasn't *being* dethroned; he'd *been* dethroned. The train had left the station, as it were, and *he* wasn't on it.

Cupid's ears twinged, and, gooey and slow as syrup, noise returned, too. There was commotion around him, people talking. Habandash. Mid-conversation.

"And the castle and limo, too. It seems like a lot, but it's not the end of eternity, Cupid, I mean, Junior. Good luck to you." Habandash shook his hand and walked away, leaving Cupid dumbstruck in a hysterical crowd. Something unlocked inside him, and Cupid felt his muscles release. Another pull on his elbow. He looked over to see Tyrone urging him to come along. Cupid allowed his driver to lead him away. Away from the crowd. Away from his life. Toward humiliation. Toward irrelevance.

"Stop it, sir. Let me take that."

Cupid felt Tyrone trying to pull the bottle out of his hand, so he held on more tightly than ever and slurred, "Why not?! 'Snot like anyone's gonna notice – er care. Everyone's too busy fawnin' ov'r th' Annointed One." He belched forcefully.

"But you've been downing this mortal drink for a solid hour, and you know how booze affects you, sir!"

"Sir, nothin'!" Cupid barked, yanking the bottle and his arm free. "I'm notcha 'sir' anymore. I'm just 'Mars Junior' now, just another love angel, so you no longer answer ta me. You go on. Get lost. Beat it. Let me have my pity party in peace." But instead of waiting for Tyrone to leave as commanded, Cupid unevenly spread his wings and jumped, shakily, into the air. If it were possible to stumble while flying, Cupid did it.

Tyrone watched his former boss' crooked flight. He scrunched his face with anxiety and must have known: there was no emotion like that of a god's, no rivaling the strength or passion of the feeling, whatever it may be. Cupid would take this hard, way harder than anyone else ever would. Tyrone ran to the limo he no longer had the right to drive and gave chase.

Chapter 4

BOOZE, BULLS, AND BOUNCERS

OR

TOSSED

Cupid landed hard. He felt his knees collapse and hit the pavement, shooting searing pain to his late-reacting brain. "Arghhhh!" he barked before jerkily picking himself up and looking around. He'd lost Tyrone, easy to do when you fly as the crow flies, and Tyrone, well, he doesn't fly at all.

Where'm I? Cupid asked himself, confused. He turned. Neon lights swirled. *No. He* was the one moving, turning in a circle.

'S dark out. How'd that happen? he wondered.

He stopped his legs from moving and focused on the blurry blue letters of a neon sign: The Blue Canary Nightclub. There was a line of people outside waiting to get in. Young people. Dancing. *Yeah,* he thought. *'At's what I want.*

He fumbled with his super white suit coat and slid it down both arms and wings. Then he struggled to put it back on, this time covering his wings. The holes he'd torn through the coat were still visible, but at least he could hide his wings and be less recognizable to another god, should one be inside during this time of disgrace.

Cupid belched again before he could stop himself and then stumbled past the line of people to the guarded entrance of the dance club. A big man – tall, heavy, clearly a bouncer – put out a hand to stop his advance.

Cupid stopped, blinked a few times, and focused on holding eye contact with the man, who unbelievably seemed to be looking back. Cupid, confused, turned to look behind him to see if anyone was standing there. *No. So who's he looking at?*

"Ya needs an invite," growled the bruiser, shaking his head. "And the way you's dressed …"

Jupiter's thunder! thought Cupid. *He sees me.*

The mortal abruptly stopped talking. Cupid watched as the man's face slackened and a glazed look washed over his eyes. Several long moments later, the man smiled broadly. Lifting the velvet rope divider from its stanchion and waving Cupid through, he cheerfully announced, "C'mon in! Ev'rybody's welcome! This here's the best club in the city, the most funktacular, most sexirific, most happy-jammy place you's ever seen! Enjoy yerselves on me!"

Cupid raised an eyebrow at the former angrypants. *How'd he see me?* Cupid wondered, muddle-brained. *S'impossible. No mortal can see me.*

It was clear two stumbling steps later, however, nearly tripping into the busy club with its flashing dance lights and screaming music, that a whole lot of mortals

could see him. A dozen heads turned his way, their owners snickering.

"Nice suit!" taunted a lanky 20-something. "All white? What are you? A snow ninja?!"

Several people guffawed until Cupid took a further wobbly step inside. Then the transformation happened again. The Getalong Gang's laughter died out. Their smiles turned feeble, their stares vacant until the tall goober who'd been taunting him interjected urgently, "Wow, man, you are soooo cool!"

"Seriously awesome," confirmed his pal.

"Fascinating," whispered a heavy-set girl so quietly that Cupid doubted anyone but he had heard it.

"Oh, please, join us!" chirped her twiggy friend.

Cupid tilted his head and nearly lost his balance. His head felt like a big melon balanced on a cooked noodle. He had to figure this out. It took so much mental effort – serious concentration – but he was catching onto it. He'd been dethroned, humiliated, stripped of his mojo, but he was still a god, so his charisma was still there. He still had *IT*, he realized. And it not only made mortals around him feel great, they could now *see* the source of their euphoria: Cupid, Sergeant Snog himself, The King of Coitus, The Master of Makeouts. Mortals would unknowingly soak up his good karma and end up seriously high off of it.

"I'm buying!" shouted the instigating mortal.

And so began Cupid's night-long bender.

Cupid saw his reflection rising and falling in the mirror above the bar. White face. Brown, curly hair. Up. Down. Someone was plucking a banjo. The crowd was waving cowboy hats. A country bar. He didn't remember getting here. *Mus' be a new place.*

He bowed his heavy head and saw his lower half astride a metal tube with a saddle on it. *'Sa mechanical bull!* Cupid realized. *Like Taurus the Bull, the symbol of virility! Like me! I'm the love god! Habbi an' Jupiter an' the res' of 'em try to replace me?! How dare they?! I'll show 'em! They'll be beggin'ta take me back!*

Cupid never got the chance to concentrate on bullriding or to beat his best time; four pairs of hands pulled him down.

Cupid fell face-first onto the shiny dance floor. *Wha-?* he asked himself woozily. *Where're the hay and peanut shells?* He looked up to see a muscular black man reach out his hand.

"Naw, man, ya click yer heels on the downbeat and

hook yer feet on the up."

Cupid grabbed the man's hand and was hoisted back to his feet. *I won't need help to get back on my throne,* he thought. *I'm da Lord of Love! Son ta Venus, da Goddess of Love! Heir ta Mars, da God of War! Got powers no one understands! This world falls tot'lly apart without me!*

Cupid swiveled around and saw his entourage growing. The rugged, windburned faces from the country bar and the fresh-faced ones from the dance club joined new faces from here – *a hip hop club?*

"Give me your hand," the man said with a fun-loving laugh. A grizzled old cow hand slapped him on the back. Everybody got along around Cupid.

The room spun. Cupid found himself in a group of more than a hundred mortals doing a line dance they called The Cupid Shuffle. The mob of humans was made of Cupid's new adoring fans, a dozen gathered at each club or bar hit by the original group. Now they danced in a converted warehouse, the walls of which were peppered with automobile parts and posters of vacationers motoring the scenic routes. Cupid stopped dancing; he felt sick. The line broke apart, but everyone kept bouncing to a techno

beat, living it up.

Cupid looked down to see himself wearing a brown overcoat over his white suit. *Where'd I get this? Who are these humans? Ach, HUMANS!*

He thought about the evening. No god or angel had come to beg his return to Olympus, even though *hours* had passed. He imagined a search party out looking for him, ready to shout for joy upon finding him, but, if the leaders of Mount Olympus wanted to find him, they could do it. And they wouldn't have kicked him out in the first place. *And hanging out with humans!* He covered his eyes and cried, "I'm history!"

"Yeah, baby, you're making history all righ'," said a short gal at his side, bouncing with the music. "No one'll ever forget tonight."

He looked over and saw a tiny, curvy, female form, her eyes closed as she tore up the dance floor. A second later, her girlfriends pulled her away toward the restroom.

Truly alone in a sea of people – and heartbroken – Cupid dejectedly dropped his drunken head into his hands and plopped down onto the dance floor. "Gods, I'm nobody!" he lamented, but his *par-tay people* didn't react negatively at his distress. Instead, they poured drinks into his complaining mouth and bounced around him on the dance floor. Their knees jerked within inches of his face; he'd get a black eye or worse if he stayed there.

His horde of humans smiled and laughed and

had the time of their lives because they just couldn't feel sadness near him – not with his powerful mojo drugging them. And they were distracted – Cupid's presence had them hooking up into pairs for the evening.

"Oh, Sugar, don't cry," came a soothing female voice. Finally, someone noticed him. "It can't be all that bad."

Oh, yes, it is, Cupid whined to himself, opening his puffy, tear-filled eyes to see very white calves in front of him and thin feet in low red heels. He lifted his back-breakingly heavy head to see a white girl with strikingly pale blue eyes leaning over him. She had loose red curls falling to her shoulders, and she put a gentle hand on his arm. He was surprised someone had noticed his unhappiness. But then again, he reasoned slowly, girls always did tend to fawn over him. *She's kind,* he thought, but she couldn't make it better. No one could. He was a god – *a god!* - yet he felt miserable.

"One more place to hit before the night's over!" blathered the boy from the first club, physically pushing the girl aside and breaking into Cupid's laments. "The Red Flag Gentleman's Club."

Cupid couldn't even properly appreciate the

bikini-clad dancer gyrating in front of him.

"Oh, Jupiter, I can't go on!" he wailed. "The hardship – it's too much to bear! Bwaaaaaaa!" he bellowed, grabbing the dancer's hips and sobbing into her belly button.

In a flash fast enough to make Mercury flinch, two sets of hands grabbed Cupid by his shoulders and yanked him back from his chair. Dollar bills stuck to Cupid's face, dislodged from the dancer's waistband.

"You're our newest and best customer, Mr. C.," said his new bouncer friend, DeShaw. "But no one touches the girls."

He and another bouncer dragged Cupid through the club, making a spectacle of him, toward the back door. *Could the night get any worse?* Cupid moaned to himself. The bouncers lowered their hold to his elbows, swung him back, and threw him hard and high out the door. The last thing Cupid remembered before everything went black was crashing into the garbage cans in the back alley and imagining wings.

Chapter 5

THE FLOATER

OR

SNATCHED

Cupid awoke to a cough. Not his own.

He kept his eyes steadfastedly shut, a precaution to give him time; he didn't know what he might find.

Internal diagnostics, he commanded of himself. *Oomph.* His head hurt badly, and he remembered why: *mortal booze.* It always had a bad effect and left him regretting at least part of its results. What he needed was ambrosia. Mortals drank coffee to ease a hangover; gods ate ambrosia.

Morning light bathed Cupid's still-closed eyelids and soaked him in warmth. *Dawn, then.* The heat felt soothing, but before Cupid dared face the day – and its possible repercussions – he opened his other senses.

He heard people walking and talking at a distance. He smelled something pungently sweet. He felt a hard surface beneath him, like concrete. *Not a bed then,* he thought, which made sense because his back was aching. His legs felt sore, probably from walking more in one day than he had in ages. His arm felt funny, and he realized there was something soft and wispy laying on it. *A woman's hair?* he guessed. *A feather?* And his fingers felt sticky.

Eyes still closed, Cupid rummaged through his memory of the previous night. It was painful; his head was splitting. He felt a presence. Cupid was fairly used to waking up next to a strange woman, even next to many strange women, but it was always an awkward thing trying to hold a conversation without letting on he'd forgotten names.

A second cough cut through his thoughts. This time Cupid was awake enough to realize that the cough was too low and barklike to belong to a female. That was probably worse news. In the past, if Cupid woke up in a strange place, that meant he was probably in the company of someone's girlfriend or daughter, and if that male could see him, that male was himself an immortal, and, if he was the jealous type, it usually meant a harrowing fight – or flight. Now that Cupid was visible even to mortals, the chances of a jealous, drunken brawl increased exponentially.

"I, yuh, don' know much," came a voice above him, a dull, thick voice that truly sounded like its owner didn't know *anything*. "But, yuh," it continued, "I know yer awake. You, yuh, betta come wit' me."

Cupid pictured a roly-poly, happily dimwitted idiot above him, and, when he opened his eyes and blinked away the immediate glare, he wasn't disappointed. His rather unfair prediction needed only a slight adjustment to fit the reality of fatuity before him.

"Cacciari, yuh, wants to see ya."

Cupid's stomach lurched. He belched and was surprised by a white feather bursting from his mouth. He sat up quickly and watched it drift onto his lap, which was draped in newspapers. *Must've used 'em for a blanket,* Cupid thought dully – *and as a napkin.* The newspapers were coated with an orangish, chunky, pungent goo that Cupid recognized as the scent he'd caught earlier. Sweet and sour sauce. Feathers and freshly picked bones littered the area. Cupid wondered when exactly over the course of the night he'd gotten ahold of a chicken, and, had he cooked it first? Eating mortal food was something he'd only done in his most desperate or drunken states.

Cupid nonetheless shrugged off concern over his cuisine and instead tore away a handful of newspaper covering his knees. He gasped, appalled.

Oh, gods, he thought. His legs were bare. His legs should *never* be bare in public. Not only that, but they were slick with some unrecognizable slime. Meat and lettuce stuck in the hair. He was a portable rat's feast.

Oh gods, he thought again. He ripped away the last remaining newspaper and shut his eyes in shame. All he had on was his *diaper* – his ridiculous, mocked, traditional diaper. All that protected the world from seeing him in all his glory was that wretched, detested thing, and even *that* was in tatters.

He *never* went out in just his diaper anymore. The whole look was so horribly cliché after mortal artists

started drawing him that way back in his youth, back when he couldn't control his invisibility. A particularly feisty seductee once told him that the diaper put her to mind of a needy infant more than a young, sexy god. Thus, he'd switched over to the hip, super-white suit centuries ago.

He already knew he was topless; his belly roll hung over the diaper's elastic band. Still, he slapped his hands to his chest, dreading, suspecting. He smacked skin. No diamond-studded necklace. His hands. No jeweled rings. His entire suit – top *and* bottom – were gone. Even his shoes!

Quickly, he swiveled left and right on his diapered bottom, hoping he might find his clothes, that maybe he'd just taken them off overnight during an amorous moment even in this dump. Instead, he was revolted all over again to see what he'd been resting in: a particularly foul trash heap consisting almost entirely of moldy food spilled from aluminum garbage cans. A memory flashed in his mind, one of him being thrown into an alleyway. He was still there, apparently, and he'd been nestling up to that garbage the whole night through.

He held back another burp – or maybe worse – and scrambled onto his knees searching for his bow and arrows. He spotted the nock of his bow peeking out from under one of the stinking piles. Diving for it, he snatched the bow, quiver, and loose arrows lying beside it. He found everything covered in sweet and sour sauce and just as

unsparkling as in his last memory, when Habandash had shaken the mojo out of them, but at least they were there, not apparently stolen like the rest of his belongings. He stuffed the arrows into the quiver, always a difficult job because his quiver was forever overflowing.

Another cough.

"Do you need a cough drop?!" Cupid asked angrily, the energy and noise of his own voice stabbing his headache. It was bad enough being seen like this but to be stared at for who knows how long by some coughing, probably plague-carrying, meandering cootie-fest was too much. He tucked his bare feet under his weight and wobbled into a standing position only to catch sight again of the rude hoverer, who was shaking his head.

Cupid stared openly. *Hmmmph,* he thought. On closer inspection, the voyeur wasn't nearly dirty enough to be called a flying disease, although his unhygienic coughing habit was annoying. He was clearly an angel, judging by the wings and bow, both of which were unusually tiny for his size. He wore a white T-shirt and blue jeans with bleached streaks on the thighs, which made them look slightly girly. Cupid looked at the angel's face. Round. Friendly-looking enough. Smooth, medium brown skin. Low, faded haircut. Was probably harmless. Still. "Who are you?"

A door to his right banged open, and a huge, muscle-bound man wearing all black stormed out. "'Nuf small

talk! Time to meet Da Boss." The bruiser grabbed hold of Cupid's arm and yanked him toward the center of the alley.

Cupid started shouting about just how important he was and how dare anyone handle him that way when another exceptionally large man emerged from the door and grabbed Cupid's exposed wings. Together, they forced him to the most open area of the alley. Cupid's bare feet slid on the slimy ground. The brutes wore black combat boots and had no trouble keeping their balance. They jerked his wings to keep him still and then expanded their own, tearing through their tight T-shirts in the process.

Cupid raged to the heavens. "You're angels! Fallen angels! How dare you touch me?"

But they ignored him. Cupid's world went black as a third person slapped a black felt bag onto his head. Cupid struggled and jerked, but it didn't loosen anyone's grip. He felt a lurch, and the ground disappeared beneath him as the criminals took to wing and dragged him along.

Through his shouts and curses and threats and writhing, several frightening things registered with Cupid: He didn't know where he was being taken nor by whom; he'd lost enough of his powers that mortals could see him; his plain-and-probably-powerless bow and quiver were left behind; and, there wasn't a thing he could do about any of it.

Chapter 6

TUSSLE WITH THE BOSS

OR

SINKING THE GONDOLA

"Ya bedda keep ya head down," warned one of the thugs. Cupid didn't know where they'd landed and couldn't see a thing through the thick, velvet bag over his head. He could hear and smell, though. Besides his own reeking breath caught in the bag, he smelled soap.

"I don't keep my head down for anyone, much less *fallen* angels," Cupid said defiantly. "I won't stand for it!"

Someone kicked the back of his knees, and down Cupid went, not standing for anything anymore.

"And stay bowed!"

Cupid tried to regain his footing, but the thugs wouldn't have it. They pressed down on him, one flattening Cupid's shoulders to keep him knelt and the other angel digging a knee into his back. After the second goon had dug his knee in good and hard, he pressed one hand on Cupid's neck and used the other to capture and crush Cupid's wingtips.

Cupid struggled uselessly. Well, it was useless *physically* but it did a lot to keep up his spirits.

It wasn't long before he heard approaching footsteps, which stopped right in front of him.

"You are ... *new* here." The voice was low and slow. Deliberate. Like its owner didn't tolerate repeating himself. "You don't know the way of things." He tapped his heel down onto the hard floor; it sounded like he was wearing spurs. "Your future depends on keeping away from what's mine and doing as you are told."

Cupid huffed, immediately incensed at both the threat and being kept under the velvet bag. He'd heard plenty of smack talk in his day, and he knew that every god protecting his or her own could ice a challenger with words, but Cupid didn't know who this jack was, and he was sure Jack wasn't a god.

"You don't know who you're talking to," Cupid snarled.

"No. It's you who doesn't know," was the bitter reply. "I am the boss here. I run things. What *you* do is fall in line like everyone else."

Cupid opened his mouth to argue but, before he could, the velvet bag covering his head was torn away and Cupid was momentarily blinded. He squinted while his watering eyes slowly adjusted to the harsh light. The room fell silent.

"Is that–?" began someone.

"Quiet!" demanded the deep voice.

Cupid looked up to see who was standing before him. The owner of that low, threatening voice was no one he knew, but the angel was powerful, judging by the

reverence shown him. Everyone obeyed him at once. A few tipped their head in acknowledgment. The stranger was taller than most, past middle-aged but, Cupid could tell, still strong and alert. He had greying hair along his receding hairline, pale blue eyes, and a crooked, once-broken nose. His pockmarked skin was noticeable but not off-putting. What unnerved Cupid was the way the angel stared hard, straight into his eyes, almost like he hated him, but Cupid was sure they'd never met before.

"Why are you here?" asked the hard-bitten angel.

"Your thugs brought me here," Cupid answered tersely, trying once again to stand. The strong hands still on him prevented it.

"No. Why are you *here*, inhabiting Earth?"

Cupid remained silent. He was not required to answer any fallen angel.

"You can be seen by mortals," continued The Boss slowly, thoughtfully.

This bothered Cupid, this sudden loss of invisibility, so he tried another of his powers, that of gathering water. He surreptitiously swirled his hand, which wasn't easy considering how he was held. Nothing. No water. All he managed to do was make his headache worse.

"You couldn't be seen before, being…" – The Boss looked towards the heavens and then back down to Cupid – "…well, being a love angel." He walked to the corner where the chunky angel from the alley floated detachedly.

The Boss stopped to touch something sitting on top of a wooden crate, and his face lit as he raised Cupid's battered bow and quiver. Cupid was relieved to see his celestial tools and wondered if Mr. Chunky brought them along.

The Boss' eyes crinkled above his wicked grin. He pronounced loudly and with obvious enjoyment, "You must have been *banished.*"

Cupid leapt to his feet but was quickly and painfully slammed back onto his knees. "I wasn't banished!" he retorted hotly through the searing pain. "I was-"

Cupid silenced himself, angry at being drawn into answering his captor. He was about to say he was "deposed" but realized he didn't know *where* he stood in the heavenly hierarchy. He wasn't sure he was *banished*, but, as he'd never accept being second string and living and working in Olympus as a lesser angel, he was *as good* as banished. Where could he go? Certainly not to ask *pretty please* for his rightful place, and Earth wasn't the place for him either. In any event, he decided it wasn't The Boss' business.

Cupid replied, "I can be where I wish." He said it as confidently as a god, but the traitorous tremors in his chest told him he did not truly believe it.

The Boss returned Cupid's bow and quiver to the crate. "You may *think* so, but you're not welcome here unless you choose to follow me. If you don't," and here he leaned down to put his face within inches of Cupid's, "I'll let my legions rip you apart, as I know they'd love to do.

Cupid's ears were pounding with the sound of his own heartbeat. He couldn't believe he was being threatened with death if he didn't submit to a fallen angel's commands. He wouldn't even obey a *lesser* angel, one welcome in Olympus, so why on Earth would he listen to the *fallen*, those flunkies banished to Earth for their failings or outright misdeeds? He wouldn't, he decided. He'd resist, even though he didn't really know how. He wished he had some ambrosia to strengthen him.

"I don't even know who you are, if anybody," Cupid said with as much arrogance as he could put into words. "You're not the boss of *me*."

His captor straightened to his full height and took his time in answering. Cupid took advantage of the delay to look around, get his bearings, maybe plan a daring escape. However, what he saw didn't offer much opportunity for heroics. He was in what looked like a warehouse with wooden walls and crates stacked against them. Those crates were probably where the soapy smell was coming from, Cupid thought. It was the sort of place you'd take a prisoner so he wouldn't know where your true headquarters were. Gods help them if this was their headquarters; they'd be even more podunk than he originally suspected.

The lead hoodlum leaned forward in a small bow and answered smoothly, "I am Vilnius Cacciari, The Boss. *Your* boss." He paused as if expecting Cupid to recognize the name. Cupid did not; he rolled the name around in his

mind a bit. *VILL nee us coch ee AR ee. Rhymes with Ferrari.*

"You'll follow first out of necessity, then out of loyalty." Cacciari raised an eyebrow, waiting for a response, which Cupid did not provide. The move seemed to insult him.

"You may have run the love machine upstairs, *Cupid*," he spat, revealing for the first time that he'd recognized his captive, "but I run it *here*. You don't know my territory, my people, and you *won't* know them the way you'd like. You will obey my orders absolutely, starting with staying away from the girl."

Cupid guffawed, trying to indicate his distaste at being given a command, any command, especially such a ridiculous one: "Stay away from the girl." *Pfft.* Cupid thought just how difficult it would be to follow such an order, were he so inclined. Staying away from a girl was almost an impossibility for him. He'd *never* made an effort to stay away from an available and receptive girl, and he didn't know if he was capable or whether it was even healthy. For a god to deny his strength couldn't be good for his longevity, he reasoned.

Cupid wracked his brain trying to remember which of the many women in his life might be the one considered off limits. The Rarin'-To-Go Romeo had been associated with so many lovely ladies and run from so many jealous boyfriends over the years that he honestly couldn't pinpoint the problem here.

The Boss must have noticed Cupid's lost look. "The girl from last night!" he hissed in disgust.

Cupid closed his eyes and tried to remember the previous night. Snippets of scenes flashed through his mind. He remembered sinking a gondola full of acrobats after fitting the boat with an outboard motor and crashing it into a bridge pillar; they'd all made it to safety. *No, that probably didn't happen yesterday.* He remembered a drinking contest in Russia that ended in a downhill ski match that triggered an avalanche. They, too, all escaped unharmed. *Hmmm, that was probably a different time, too.* He next remembered a music-filled campsite where he got quite frisky with a hairy gypsy woman. At least he *thought* it was a woman.

Cupid shook his head. *Focus!* he chided himself, trying hard to remember members of the fairer sex he'd met last night. He could see two girls dancing, Miss Twiggy and a curvy Hawaiian. There was a bunch more by a mechanical bull. A final flash of memory showed him grabbing the hips of a girl dancing for him. He gasped. *The stripper!* She was the only girl he remembered getting close to last night, and he wasn't even all that close. *She's his girlfriend?*

"Ah, I see you remember her now," The Boss said in a cool tone. "She *is* difficult to ignore."

Cupid thought this over. It was not unusual for a love angel, fallen or not, to actually fall in love, be it with a

princess or a pauper, a respected artisan or an overworked seamstress, a celebrated ballerina or a jeered-at stripper. It could be anyone. So it wasn't that Cupid, that King of Caresses and Knight of Nights, was judging Cacciari. He was merely surprised that Cacciari didn't try to keep her from dancing all over other men. All males get territorial, even angels. It's in their core.

Cupid wasn't at all interested in that girl. He couldn't remember a single feature of her face. In fact, he was pretty sure that he could recognize only her hips were he to have to pick her out of a line, but this issue wasn't about the girl. It was about a god's pride, and Cupid, that Dangerous Don Juan, wasn't about to let any fallen angel tell him whom to see. Cupid decided rather spitefully to steal her away – or at least make Cacciari think he had.

"Oooh, yes, her," Cupid sung in an ethereal, lost-in-thought sort of way. "She's lovely. Smells like vanilla milkshakes."

Cacciari's cool demeanor faulted for the briefest fraction of a second, long enough for Cupid to see concern. *He* should *be worried*, Cupid thought smugly. There'd never been a girl Cupid couldn't charm – or at least intrigue for a time.

The Boss shifted, turned to the floater, and called for his scissors.

The large bruisers grabbed Cupid again, held him tightly, and pushed his face so flat to the ground that Cupid

could have licked the dust between the floor's wooden planks.

Cupid struggled uselessly, demanding to be freed. He had a terrible feeling about this, and, for the first time in centuries, chose to evoke his more primal heavenly powers. Besides being able to spark love in mortals, which was his most often used gift, Cupid had the power to exude *Peace and Goodwill.* With great mental and physical effort – it was sort of like bearing down for a bowel movement – he could create feelings of harmony and oneness, even among the greatest of mortal foes.

It was a power he was loathe to use after some hard-learned lessons from his youth. He realized early on that he couldn't prevent war with it; he could only increase the likelihood of war and double the animosity between enemies once the mist wore off and the two combatants realized they'd almost conceded out of some strange sense of sentimentality or "oneness with humanity." Neither leader would want to be seen as weak by his subjects (or constituents, as the historical era might allow). Neither warrior wanted to be caught simpering and singing odes to the milk of human kindness. In other words, the *Peace and Goodwill* aura worked well on *open* hearts, not hardened ones.

This group, it turned out, was the hardened type. Not only did they balk at the mere scent of *Peace and Goodwill;* they mocked it.

"You think *P&G* will work on us?" taunted Cacciari to a howl of laughter from his goons. "Well, you don't know much then. We're wise to your tricks, and we gave up on peace when we were booted from the *Land on High*."

These supposed love angels mocked love. Cupid briefly wondered, as he stopped pushing P&G, what had happened to them to cause their fall and subsequent anger. His curiosity lasted but a moment before he was further humiliated – more so than by being kidnapped, more so than trying to defend himself while in his detested diaper, more even than being ordered about by a fallen angel.

As Cupid struggled and shouted and the chunky angel covered his eyes and begged for it to stop, Cacciari, scissors in hand, snagged the tip of one of Cupid's wings, pulled it away from his torso until it was fully extended, and slashed six strategically spaced flight feathers. He cut them mercilessly close to the shorter, protective, covert feathers and drew blood, then repeated the appalling act on the other wing.

Cupid roared and writhed in near hysteria. Clipping an angel's wings denied him flight and balance and *forced* him to walk like a common mortal. Cupid had eleven flight feathers per wing. Clipping six on each was more than half the total. He wouldn't even be able to glide. New feathers would, of course, replace the old during the next molt, but being cut so close, the new ones would take a long time to come in, and the act of the clipping itself

has been known to seriously damage an angel's psyche; in a god like Cupid, the emotion could be much worse.

When the despicable act was done, Cacciari's thugs released their steely grip. Cupid fell in a heap. He felt sick. His heart raced.

There was silence for a long while.

Floatie was the first to make a sound – a cough, naturally – after which he cleared his throat and said gravely, "Yuh, Boss, yuh, dat was … unnecess'ry."

The Boss scorched him with a look before addressing Cupid once more. "You've been kicked downstairs. You'll learn to obey. The work here isn't so different than what you've been doing for millennia, from a certain point of view." He chuckled at that, and his beefy gang followed suit.

"What I've been doing for millenia is matching ideal mates!" Cupid spat, wanting to imagine old couples holding hands. Instead, his mind's eye brought up the severe-looking woman whom he'd failed to hit and a male silhouette representing her nearly-escaped landscaper husband, neither of whom he'd been terribly concerned with. Cupid felt convicted but went on, "I spread perfect love!" This time Cupid wanted to imagine a huge wedding with smiling family all around. Instead, he pictured dozens of love angels with orders to correct his mistakes.

"Perfect love?! Your kind knows nothing of love! Take him out of my sight!"

Someone pushed the velvet bag back down over Cupid's head. It didn't douse the retreating sound of Cacciari's spurs. One strong pull on each arm and Cupid was hauled anew into flight. For the first time ever, Cupid was terrified to fly; if the goons lost their grip, if he fell, he wouldn't be able to stop himself from becoming a Cupid Crêpe.

Soon enough, though, The Love Lord felt their descent. His feet hit grass, then, a few steps later, flooring. The thugs ripped off the velvet bag to show Cupid his new, dreary, poorly-lit surroundings. They were inside a dusty, old house. The thugs flew off again, and only Float Boy stayed in the new place with him, clutching a shoebox and clothes procured who-knew-when – or maybe the clothes were already there in some corner closet. At any rate, the angel wore a heart-wrenching look.

Cupid settled to the floor, and the clothes-carrying angel fluttered down and sat next to him. It was … unexpected. Generous. Angels with working wings didn't typically deign to sit where mortals tread their filthy shoes, but the angel pushed the gear next to Cupid, folded his legs to sit criss-cross, and settled in to a sympathetic silence.

Chapter 7

THE SAFE HOUSE

OR

FASHION FLUB

"Thanks," Cupid said after an hour of silence. It was as sincere an expression of appreciation as the fallen angel's gesture of sitting on the floor, but Cupid's act was more generous, at least to *his* way of thinking. A god doesn't often thank a lesser being, much less a fallen angel, but, then again, a god doesn't often appreciate company like Cupid did just then.

"Yah welcome – for da clothes. I'm, yuh, sorry 'bout da rest. I, yuh, thought Cacciari wanted to talk, not to, yuh, hurtcha. And he kept yer bow 'n quiver."

Cupid schooled his face to show no reaction to the awful news that someone had his precious tools. There was nothing he could do about it now. He didn't know where Cacciari was, he was sure his companion – or jailer, as the case may be – wouldn't tell him, and he couldn't get there even if he did know.

Cupid turned his head to take a better look at the place. The house was dreary and poorly-lit, and, he came to realize, completely empty. Not a stick of furniture broke up the expanse of flooring. No chairs, no tables, no lamp nor knickknack graced any nook. There was no marble, no

fountain nor garden visible through the uncurtained windows. It was all dirty beige drywall and dry hardwood floor, the latter whitened in streaks by decades of dragging feet.

"Yo'r in Da Safe House. It's, yuh, where Da Boss takes new recruits to settle down. You supposed ta ask around, git a feel for *real* life here on Earth, and, yuh, eventch'lly give in and wanna see him. Yer ta use a remaining remige –"

Cupid swiveled to glare at him, and the messenger angel clarified, insultingly, as if Cupid, a winged god, didn't know what the word meant.

– "use a remaining *flight feather* to call 'im, and, yuh, Cacciari'll 'grant ya an audience', as he likes ta put it."

"Who *are* you?" Cupid asked with renewed bitterness. "And what is it you do for him?"

"Name's Jarel. Jarel Wright, and I, yuh, do what ev'rybody else here do. I gopher and shoot arrows."

Cupid balked. "You? You can't shoot arrows. You're *fallen.*"

Jarel's eyes fell, and Cupid knew he'd insulted him. He wasn't ready to apologize to a captor, even a crony one, so he merely mumbled, "I've offended you."

Jarel raised his eyes again and replied, "Yeah, I'm fallen, as is, yuh, all'a us down 'ere, but Cacciari got us doing da work, yuh, da work we's meanta do, shootin' arrows, so he's gotta lotta loyalty, enough even ta obey his command to, yuh, clip a fellow angel's wings." Jarel picked up a bit

of feather that had fluttered down from Cupid's left wing. Cupid snatched it away, furious that Jarel dared touch it.

"So you're Cupid, huh?" asked Captain Obvious.

"Of course I am." Cupid snapped. He was sorely tempted to remind Floatie that the angel had surely seen Cupid in the flesh at some point or other because nearly every love angel had. Every half century, Habandash organized a gathering of love angels with Cupid as the honored guest, always seated at the main table. Thus, every love angel had at one time or another seen him, and, even if Jarel had fallen from grace in his first fifty-year stint and missed the gathering, surely he'd seen Cupid's image somewhere in Olympus.

"Ya got the right outfit fer it, yuh, dat's fer sure," he said, pointing at Cupid's diaper. "So if ya really Cupid, why ya here, yuh, 'stead 'a up there?"

Cupid glared. He didn't want to get into it. He grabbed the clothes next to him and started pulling them on. The jeans fit too loosely, but the brown leather belt kept them up, bunching them like a drawstring potato sack. The grey trench coat smelled musty but covered his still-tender wings well enough; he winced when a jagged quill pierced his back. Next, Cupid opened the shoe box to find black wrestling shoes. Cupid was pretty sure Jarel had stolen them because they looked brand new and were just his size.

When Cupid finished pulling on the second shoe,

he looked up at Jarel and waited. Several uncomfortable seconds passed before Cupid demanded, "Well?"

"Well, what?" asked Jarel, knitting his brows.

Cupid huffed petulantly and stood. "My shoes. They need tying."

"So dey do," observed Jarel, straining his neck as if trying to see something hidden from view. Cupid stuck out his foot and pointed. Jarel didn't move.

"I'm not accustomed to dressing myself, yet I've already done most of it."

"Say what?! You, yuh, ain' accustomed ta dressin' yuhself?" Jarel stared at him incredulously.

"No," Cupid answered curtly before adding, "So?"

"So what?"

"So I expect a little service here," clarified the Pampered Prince, crossing his arms.

"You 'spect wrong," Jarel answered, crossing his arms in turn.

"Aren't you supposed to tend to me?"

"No," answered Jarel with an incredulous laugh. "My job, yuh, was to getcha here. I, yuh, took it upon maself ta getcha clothes an' tell ya how to reach Cacciari when da time come cuz I'm nice dat way, but I, yuh, certainly ain' gonna dress ya."

Cupid seethed but, wanting to get out of there, bent down and put both hands on his laces. He tried to remember: something about crossing bunny ears. He

fumbled with the loops and dropped them several times.

"Oh, my gods!" Jarel exclaimed. "You, yuh, don't know how ta tie yer laces, do ya? How'dya git yo' shoes tied all yer life?"

Cupid flung the laces to the ground and spat, "I've never had to tie my own laces! I've never woken up alone! The ladies love to dress me, and if they're not around in the morning, my driver does it. I'm out of practice!"

Jarel looked sideways in an I-can't-believe-this way before kneeling down to tie Cupid's shoes. As he did so, he noted, "You didn't answer ma question. If yo' Cupid – and not knowing how ta tie yer shoes would be right in line wid dat – then why're ya down here?"

"I don't want to talk about it."

"Huh! Well, I, yuh, ain't callin' you Cupid 'cause, first, the real Cupid'd be lordin' it on high, only comin' down here to arrow up the humans, and you, yuh, you clearly ain't lordin' ov'r nuthin'. Second, even if Cupid wanted ta slum it a bit, ta visit da lower classes a' angels, he'd be too pow'rful to allow Da Boss to do what he done. So, yuh, if ya don' give me yer *real* name, I'll jus' call ya *'D'* for diaper."

There was absolutely no way in Titanic Creation that Cupid was going to allow the use of a nickname that constantly reminded him of his most infamous possession, so he relented to give another name. *But not because* he *wants it,* Cupid told himself. *It's because* I *determine my name.*

"I'm Mars Jr., of course."

"Right, 'cuz Cupid's the son of Mars. Yuh, well, yo' mama mighta really named ya after the god of war even if ya ain't Cupid, 'cuz I 'spose yer mama hoped it'd grant ya some strength." Jarel looked Cupid over before adding, "Well, ya can't fault her fer trying."

Cupid's jaw dropped. He was pretty sure he had enough strength to level the flatulent floater with one strike. The smart aleck angel must have sensed violence; he fluttered out of Cupid's flightless reach.

"Anyway, *Mars Junior – M.J.,*" he stressed sarcastically, "I dun believe ya one bit. No matter. I'ma go get some mortal food. It'll taste terrible, but, yuh, it'll keep ya alive 'til ya give in to Da Boss. He's got the only ambrosia hoard outside of Olympus, so that's the main reason we, yuh, start working for 'im. Event'ally, ev'ryone gets hungry enough ta give in. See ya." And off he flew, leaving Cupid in a disheveled, wounded, and absolutely famished state.

Chapter 8

THE UNSAFE STREETS

OR

MODERN CHARIOTS

Cupid buttoned his coat and charged out of the house. The sun hadn't advanced far since Cupid awoke in the alley. *Apollo's chariot is only a few hours into its sky-wide journey,* thought Cupid. *So, mid-morning.*

Cupid didn't recognize the dingy, littered street on which he found himself, but he didn't recognize many mortal streets even in the best of circumstances. Sure, he knew Paris', Tokyo's, Buenos Aires', and New York's main thoroughfares, but those places were as sexy as he, he reasoned, so of course he'd be familiar with them. This place was decidedly unsexy.

He sniffed the air tentatively, hoping to smell ambrosia somewhere, anywhere, or a trace of something or someone he'd recognize so that this mortal world wouldn't seem so horribly foreign. He immediately regretted it. His senses were stronger than mortals'. The stench of stale beer, dog doo, and human indifference was nearly overpowering.

He'd always been able to smell human emotions, especially if there were lots of the same in one place. This is what led directly to his youthful failures in pushing Peace and Goodwill; groups of political leaders with strong

feelings of hatred and envy were a powerful draw to someone hoping to spread love nigh.

And this poor, wretched neighborhood suffered a lot of human indifference. The apathy was visible even in the untidy lawns and unchecked piles of garbage. People who care about others, Cupid thought, generally don't let their neighborhoods suffer such decay if they're at all capable of cleaning. Nor will they watch them silently go to seed and become cozy dens of malevolence. No, the people who lived here were poor and desperate. He could smell it. They chose survival over niceties.

This place would need a thousand arrows to re-infuse love, thought Cupid bitterly. He could do it, too, if he had his ancient, glittering tools back. He used to do it regularly back in the day. Cupid smiled as he remembered details of his long ago Love Hunts.

Hunts always started the same way. Cupid would summon Tyrone. Together, they'd stalk through the seediest parts of whichever town they chose that day and find some of the most impoverished, hopeless people they could. Then Cupid'd find their Love Connection. Right then and there. Put them at the top of the Hit List. His pride swelled at the thought. It brought those poor souls a happiness they never expected to find, with the added bonus of flouting The List. Cupid pictured Tyrone's smiling face, his laughing, just thrilled to be a part of it. Cupid's own smile at the memory faded, however, when he realized that

it'd been decades since they'd done that. Lately, Cupid had only worked the names on The Hit List. And now he wouldn't be doing even *that*, much less with the splintered, plain, unspectacular tools he now owned.

Newly depressed, Cupid decided to plunge forward. He didn't try his useless wings. Instead, he put one foot in front of the other, each step sticky thanks to the oddly superb traction of his new wrestling shoes. He walked in the middle of the road, preferring the open space to the littered and cramped sidewalk. His coat was warm. The breeze created by passing cars felt good. Cupid decided to inch closer toward an oncoming taxi cab. A sudden long blast rang out, and Cupid turned to see the driver's eyes widen. The man was laying on the horn. He swerved. Cupid, confused, arched his back but still felt the taxi's side mirror scrape across his back. *Mercury's Menace!* Cupid swore to himself, realizing he'd nearly gotten sliced in half. *I'm not impervious anymore! Curse my ridiculous condition!*

He stumbled off the roadway toward safer ground and collided into a young man walking past a light post.

The offended – or offender, depending on how you look at it – shouted an obscenity. Before Cupid realized there was a problem, he found himself on his back; he was pretty sure he'd been knocked flat.

The affronted young human stomped away, cursing about Outsiders not respecting him or his 'hood, and Cupid realized he would have to once again pick himself

up off the filthy ground. The Know-Nothing Nitwit put a hand down, unfortunately on a crushed beer can, which slid and crashed his elbow painfully to the pavement.

"Jupiter's Rage!" cursed Cupid. He leapt to his feet and looked around for witnesses. Sure enough, a couple of curtains fluttered behind closed windows.

The Mortified Monarch scurried off in haste, angry at everything and everyone. For several fast blocks, he simply put distance between himself and anything having to do with Cacciari. He looked up to see his uncle Apollo spur his sun chariot across the sky; Apollo looked serious and determined, his horses lathered. *At least someone still has a job,* Cupid thought, sulking. He kept walking.

At each block, he came across heart-sick scents and felt their owners' keen sadness, their deep, sincere desire to find love in their lifetime, to find someone with whom to share their highs and lows and with whom to grow old. He wanted to help the poor, powerless souls. Their misery nearly broke his super-sensitive heart, which was oddly more sentimental here on Earth. Maybe palace life put too much distance between himself and the people, he thought. Cupid vowed to remember them, the poor, powerless souls, and grant them their deep desire. Somehow. Some way.

When the pain of these sad beings became too much for his tender heart to bear, Cupid broke into a run. He could cover more territory than any human, and, by running, he'd be less vexed by the love-wanting. Also, he

figured he'd eventually hit a major metropolis, and perhaps run into someone he knew. Maybe he'd hit an ocean and call on Neptune to fetch his mom. *I certainly can't spare a single flight feather to call her myself,* he thought bitterly. *And maybe they'll have some ambrosia,* he went on.

He was starving. Famished. He imagined himself wasting away to nothing but then looked down at his fleshy belly and realized that might take awhile.

Our Flabby Infatuator didn't have to run so far as to hit a metropolis or body of water, though. At the city border, he spotted salvation: a lingerie shop. He skidded to a halt and stepped into the street. A speeding BMW nearly ran him over.

Mortals and their gods-forsaken mechanical chariots! he cursed. Checking both ways this time, he skittered across the rest of the pavement, reasoning that the risk was worth it. He would go in, and all of this would be taken care of.

Chapter 9

THE LINGERIE SHOP

OR

UNDIES AND OTHER UNMENTIONABLES

Cupid approached the dented metal door of the lingerie shop and pushed it open. It creaked back and hit another door fastened tightly against the wall. This second door featured prison-style, vertical bars, no doubt meant to keep thieves from pilfering the esteemed booty within.

The sole worker was a thin, elderly, white woman. She stood beside the counter with one arm crossed in front of her holding the elbow of the other, the hand of which propped up her chin. She swung a lazy glance toward the entry with bulging, grey eyes that made her look like a human-lemur mix. She wore her long, silver hair in a bun at the very top of her head and a tight, long-sleeved, high-necked-to-low-ankle dress that covered what Cupid decided had to be a form-enhancing undergarment because no one that skinny could have such curves naturally. She only half monitored a group of middle school girls who were huddled together giggling at some scandalous item.

Cupid stepped fully inside. The Corset Captain dropped her hand, forcing her neck to bear the burden of all that grey matter.

"Are you looking for something in particular, young

man? Perhaps for a gift?" She asked this with such haughtiness that Cupid got the distinct impression men weren't allowed, although that didn't jibe with his past. He clearly remembered his mother, Venus, dragging him to every celestial store ever opened when he was a lad and making him wait around *forever,* him wondering just how many girdles a female had to try on before picking one. The store matrons never looked down their nose at him back then. *Maybe because I was just a boy then and not an adult leering at pantyhose.*

The all-grown-up Master of Mojo ignored the governess and instead took a quick glance around. The shelves overflowed with bras, bandeaus, and shapewear of every size, color, and durability. None of it surprised Cupid; he'd seen it on actual ladies. He was, after all, the god of erotic love and a randy rake himself. He knew this was the place to be.

Cupid walked over to the group of girls and heard one gal ask another whether she should get something for the school dance. When Cupid stepped into their midst, their laughter died and their shocked faces rose. Cupid yanked the electric blue push-up bra out of the instigator's hands, much to her chagrin.

"Darlin'," advised Cupid, "if you make friends with this, neither you or anybody you're trying to impress will ever be happy with the real thing. Best to just let it go."

With that, Cupid yanked the blue monstrosity

off its hanger. The girls, suspecting trouble, ran out of the store just as the indignant proprietress shouted about scaring off customers. Her hand had nearly reached the phone (presumably to call the police and protect all the parlour's precious panties) when Cupid swung the blue wonder around and around over his head and called,

"Mother Venus,
Most fair of all,
Please come to me!
Please hear my call!"

The proprietress squawked into the phone while Cupid swung the frippery in his divine, outstretched hand. He might have looked like a sports fan twirling a towel had his swinging material not been lacey and electric blue. He squelched his shame and ignored the proprietress' continued complaints, knowing that the unmentionable bauble was the most effective way to invoke his mom. As the goddess of love and beauty, she was always drawn to whatever led to either love *or* beauty.

Sure enough, the sound of waves and surf arose from nowhere. The center of the shop glowed like dawn itself and then flashed the most lovely, blinding light to ever grace that froufrou place. When the flash ebbed, there stood his mother, Venus, naked as the day she was born and standing in her giant clam shell to boot, the same shell famously depicted in Botticelli's painting. Botti was one of Venus' boyfriends for awhile, and he liked her entrances

so much that he captured them in paint.

It was an odd painting, though; Cupid never thought it really looked like his mom. Her hair was a deeper red in real life, her jaw more square, and her figure more robust and curvy, the perfect hourglass. Cupid noticed over the years that people had described her differently, and he suspected she might look different to each male, taking on the distinct image of his ideal mate, perhaps even unknowingly, but Cupid never bothered asking anyone about it. The subject of his charming mother always brought on a glassy-eyed hypnosis in man and god alike. They all became mushy and useless. *You just can't talk to people after they'd seen Venus.*

Cupid didn't change appearance to each woman as far as he knew but, then again, he was only her son, so only half of her genes resided within him; thus, it made sense that he'd not have all her godly powers. He looked at Venus again, still glowing from her grand entrance.

The proprietress, queen of corsets that she was, was looking, too, awed.

Cupid shook his head, amused. Men who saw Venus' opulent theatrics usually fell over themselves with desire. Wide-eyed and seduced, they'd lift their hands in reverence to the goddess of pleasure, scrunching their greasy faces with such longing as to make heaven itself weep. Women were usually much better at her entrances. It was evident in their faces. They felt empowered by Venus'

beauty, intrinsically understanding that while they may not look exactly the same as the goddess, they *did* look just as good to the person destined to love them. Too bad the girls who ran out didn't get a chance to learn that; they'd have left the shop feeling no need for a push-up anything.

Venus slowly stepped over her clam shell. The sea wind swept back her hair and raised her arms in mock embrace. The surf sung odes of love. The dawning light caressed her bosoms. And the sole mortal in the room was transfixed.

"Gods, Mom! Cut it out!" Cupid cried. "Stop letting the human see you, and put some clothes on. We've got to talk."

Venus bent low, grabbed some surf from her feet, and blew it onto the woman. When the spray struck true, the mortal froze. She'd not remember Venus being there but would for days feel generous to those she loved, a gift to both her *and* them from the goddess of love.

Venus snapped her fingers and was instantly clothed – just barely – in a tiny, slick, light blue leather dress corralled by a red belt. Actually, the whole dress wasn't much more than a belt; it barely reached her chest and hardly covered her bottom, but it was the best Cupid could hope for from his mom, who was also the goddess of sexuality.

"Thou callest?" she asked in a still sexy yet mocking tone while grabbing and slipping on a pair of red silk heels

with faux feathers at the toes. She then strode over to a candy dish, snagged a fistful, and popped a chocolate into her mouth. She dropped the others down her cleavage, where they disappeared.

"Mom, I can't believe *I* had to call *you* after all that's gone on the past 24 hours," Cupid began, setting his hand at the small of her back and steering her out the door onto the sidewalk. "Where have you beeeeen?"

"I have been nigh, fair child. 'Twas I who steeled thee on the tally stage lest thou disgrace thy good name."

"What?! *You* froze me on stage?!"

"Aye, son."

"Mom, that was so embarrassing! I couldn't move! And why didn't you plead my case to Jupiter? You're older than him. Pull rank!"

"Age holds no higher rank than position," she gently retorted.

"Soooo," hedged Cupid, not entirely understanding her all the time, "you're saying age doesn't matter?"

"Truly, child. Thine honor was stolen that ill-fated day when the fair, young Mandre came your way."

"No poetry, Mom, please." Cupid noticed several handsomish men stop dead on the sidewalk and look longingly their way. "And concentrate, Mom, please! Turn off the whammy for awhile!"

"Yes, Lamb," she replied with thinly veiled disappointment. She was not often asked to cease her flirty

games. "But thou shouldst not plea for deliverance. Thou shouldst have conquered thine own enemy. Thou art the son of Venus and Mars. Thine arrows should strike strong and sure, thy duels e'er won."

Cupid looked down at his feet and swallowed hard. Hot, angry tears pricked behind his eyes, and his hands balled into fists. In his younger years, he'd have thrown a tantrum for sure, but he stopped throwing them the day Mars heard about it and dragged him to a fresh and bloody battle scene to "show him something really worth crying about." Ever since, Cupid was wary about showing his emotions too openly – a bender was one thing; bawling to his mama was another. He expected help from her, not chastising.

He looked up again to find more mortal men sniffing the air and looking 'round to spot the source of such enchantment.

"Mother, please, stop letting passersby see you – or smell you," he added at her look of mock innocence. "It's very distracting."

"'Tis the word of Jupiter and the labours of the angels that bestoweth the noble honor of *Cupid.* Neither Mars nor I may interfere in the naming of said title, Junior." She started to become transparent, and Cupid knew she would soon disappear.

"Wait, Mom! There's more!" he called, and the ghost of her solidified once more. "I've been accused of

mingling with a girl, but I didn't."

"Tall tales for the fainthearted," answered his mother.

"You don't believe me?!" Cupid realized that for the first time in his life he was in the odd position of trying to prove his innocent intentions with a girl.

"No," she practically sang, laughing. "I further ask why thou wouldst hope to prove thine innocence – and why, prithee, thou wouldst want to actually live through such innocence? Art thou not the god of desire?"

"Mom," Cupid huffed, both offended and ashamed at the same moment. "I've been threatened because of this girl, and my powers aren't what they once were."

"In matters of combat, thou wouldst do well to consult thy father."

Cupid was aghast. His lower lip trembled in incredulity. "Love can't help here?" he asked, stunned.

"Love e'er helps, son. The mere scratch of thine arrow changeth worlds."

A chiming ringtone broke in, and Cupid watched Venus pull a cell phone from her cleavage. *How much can she fit down there?* he wondered. She hit a button to see a strapping young stud wearing nothing but jeans and a cowboy hat.

"Hale be thou," she answered. Cupid rolled his eyes and wondered when she'd modern up and say *hello*, not to mention drop the *thou*s.

She covered the mouthpiece and turned to her son. "I depart. Booty call." And with that, she allowed the whole street to see her before disappearing in a ping of white light. A squeal proceeded a car crash, a whistle proceeded a stampede, and Cupid was suddenly rushed by a dozen men asking where the beautiful lady had gone. He shooed them away and only then, when his stomach growled, did he realize that he'd forgotten to ask her for ambrosia.

He was famished and losing strength by the hour. Ambrosia not only fed the gods but ensured their immortality. Cupid wasn't exactly sure he could stay immortal without it; yes, he was a god, but he was lacking his rightful position in Olympus. He just didn't know anything for certain.

Cupid turned and surveyed his surroundings. *What now?* he wondered. He turned north but had no desire to suffer an eventual cold season. He turned south but felt immediate boredom; he'd spent so much time vacationing in Puerto Vallarta, sweating like a pig, that the idea of more heat lacked all appeal. He was pondering heading east when another squeal of tires thrust his thoughts aside. He looked up to see his old limo skid through a turn and bear down on him. Tyrone was wide-eyed behind the wheel.

Chapter 10

THE STASH

OR

THE MEMENTO

The candy-apple red love machine screamed to a halt within an inch of Cupid's knees, and Tyrone leapt out of the driver's seat. He scrambled to the front of the vehicle and started pawing Cupid hysterically.

"Sir, sir, are you alright? Where've you been? I've been looking everywhere for you. I finally caught the scent of sea foam and thought Lady Venus might be near."

Cupid immediately wondered whether Tyrone hoped to find *him* alongside his mother or just her alone. His mother had every man on a string. She couldn't help it.

"Tell me, Tyrone. What does my mom look like?" Cupid tried to keep his face neutral. "Describe her."

Tyrone stopped his pawing and stood tall. Dropped his hands. Looked wary, like a soldier facing inquisition. "I never touched her."

"Don't get paranoid," Cupid quipped.

"But I never did anything to her! Is she hurt?" His hands fisted at his side. "'Cuz if she is, I'll be just as angry about it as you, and we can go hunt down the rat who hurt her."

Cupid paused for patience, then replied, "Just

answer the question, T. What's she look like?"

Tyrone relaxed his hands and sighed, satisfied that he wasn't being accused of anything. He looked skyward, then back down. His eyes softened, and he spoke gently and reverently. "She is the most beautiful living thing I have ever seen. She is womanhood itself. She is love incarnate – and beauty and grace – all mingled and bound in one. She is ... exquisite." Tears beaded his lashes, his soul weeping for want of her.

"No, no. I know all that," Cupid insisted with a sweep of his hand. "I mean, what color is her hair? Her skin. How tall is she?"

Tyrone stepped back and eyed Cupid cautiously. Finally he asked, "Are you still drunk?"

"Just describe her!" ordered Cupid, resuming the usual bossy demeanor he reserved for his former driver.

"Black, curly hair. Brown eyes. Brown skin. Short. Big-bottomed. Perfection," he ended with a sigh.

So I was right, Cupid thought. *Her appearance does change. Interesting.* He returned his attention to Tyrone's first question. "I've been better. I–"

But Tyrone wasn't listening. He was sniffing the air slowly and dreamily, ensnared by the lingering smell of – and talk about – Venus.

"HELLO, Tyrone!" Cupid snapped his fingers in front of his friend's eyes. "She's gone. Now why are you here – and in my limo?

Tyrone shook off the enchantment and suddenly remembered his quest. "Oh, sir! Mr. Habandash caught up with me about an hour after you left and told me to surrender the limo immediately to the new Cupid, but I begged for another hour. He knows I've worked with you for a long time, so he granted it, but I'm way overdue. Then Pip came to collect it. I dodged him once, but I can't evade him forever. Anyway, sir, I wanted to tell you the reason Mr. Habandash searched me out. He told me he still considers you a working angel and expects you to report for duty tomorrow – er, today. You're about three hours late now, so you could expect grief about it, but, sir, here's your chance to right this terrible wrong. If you work hard, maybe after a few years of proving yourself to be serious again, you could regain the title of Cupid!"

"I *am* Cupid!" he forcefully asserted while not knowing whether to be thankful that Tyrone was trying to keep him employed or incensed that his faithful driver-slash-assistant thought it would take him years rather than days to resume his rightful place. "Tyrone, what are people saying?"

Tyrone took another step back and began studying his shoes in earnest. *So,* Cupid thought. *It's that bad.*

"Tyrone," Cupid prodded.

His friend raised his eyes, which looked tired and saddened. "Well, sir, Olympians like drama, as you know. The gods especially seem to feed on it, no offense meant to

you, sir. So they seem to be enjoying the new man, sir, and don't appear to be in any rush to reestablish the status quo."

"Soooo," Cupid began, processing the information, "you're saying, they don't *miss* me?"

Tyrone cleared his throat. "Not yet, sir, but they will. He's no match for you, sir. There's never been a better Cupid, and there never will be!" Tyrone pounded his fist into his palm for emphasis.

"For a fact," Cupid agreed, nodding once. He glanced at his limousine and suddenly remembered. *My stash!* "Tyrone, tell me you haven't cleaned up in there!" Without waiting for an answer, Cupid ran to the limo, wrenched open the back door, and dived inside.

Tyrone hustled over. "What are you looking for?"

"Ambrosia," Cupid answered over his shoulder, digging his hands into back and side compartments before thrusting his upper body through the partition separating front and back. "I usually keep a few squares in here for an emergency." He opened the glove compartment. Nothing.

"The girls cleaned you out yesterday," Tyrone answered, "and I wasn't about to restock it for anybody else."

Cupid stepped out of the limo. He felt his cheeks go ruddy with rage. "So Habandash expects you to hand over my limo to the new guy, does he? Well, then, let's make a gift of it!" Cupid slammed both hands on the trunk, hopped onto the back, and scrambled to the roof. When he found his footing, he stood astride the sunroof

and dropped his pants.

"Sir!" exclaimed Tyrone.

Passersby stopped in their tracks. To their mortal eyes, eyes that could not see the limo nor its driver but that *could* see Cupid, this was an impossibility. A floating, slovenly dressed man was squatted mid-air and relieving himself into open space. Equally impossible, his feces plopped not on the ground but two feet above it.

"Ha, ha! A little gift for the false idol! You want my limo, Pretty Boy?!" he shouted to the heavens and, presumably, an absent Mandre. "Well, here it is – with a happy memento from me! May it leave its stench for the ages!"

As Cupid crapped into his own personal Porta Pottie, a city bus rounded the corner and headed their way. Tyrone focused his sharp eyes into the oncoming carrier and spotted the familiar, flowing, white and black robes of nuns' habits.

Moving faster than the collection plate, Tyrone jumped to snag the corner of Cupid's trench coat and pulled as hard as he could. Cupid tumbled off the roof. Turds flew everywhere. The Prince of Poop rolled, leapt to his feet, and, pleased as punch, smiled broadly for the crowd. The witnesses gasped, covered their eyes, or scattered, and Cupid hoisted up his pants just in time for the devoted to pass untroubled.

A light flashed behind them, and both Cupid and Tyrone whipped around to face it. The glare ebbed,

bringing into view that disloyal little zit, Pip, and, even worse, the newly-employed *Cupid* Mandre, arm in arm in arm with three escorting angelettes.

"There you are, Mr. Tyrone! Oh, goodness, why are you with *him?*" Pip said "him" as if the very pronoun offended him as much as he to whom it referred.

Cupid grinned and thought, *Yeah, you'll be a lot more offended pretty soon. Step into the limo, why dontcha?*

"I've been searching high and low for you, on Heaven and Earth," Pip went on. "You and that vehicle are to report to its *new* rightful owner. Cupid needs it for his traveling comfort."

"Cupid is–" Tyrone began, and Cupid was sure he would have continued to say something like "Cupid is right here, and he's not that slimeball standing beside you," but Cupid – Mars Jr., that is – put a hand on Tyrone's shoulder to stop him.

"Oh, *Cupid's* going to need a buggy, to be sure," Mars Jr. completed. "He'll want to keep the ladies comfortable, and I should know. They'd been faithful to me for years. I suspect"— and here he threw the angelettes a scathing look — "that they'll prove themselves as faithful to the *new* Cupid as they were to *me.*"

The angelettes didn't appear abashed; in fact, one retorted rather harshly, "Oh, you mean the same way you were so faithful to us, do you? I don't recall getting invited back into your limo more than once, and neither have

the other ladies I've talked to, so don't preach to us about loyalty."

Mandre smirked, and Mars seethed. It was not in his nature, as the son of both the god of war and the goddess of love to have peaceful, lasting relationships, but he'd heard once, talking to his dad, who didn't want his son to spend nearly every waking moment contemplating war like he did, that a person's future isn't immutably tied to his past. A man *can* change his destiny, he'd said, if he was so inclined. It just so happened that Mars Sr. was so good at and interested in war that he had little thought for anything else.

Tyrone pulled from his pocket the shining silver car key on its diamond heart keychain. Mars leaned in to whisper in his ear, "Don't lose your job for me, T. Just make sure to lock their windows shut."

Tyrone chuckled and stepped to his door. He simultaneously hit the partition-up and windows-lock buttons and then opened the back door for his new charge, the lady escorts, and Pip, who stepped toward the luxurious black leather with obvious satisfaction. Tyrone quickly snapped the door behind them and sprinted into the driver's seat. Mars heard screams and shouts and banging on windows before Tyrone peeled away.

Mars burst out laughing and, smug for the moment, looked up once again. Apollo was more than half way through his daily sprint. Mid-afternoon. Now what?

Mars needed a plan and sorely wanted to call on his dad, but he knew that would be even more futile than calling his mom. *If Mom scolded me and offered the whoppingly super advice that love helps, imagine what dad'll do. He won't just scold me for losing a duel, he'll drag me off to Sparta to learn how to fight like a real soldier.*

Mars stood there, not knowing what to do next until he heard small wings flapping furiously above. He looked up to see Jarel drop out of the sky, plummeting towards him.

Chapter 11

HIS AND HER BELLIES

OR

LOVE MISLED

Mars Jr. took one long step to the right and slid over as gracefully as if he were dancing The Electric Slide. Jarel's tiny wings flapped frantically, and Mars couldn't help but think that those poor little limbs were perpetually overworked. Jarel landed with a thud on the very spot that Mars had vacated.

"Got ya some food, M.J.," Jarel said, huffing and handing him a cardboard box with wet-looking stains at the bottom. "They call this stuff 'pizza'."

Mars had been to Earth enough times to have heard of it, along with many other foods, but he wasn't exactly sure what "pizza" was, so he let Jarel explain.

"There're, yuh, lotsa diff'rent kinds. This here one, yuh, is whatcha call, 'veggie pizza'. It's plant growth an' fermented milk bits on a baked grain mass. Di'nt wanna getcha the 'meat pizza'. The mortals put dead animal chunks on it."

"Ugh," groused Mars, who conveniently forgot that he'd possibly eaten a raw chicken the evening previous. The stuff smelled ghastly compared to his usual fare, but anything would. *Ambrosia's incomparable,* thought Mars,

and he could swear he smelled it even now. Grimly, he realized the smell was probably lingering off of Jarel, who no doubt got his regular share while working for … *that foul beast who would remain unnamed.*

"Yeah, pizza 'snot great, yuh, but it'll keep up yer strength. I can survive a coupla days, yuh, maybe a week on this stuff, but, yuh, a god, if that's what yer still claimin' to be, yuh, prolly couldn't go past a day wi'out ambrosia."

Junior thought back and realized he was coming up on 24 hours without the food of the gods. The Woefully Weakened Wooer waited until Jarel prodded him. Then he pulled a triangular wedge out of the circular, granular mass and pushed it into his mouth. He bit. *Soft and tearable,* he thought. He chewed. *Make that terrible. And greasy. And salty.* He swallowed and felt the foreign lump descend jerkily, forced down by every uneasy, protesting esophageal muscle he had. It was entirely different than the airy, melt-in-your-mouth, caress-your-throat, smooth sweetness of ambrosia. Mars, nauseous, nearly vomited the chunk back up.

"Finish it, M.J., or you won't have the strength for our trip. And I got a surprise fer ya, too."

Our Object of Worship did as he was told, too grateful for food – *any* kind of food – to keep up his usual, haughty air. He choked down every bit of it and was surprised to feel marginally better afterward – well, stuffed, anyway.

"Here." With that simple word, Jarel offered a square inch of ambrosia wrapped in thin, gauzy cloud. It looked and smelled heavenly, and Mars, that Edacious Deity, seized it. It slid down his throat so easily, so softly, yet its effect was powerful. He rolled his neck in almost obscene pleasure and instantly felt more alive, more vigorous, more determined. Another ten or so squares and he'd have felt invincible.

"Ohhhhhh, yeahhhhhhhhhh," Mars moaned unabashedly. "That's the stuff!"

"Don' get use ta it," warned Jarel. "I can't, yuh, sneak ya no mo'. Yer only option is to, yuh, join Cacciari."

"Not a chance," Mars chirped energetically, happy on ambrosia. "I want to go back to the spot where we met."

"Da alley?" asked Jarel.

"The very same," Mars replied, and, to show he meant business, The Revved Rapscallion walked around behind Jarel, grabbed hold of his white T-shirt with both hands, and commanded, "Mush!"

Jarel looked over his shoulder and frowned. Nonetheless, he spread his tiny wings – smacking Mars in the face in the process – and flapped furiously, breaking gravity's hold.

Jarel, puffing and straining under the exertion of the added weight, still managed to ask, "Why da alley? S'nothin' there."

Mars smirked. "I know that's where she works, so

that's where I'm going."

"S'where who works?"

"The girl. Go higher," Mars commanded.

Jarel climbed into the clouds, getting them both coated in mist, before stating the obvious. "Yuh, lotsa girls work der, M.J. S'a strip club."

"Yes, well, it's also where a very particular girl works, now isn't it?" Mars teased knowingly. "You don't have to cover up for him, you know."

"Who?"

"Whom," corrected Mars.

"Dat's what I'm askin' you." Jarel's forehead corrugated in confusion.

"The Boss," replied Mars impatiently.

"Wha' about him? He, yuh, don' work der."

"But he doesn't want *me* there, now does he?" Mars teased again, shaking Jarel's shirt for emphasis.

"How would I know?" asked Jarel. "Hey, are you still drunk 'cuz I ain't got no mo' ambrosia to fix ya."

Mars rolled his eyes and scanned the city below. It wasn't easy to tell one square roof from another, but he spotted the giant red flag after which the club was named billowing atop a red brick building that towered over a garbage-strewn alley. Zeroing in, he spotted white feathers among the rubbish.

"There it is. Down, Jarel."

Jarel stopped his forward-moving, horizontal flight

to hover vertically above the bar. He crossed his arms and looked over his shoulder again at Mars.

"Now, you didn' say the magic word."

Our Divine Romeo, spoiled as he was, only scowled.

Jarel lowered his chin. "You want me to move again, you, yuh, gotta say 'please'."

"I didn't have to say it before," countered Mars.

"Jes' cuz I do as ya say once, yuh, don' mean I'm, yuh, gonna keep doin' it. 'S *me* doing *you* the favors here."

"You were somewhat ... compelled to obey, weren't you?" asked Mars, thinking it was his godly powers – infused with ambrosia – that forced Jarel's obedient flight.

"Whatchoo talking 'bout?" asked Jarel incredulously.

"Well, me being who I am and commanding you to fly. You really hadn't any choice but to obey a god. Plus the ambrosia and all."

Jarel barked a laugh, which Mars chose to hear as another cough. "If'n that was the case, oh-god-of-one-if-you're-any-god-at-all, we couldn'ta taken ya to see Cacciari in the firs' place. You was, yuh, hollerin' and squirmin' for it ta stop."

Mars frowned, seeing the logic there.

"I flew jes' now to be agreeable, 'cuz I don' like confrontation, but I also don' like being ordered around. I only obey Da Boss 'cuz I, yuh, ain't got no choice lessin' I wanna curl up 'n die widdout ambrosia. Now, you, you say it 'er I'll drop ya righ' here and be done witcha. Da

boss'll be a little mad at me but not all *dat* much."

Mars stared at Jarel, who stared right back. Sensing a stalemate, Mars closed his eyes and breathed deeply. He felt ego-deflating humiliation pressing down, flattening him like a cold, wet blanket. He let the air out with a heavy sigh.

"Fine," he murmured through gritted teeth. "Please. Pleeeeeease down right here."

"Dere now. Dat, yuh, wasn't so hard, now, was it?"

Mars thought it was harder than defeating a Gorgon.

Jarel lowered his head and slowed his furiously fluttering wings. Gravity pounced at the chance and yanked its captors back to Earth. They landed in the alley – harder than Mars was accustomed – but at least it wasn't the threatened free fall.

"Okay, yuh, so we're here. Now whatcha want?"

Mars let go of Jarel and stepped to the club's back door. He had no trouble maneuvering the slimy alley this time, thanks to the traction of his wrestling shoes. Jarel slipped around in worn sneakers. *Heh heh.*

Mars waved a hand over the deadbolt and heard the latch slide.

"The place'll open in a few hours, M.J. No need to, yuh, break in."

"I'm not breaking in," countered The Gotta-Get-Some God, stepping into the gloom of the posterior

hallway. "Well, not to steal or anything. The girl from yesterday, she's—" Mars sniffed the air and turned toward a wall to his right. "The girls are gathered together farther inside."

He turned back toward the darkness and strode confidently in, turning right and then left until reaching a hallway speared by thin rays of light escaping around closed dressing room doors. At the final door were two large men, milling about, no doubt waiting for the club to open and for their daily duties to begin. They startled at his appearance, but their faces soon turned lax. Mars' mojo washed over them. They smiled and quickly accepted his presence.

Mars nodded their way and kept walking. The hallway slanted downward and then reached a small stairway leading right, onstage. Mars veered left, continuing down the slanted walkway to the empty and unlit patrons' gallery. He sat at a small, round table just out of reach of the stage lights. Jarel joined him.

"Okay, Ladies. Line up for rehearsal," shouted a raspy male voice from offstage. The ladies, dressed in shorts and tiny tops, lined up. Mars slowly scanned the row of exposed abs, his eyes lingering over each mid-section, conducting an unquestionably accurate umbilical ID. When he spotted the right belly button, his eyes lit up.

"And there she is," he whispered.

"There who is?" asked Jarel.

Mars ignored him and stepped forward to reach the tables bathed in stage lights.

The crowd onstage stopped moving. The noise backstage lessened, and everyone slowly, oh, so slowly, broke into a drunk-with-Mars'-mojo smile.

"Well, if it isn't my good friend, Mr. C!" exclaimed one of the bouncers who'd yesterday tossed him out on his rear. Mars vaguely remembered him introducing himself as DeShaw. "Glad you're back. Hated to send you packing yesterday, but – " he touched his finger to the side of this nose in a knowing manner – "you can't be touching the ladies."

"Well, not when we're working, anyway," cooed a 30-something redhead with a Southern drawl wearing a sparkling blue glitter bikini top, red shorts, and clear plastic platform wedges. "But, Honey, we can choose to see who we want off hours, and I get off work at three. I'd love for you to walk me home."

Mars smirked shamelessly, that Flighty Philanderer. "Cupcake, you are lovely, and an evening with you would be sublime, I'm sure, but I've got business with *her* tonight." He pointed at the girl whose belly he'd identified. Their eyes met. "My dear, would you come with me?"

All faces turned to an emaciated, dishwater blonde with high cheekbones and light brown circles under her eyes. Perhaps the circles were the result of dehydration, Mars thought. She wore a blue denim tube top and

matching shorts, which barely managed to stay atop her visible hip bones, and the whole of her teetered on high, white stilettoes. She wobbled like a reed in a windstorm, but her eyes soon revealed that she remembered him, and now the dashing man chose her.

"I … I'd love to … but I'm working … and I can't … "

"Aw, you can go say hello to my buddy," slurred DeShaw. "Can't she, boss?"

For a moment, Mars thought Cacciari might make his presence known, turn the corner, and put up a fight for his girlfriend, but the only one to show himself was an older, bushy-mustached Middle Eastern man with the same glazed look as the rest of them.

"It is good, Rachel," he reassured her, bobbing his head and lifting his palms in peace. "You take break and be back for show. It is good."

Mars took the final steps toward the stairs and extended his hand to help her down.

"I'm Rachel Kiskis," she squeaked.

"And I'm confused," Jarel hissed behind Mars. "Ain' you, yuh, suppose' to be gettin' a feel for life here, away from Olympus? Ain' you, yuh, supposed to be askin' around, makin' up yer mind ta join Da Boss widdout a fight?"

"He'll come to me once he sees who I'm with," Mars answered, not taking his eyes off Rachel, who'd descended the stairs slowly, amazed at her luck. "The Boss may have scissors, but I have the power to keep a

girl's attention for a very long time."

"Yeah? So?" asked Jarel.

Mars was directing Rachel out the front door of the establishment. "So, Dollface, what can you tell me about The Boss?" he asked as they reached the street.

Dollface – Rachel – answered promptly. "Well, he wants us girls to stick with him." Her voice was unusually high, falsetto even, like she was trying to sound even younger than she was. "He doesn't want us going anywhere else."

"Hmmm," was Mars' neutral reply.

"He's nice enough to me, though, I guess. I think he likes blondes."

They'd only walked half a block, during which Mars hadn't gotten much useful information out of her, when he heard it: the familiar, air-slicing zings of arrows in flight. Zing, zing! One rapid-firing arrow after another.

Mars decided in a moment. Placing his hand on the small of Rachel's back, he steered her back toward the club.

"Where're ya goin' now?" demanded Jarel.

"Is that all the time for our date?" asked Rachel sadly. "It was so short."

"Oh, believe me, a lot can happen in a short time," answered Mars. "You just tell the other girls that if they tease."

Rachel laughed and walked through the club door

that Mars held for her a second time. She stopped when he offered a conciliatory, "Perhaps we'll meet again, ma chère." His French brought a smile to her face. She turned again and disappeared into the interior darkness.

"Now, what was da point in dat?!" asked Jarel when the door closed behind her, but this question went as ignored as the previous.

Mars turned and broke into a run, chasing the sound of rapid-firing arrows. *Maybe the love angel firing them would have more ambrosia,* thought Mars, *or news of Mandre's Adventures in Excrement. Heh heh.*

Mars ran three city blocks in mere seconds. Turning a corner, he caught sight of an arrow in flight.

The arrow should have been shiny, nearly blindingly gold, so glistening and brilliant that it would give off rainbow-colored shimmers as it cut the air. But this arrow, Mars saw immediately, was different, odd. The gold was muted, almost dull, and it looked fatter and heavier. It surely wasn't as aerodynamic as *his* arrows because it wasn't going far. It would only just reach the couple which was its target. And the sound it emitted was somehow … off.

Mars quickly turned to see from where it had come. The opposite of its trajectory led to … *GRRR* – his old limo with Mandre's top half sticking out of it. Mandre wasn't holding his nose or gasping for breath, so Tyrone must've had to clean out that limo in record time. Mars would have felt sorry for Tyrone, maybe, but just then Mandre spotted

Mars and taunted him in a way that no god should have to endure: he flicked his fingers outward from under his chin. The gesture was as childlike as blowing a raspberry, and it worked.

"You job-stealing fraud!" Mars shouted, enraged. "How dare you mock me, riding around in my limo with my girls and my driver, pretending to be as skilled as me?! I challenge *you* to a duel! And *this* time, we'll see who wins!"

"But we *have* dueled," replied Mandre in his deep, soothing voice; it was far sexier than Mars' whining, shouting one. "And you lost. Spectacularly." The words carried all the way across the street and echoed cruelly. "How could we replicate that historic defeat? And why would you want to?!"

Mars heard girly laughter from within the limo. Soon, hands jostled at the edge of the sunroof, and one girl squeezed her way up to stand alongside Mandre. The two had to press together to fit, and Mars caught Mandre's satisfaction over it. *The pervert,* judged Mars before recognizing that he'd have relished the tight squeeze, too.

"Those girls only think you're better than me!" declared Mars, to which the angelette laughed. "But they'll learn better!"

"Well, I'll spend time with each one of them, I promise," retorted Mandre. "And when I've proven to them that I'm superior, I'll prove it again so they're sure."

"Ha!" laughed the girl before singing to Mars, "Oh,

exxxxxxx-Cupid! You are sooooo yesterday! And you smell! Ha, ha, ha!" And down she ducked, back into his old transport.

It was one thing for *Mandre* to taunt him, but quite another for an angelette to do so. He'd remember her, her insults. Just a day before, she'd have likely bowled over another girl for the chance to sit beside him in his famed limo, and he'd have loved her enthusiasm. Mars thought back to the thousands of angelettes who'd graced his backseat. None really set off great, heartfelt memories. They were all pretty interchangeable, all seeming to want to feed off his celebrity as much as he fed off their passion. None intrigued him, and now the Self-Absorbed Caesar knew why. *They're takers,* he judged, before again recognizing their shallow actions reflected in his own behavior. *But Mandre too will earn the harsh lesson of "celebrity love" and celebrity lost.*

"Nothing to say, *Mars Junior?*" queried Mandre loudly. "No pithy jab? I'll tell you what. I know you miss being a part of the action. I'll hire you. You can clean the seats in *my* limo."

Laughter burst from within the vehicle, and Pip popped out.

"Mars Junior," he pronounced as loudly as his tinny, mini-voice would allow. "If you interfere once more with the duties of the duly appointed Cupid, I'll report it!" He crossed his twiggy, little arms and bobbed his head once

importantly. "You have been warned."

"*You* interfering wid *him?*" Mars heard beside him. He looked over in time to see Jarel pick up a stone and launch it toward the vehicle. A second later, that magnificent mouse of the skies, that pesky Pip, got pebble-pegged right in the head; he dropped into the sunroof, presumably knocked out cold. Mars heard ladies' screams.

"Augh! It's dead!"

"Ew, it looks like a bug! Open the door! Kick it away!"

But before anyone could drop Pip outside, the limo peeled away. Mars caught sight of Tyrone in the driver's side mirror, laughing his head off and waving goodbye.

Mars turned to Jarel. "Why'd *you* get involved?"

"We Fallen got some'n aginst the higher-ups, and I, yuh, don't appreciate dem comin' down here insultin'."

Mars watched his angry face for a moment before asking, "What is it, exactly, Jarel, that The Fallen have against Olympians?"

"Not all Olympians, but most, I suppose, for not speaking out. I'll 'splain. Come on."

Mars did plan to follow but was momentarily drawn to look toward the couple to whom the arrow had been directed. They had been holding hands and looked reasonably happy together before, but as Mars watched, a change came over them. They let their hands slip apart, and they stepped back from each other. As they increased

the distance, one said something about a weekend spent apart. The other voiced suspicions that something had happened. Before Mars' eyes, the once-content pair were in a sudden and heated argument. The girl threw her hands up and stormed across the street. The boy shouted and stomped the other way.

Mars' brows furrowed. He walked cautiously to where they had stood, perplexed at the strange reaction. His arrows had never malfunctioned that way. He looked around. There, on the grass beside the sidewalk, lay the arrow. Dull gold with black fletching. Mars picked it up, careful not to prick himself with the tip, and turned it over in his hands. *Strange,* he immediately thought. *Too light for real gold. Too heavy for wood. And … hmmm. Not right. Not right.*

Mars eyes widened. He gasped in shock and threw the terrifying thing to the ground. He wiped his hands frantically on his coat and stomped on the arrow at the same time, desperate to break it into a million pieces. It bounced slightly under Mars' shoes but wouldn't break.

Jarel caught up and grabbed Mars' shoulders, turning him to look eye to eye.

"It can't be," Mars said, feeling his own face contort with disbelief. "No! No! No!"

"Yeah, M.J.," Jarel answered, sadness in his own eyes. "You, yuh, see what we've become."

Chapter 12

THE TRIO

OR

THE FAINT AMONG THEM

Jarel steered Mars away and whispered, "We, yuh, can't talk here. We goin' ta see some people. Grab hold and think light thoughts 'cuz I'm, yuh, gettin' tired 'a carryin' yo' dead weight."

Mars bristled and intentionally thought *heavy* thoughts: *Anvils, pianos, marble temples.* Notwithstanding, the ground fell away, and the air around him changed as they took flight. It was unsettled, and turbulence occasioned another terrifying flight with deep dips and shoulder-numbing shakes. Soon enough, his feet again touched the back yard of the dilapidated Safe House.

His sweat-soaked and starting-to-smell tour guide led the way in. Mars gave him a 10-step head start and then followed. The way in from the back of the house was as bleak and fusty as the front, Mars decided. When Jarel entered the main room ahead, Mars heard commotion.

"Jarel! Gods, where have you been?"

"We been lookin' everywhere fo' you, man! We heard da stupidest rumors goin' 'round dat-"

But whatever the rumors were, Mars, crossing the room's threshold, didn't get to hear.

Someone gasped, and a female angel cried out, "So, it's true! You're hanging out with Cupid!"

Mars focused on her as the fairest sight in the room and the only angel there that he'd ever feel comfortable around. He offered a tiny bow of the head in appreciation. She had a coffee-and-cream complexion with graceful cheek and jaw bones. Her shoulder-length, black, wavy hair complimented her, and she'd chosen to drape a light green, spaghetti-strapped summer dress over her sculpted shoulders. It was a good choice.

Next, Mars noted the wing-bots flanking her: two pudgy males who raised their eyebrows and broke into madcap grins. Mars had the strong impression of a couple of class clowns who'd found comradery and appreciation for their own and each others' hijinx in the pairing.

The first court jester was white – bordering on pink – with blue eyes and dark brown, curly hair that rioted against any sort of style whatsoever, mimicking the clownishness of its master. He wore purple pants and a red T-shirt. It was a *bad* choice.

The second farceur had gravy-brown skin with cropped, tidy hair and a thin, well-kept mustache. If it weren't for the look of mischief in his jet black eyes – and the wings, of course – Mars might have thought him a salesman who'd simply enjoyed too many doughnuts in his day. His brown dress pants and blue V-neck shirt weren't so bad.

Mars' immediate impression was that the three didn't seem to belong together. He said nothing. The female angel was holding her breath. Jarel broke the silence.

"Well, M.J., they seem to think you're Cupid even if I don't."

"M.J.?" asked one of them.

Mars wasn't going to be bothered to *tell* anyone who he was when he wanted to prove his identity more dramatically and, at the same time, test his old strength. The other angelettes might think he was all washed up, but Mars wouldn't believe it. He stepped lithely over to the waiting angelette and kissed her gently on the cheek.

She fell in a heap, no one being quick enough to catch her.

"Neptune's nads!" shouted the croppy-haired angel, who squatted beside her and patted her hand, trying to rouse her. "She fainted!"

"Yeah," drawled Jarel. "He, yuh, sure gots a funny way wit' da ladies, but he *is*, yuh, a love angel like all'a us. Him? Cupid? Pfft. I dun believe it." He yawned widely.

"Oh, no, sir. It is he all right," confirmed the curly-haired one, who wasn't bothering to bend down for the girl now that she had a nurse. He turned to face Mars. "I remember seeing you, sir, at the last banquet. It's an honor, Mr. Cupid. A true honor."

It seemed he was the proper one in the group, Mars thought, although any tendency toward propriety did not

extend to regular haircuts. He looked like he was wearing a huge brown loofah for a hat.

The fluffy-headed angel turned again and bent toward his friend, who was still patting the girl's hand. "You were there, Tommy, and Tamara, too. *She* obviously remembers seeing the God of Love – and surely never imagined getting that close to him. Oh, look," he said, pointing. "She's coming around."

She stirred, and all eyes turned her way.

"Tamara has never fainted in my vicinity nor have I heard of such an occurrence," the angel continued, as if Mars needed assurance that a girl could faint at his kiss. "Jarel," he added, turning to face his fellow Olympic outcast, "this is Cupid, no doubt about it, and I hope you've been treating him accordingly."

"Pfft," answered Jarel with a roll of his eyes.

The angel named Tommy took hold of Tamara's elbow and helped her to her groggy feet. He didn't let go of her as he extended a hand to shake Mars'. Mars wasn't accustomed to touching everyone who wanted to meet him – unless they were ladies – and so did not extend his hand in return. He did, however, nod his head in acknowledgment. For the Prince of Pompishness, it was *something*.

Tommy nodded his head in return, seemingly unoffended, and offered, "I'm Tommy. Tommy Redding. Nice ta meet ya. Dis's Cornelius Brewster, the most straight-backed, correct angel ever to grace the skies, and

the gal you knocked out is Tamara, Tamara Rumavina, and I sugges' you not do it again 'cuz while you a god and all that, I'm pretty protective of her and don' wan' her hittin' her head or gettin' hurt some other way. She's smart and capable and ain't jes' another perty face fo' ya."

Mars raised an eyebrow, registering the veiled threat, but he was too irritated by the arrow he'd found to retaliate against nobodies. *Who are these people?*

Still, he wasn't about to ignore a woman. "Are you all right, Miss Tamara? I see that I startled you, and for that I apologize. But, in truth, it is your beauty that startles all who have the good fortune of beholding you." The smooth talker.

She struggled to regain sentience.

"Ahem," coughed Jarel. "Time to, yuh, get dis party started, as dey say. M.J., – that stands for Mars Jr., as he claims to be, in case y'all was wondering – I, yuh, brought ya here to give ya a chance to, yuh, talk wit' a few of The Fallen – the reasonable ones, anyway – about what yo' up aginst. You, yuh, really ain't got no choice but ta join da crew."

"What *crew?*" demanded Mars. "What is this *hold* exactly that Cacciari has over you? What does he have you *do?*"

"Well, I, yuh, awready told ya he's got da ambrosia," Jarel answered quickly. Tommy and Cornelius looked at each other nervously and shifted their considerable weight.

Tamara looked at her feet.

"And what must you do to get that ambrosia?" needled Mars. *Hercules' Knots!* he thought, exasperated. *It's like pulling teeth around here to get some solid information.*

Tamara sighed. Tommy swallowed hard. Jarel looked to his companions for some back-up. It was Cornelius who finally lifted his chin and spoke up.

"We do many odd chores and errands, but we primarily shoot arrows as directed by Mr. Cacciari."

"But The Fallen are no longer love angels," hissed Mars, demanding more, "so they haven't the right to shoot arrows."

"No, sir. We're not love angels … not anymore. Only Cupid, under Jupiter's blessing, and those angels under heavenly direction have the honor and privilege to shoot *love* arrows and thus bestow or strengthen *love* among couples."

Mars didn't like the emphasis put on the word *love* and felt uneasy once more. He dreaded continuing the interrogation and was sure he wasn't going to like the answers to any more questions he'd ask, but he had to do it. "And so," asked Mars, "what kind of arrows are you shooting?" Mars remembered touching, holding, mere minutes ago, the fake, foul thing that passed for a love arrow, the poisonous dart that came from that shyster Mandre that was coated in gold but was no more pure and wholesome than the most aphotic depths.

Cornelius took a deep breath and answered matter-of-factly, "They're leaden arrows. Touched by Pluto. Infected – made evil – by The Lord of The Underworld."

Mars suddenly felt sick and the room seemed smaller. He didn't want to hear any more.

But now that Cornelius had found the bravery to tell the truth, he wasn't stopping. "The lead arrows," Cornelius went on to Mars' dismay, "inspire hatred rather than love. They undo your work, Cupid. They're Pluto's revenge. And we shoot them to stay alive. And the reason we're forced to do so is because of *you.*"

Mars didn't know if he was losing his strength and needed more ambrosia or whether it was the horrific news that made him suddenly feel sick, but the room was spinning. Nothing was making sense anymore. He fell to his knees and then saw the floor come suddenly towards him.

Chapter 13

LOATHSOME LEGACY

OR

WHAT GOES AROUND COMES AROUND

Mars opened the sunroof of his limo, now painted in yellow glitter, and raised himself into the brilliant sunshine. The light sparkled and cascaded and turned everything around him into glee and gaiety.

He plucked a particularly pretty arrow and set it aloft toward a nearby couple. They were stylish in white gown and suit, and their radiant smiles gleamed with joy. Butterflies sprung from the arrow's wake, and birds twittered of impending love.

Mars lifted his arms and spun in a wave of delight. He thrilled at his métier. His life's work was a pleasure to last for all time.

A sudden blow across the face left him struggling to understand why the butterflies were battering him.

"Cease striking him immediately!" Mars heard one of them say. "I cannot believe you just did that! One does not strike Cupid! It is simply appalling!"

A giant, angry butterfly zoomed to the other side and slapped his other cheek so hard that Mars jolted. His eyes shot open, and suddenly there was no brilliant sunshine. No sky. No rainbows or even butterflies. There

was only a dingy ceiling – made from rotting, greyed-out, wooden planks.

Mars had been dreaming.

Aw, nuts, he thought.

Jarel's angry face emerged from his haze of sleep. Jarel had a hand raised, ready to strike again, but lowered it when he caught Mars' confused gaze.

"'Kay, now, see? He's waking," said Tommy. "You can both have yo' way. Jarel, you stop hittin' 'im, and, Cornelius, you won' have ta worry no mo' 'cuz he's not gonna be disrespected, although fer the life of me, I can't figure out no reason why you're not angry wit' him, too. I think we all are, even if we do still sorta worship him."

"Right. Well, wakey wakey, Cooopid," Jarel commanded angrily.

Mars sat up and rubbed his cheek, angry but not too out of sorts to notice that Jarel used his godly title. "I'm glad you've come to terms with that," Mars grumbled. "I've been telling you who I am since we met."

"But you ain't, so I'ma still call ya M.J."

"At least until I've regained the title."

Jarel squinted, and Mars got the strong impression that Jarel wouldn't mind getting in one more blow. *So much for not liking confrontation.*

"'S time you, yuh, heard how yo' decree got us all kicked offa da job."

Mars looked from face to face and saw no friends.

"What decree are you talking about?"

Cornelius stepped forward again as group spokesman. "The Deadly Dictator Decree, sir, put forth by Jupiter and seconded by you in the late 20s." He flapped his hands jazz style. "You know, The Roaring 20s."

Mars thought back in terms of human history. He pictured flappers with short hairstyles and scandalous, knee-length skirts. He smiled inwardly at the advances in feminine freedoms; they gave him more to look at.

"Yes, I amuse you," Cornelius said with a hint of coldness in his tone. Mars thought better of clarifying what he'd been thinking about. "My story won't, I assure you."

So Mars got to his feet and put on a somber face, preparing himself for what he was sure wouldn't be a happy tale.

Cornelius, with his audience now properly attentive, took in a large breath and continued speaking. "The First World War had ended, and much of the world was happy again. It was a good time to plant love everywhere. People were receptive. But Jupiter sensed more trouble ahead for Europe and urged you to keep love flowing."

Mars' jaw clenched. *No, he hadn't,* Mars thought. *Jupiter didn't warn me. I've never even* seen *him.* Mars did remember speaking to Mr. Habandash about it, though. Habandash had called him to a room where a heated discussion with a handful of love angels had just ended. Mars

heard the argument through the door but plowed in anyway. He ignored the lot of them except for his boss' assistant.

"Ah, Cupid," Habandash called upon seeing him, effectively ending all other discussion. Mars was used to that, getting all the attention when he entered a room. For some reason, Mars also remembered Habbi's outfit that day, a ridiculous blue and red plaid suit. Mars had decided that Habbi probably switched suits about once a decade. With a grimace, Mars recalled that his own white pants at the time were Oxford Bags.

"Jupiter says that Pluto is circling Europe again," Habandash had gone on to say. "Hate and envy are rearing their vile heads, so Jupiter wants you to see to it that love is generously dispersed to prevent another war."

Mars remembered replying snarkily as always, something to the effect of, "I always bestow love generously. What's your point?"

Habandash had glowered and continued, "Jupiter will allow no wasted arrows."

"I don't waste arrows." It may not have been entirely true even then, Mars admitted to himself, but it was mostly true.

"*Some* of your love angels do."

"So get rid of them. I can do the job of a hundred angels myself." Mars' eyes widened as he realized that his words to Habandash may have not only sanctioned immediate firings but may also have planted the seeds of

his very own dismissal nearly a century later.

Cornelius cleared his throat to re-harness Mars' flighty attention. "Jupiter demanded accuracy, and you, apparently agreeing, moved ahead with the dismissal of thousands of angels. You weren't the only ones in the room, you and Mr. Habandash. There were five others there. One of them was Vilnius Cacciari. You may not recall; The Boss always said you didn't so much as acknowledge their presence, much less their outrage."

Mars wanted to be angry for being blamed here but could only stand there blinking. He knew that, no, he hadn't paid any attention to anyone other than Habbi. And, no, he hadn't wondered if he might be offending anyone. And, finally, no, he hadn't looked around for reaction. But, really, he was the god in the room. Why would anyone pay attention to somebody else?

"Anyway," Cornelius went on, stuffing his beefy hands into the pockets of his baggy, purple pants, "many of us were dismissed. With no job, we didn't linger in Olympus. It wasn't long before we were starving for ambrosia, and then Cacciari found a way to feed us."

"A way to feed you?!" asked Mars, astonished. "He's a middle man, isn't he? It's Pluto providing the ambrosia, right? And Cacciari is feeding you to do Pluto's dirty work!" His angry wings expanded as much as they could under the musty trench coat. "How could you?! That's the antithesis of your being! Your whole purpose!"

Cornelius coolly stared Mars down and answered calmly, "If you cared, you could have done something about it."

Mars forced his angry wings flat. "I care about all my love angels. I'd never do anything to … hurt … " The words died in his mouth as he remembered wanting to plow his limo through the crowd in Paradise Plaza. *Yeaaaah,* he thought. *That wasn't very loving.* Nonetheless. "I couldn't have done anything back then but work, and still Pluto got his way."

There *was* a second world war, and Mars had worked non-stop through *it,* as well. He'd noticed his increased workload but loved his work so much that he didn't give it a second thought. The war ended, and still he worked. The Era of Free Love, as the 1960s came to be called, was almost exclusively his doing and a testament to his prolific abilities.

Mars looked around at his companions then. They stared back coldly. *Are they friends or enemies?* he asked himself. Either way, he wasn't about to fall on his sword for them.

"I did not do the firing, but I did support The Deadly Dictator Decree. We had to prevent haters from taking over the world. It was our job as love angels to prevent hate and to spread love."

"And we *was* doing that job," answered Tommy angrily and crossing his arms – possibly to prevent himself

from taking over Jarel's job of slapping any disgraced gods in the room. "But Jupiter o' Habandash o' you o' somebody got it in dey head ta get rid'a ev'ryone whose accuracy rating was b'low 90 percent. We all'a us had ratings'a 85 percent o' higher, but somehow dat wasn't good enough? Jes' *think* how history mighta been changed if we'da been working. That second world war dat was comin' might not'a happened if'n we'd been dere to help."

Mars grimaced. He didn't want to acknowledge aloud the truth there, especially if some of this situation was his doing.

Jarel coughed, readying to pipe up. *Great,* thought Mars. *Another one.*

"We all thought, M.J," Jarel said, "and some of us still do think, mind ya, that ya jus' got greedy, dat da Ol' Pervert Cupid jes didn't wanna share his work with othas. If he do all da work, he get all da glory. If he's number one, he gets hisself da castle and da girls and Olympus all to hisself. And it do make sense, now don' it? If dey's one thing ever'body knows, it's dat, for Cupid, enough's never enough. Yo' Enemy Number One down here, M.J., and you oughtta be thankin' yo' lucky stars that Cacciari be offerin' ya work an' protection, cuz you might not be safe widdout it."

Mars shook his head in disbelief. "Wait a minute. Me?! I'm the bad guy here?! Catch-a-crap-ee makes you Pluto's Pain Pushers, and I'm the one who needs

protection?!" He turned, ripped off his trench coat, and thrust out both mangled wings. "Is this the kind of protection 'Da Boss' offers? Mutilation if there's no compliance?" Mars' mouth was spitting with each angry word he spoke. "I look like a plucked turkey!" He puffed out his chest more like a preening peacock than a turkey. "Even my sex appeal is tested with these scrawny appendages."

"Don't you talk about sex appeal now, you traitor!" scolded Tamara. It was the first time she'd spoken since fainting, and the reverential awe she once had on her face for Mars was well replaced with distemper.

Typical, Mars thought. *You can't hold 'em forever.*

"How was I to know," Mars challenged, "even if I'd known you were fired, that you'd all go to The Dark Side? Seriously, don't pin your inadequacies on me! If you'd been more accurate, you'd still have a job!"

"So would you from what I hear," Tamara answered bitingly. "Rumor has it that you've been outdone by that Mandre fellow, who's now the new Cupid. Taste of your own medicine. It's bitter, isn't it?"

Chapter 14

WAR

OR

MOJITOS

Mars didn't find Tamara so attractive anymore. Well, that wasn't true. She was supremely attractive but her rebuttal was a little too feisty for his comfort. Mars was … conflicted.

"I had an off day," he offered.

"More like an off decade," she rebuked. "The word on the street is that Habandash gave you an awful lot of chances."

He turned away from his latest sharp-tongued interrogator to address the others.

"So let me get this straight," he said. He pinched the bridge of his nose in the hopes of dispelling the ugliness of the situation. No such luck. "In your minds, I've got two options." Mars ticked them off his fingers as he spoke. "Join Cacciari in his bid to undo all the work I've ever done and in the process humiliate myself by bowing and scraping to someone who once answered to me *OR* don't join him and be hunted down like Diana's stag."

"By Jove, I think he's got it!" sang Cornelius in a British accent.

Tommy rolled his eyes before addressing Mars.

"Look, it's not so bad workin' fer Cacciari and Pluto. S'kinda like the first time ya disobey yer parents. Ya really don' wanna do it, and ya feel guilty after s'done 'cuz ya got that pit of disappoin'ment in yer stomach fer havin' failed 'em, so ya wanna take it back, but it's done, and if dey or da system makes ya do it often enuff, ya get used to it. Ya learn to shake off yer pride and just survive."

"You mean shake off your honor," retorted Mars. No one answered, and Mars wasn't going to waste any more time: Jupiter had to be warned of Pluto's deception, and Mars needed guidance. He looked at all four fallen angels to decide which would be the best one to fight, someone who was quick to aggravate yet not so aggressive that the whole thing became serious. Tamara was out of the question, of course, because women are meant to be adored, not hit. Cornelius? Too proper for a rumble. Tommy? Hmmm. Mars looked at Jarel and realized he'd known before he began. Jarel was his patsy, although he almost regretted it, seeing as how Jarel had clocked Pip for him, but, alas, it had to be done.

Like a schoolyard bully, Mars walked up to Jarel and stomped down hard on his foot. It wasn't the classiest way to start a brawl, but Mars was inexperienced in intentionally starting fights, even though they seemed to sprout around him all the time.

Jarel howled. He hopped on the unwounded foot to massage his other. "Ow! Man, whatchoo do dat for?!"

Mars was committed. He captured Jarel in a headlock.

"What da – whatchoo doin', M.J.?!" Jarel dropped his leg and struggled to keep his footing.

"I'm getting help," Mars answered obscurely.

Tommy and Cornelius stepped back, agog.

Mars moved on to noogies, struggling to keep Jarel off balance and upset.

Cornelius squawked about this not solving any problems.

Jarel swung a fist and connected.

Our Gut-checked Gladiator sputtered and thought, *Gods, who'd even want to fight?* But he had to make this genuine to summon his reluctant father, so he grabbed Jarel's wings and yanked out a handful of soft, white down.

Jarel shouted, aghast, as the fluff cascaded to the ground. Down, unlike regimes, wasn't critical for flight, but it keeps angels warm, and Mars knew it was generally off limits. To finish the goading, Mars taunted, "And there's a taste of *your* gang's own medicine, taking out feathers! If you don't like it, come and get a piece of me!"

Jarel didn't need to be offered twice. He spread his tiny, dented wing and launched himself at Mars. The take-down was clean and hard. Both expelled air with an *"oof!"* before rolling onto the bare, decrepit floor.

"Stop it! Stop it, you two!" screamed Cornelius, flapping both his hands and his wings.

"Fight! Fight! Fight!" urged Tommy unabashedly.

Tamara didn't say a word. She merely stepped out of the way while the combatants tumbled across the floor.

Jarel shouted not-so-angelic things. It was in the middle of the tussle, while they were still rolling and slapping, that Mars chanted:

"Oh, Fighter Supreme,
So feared through the ages,
Your son comes to blows.
Mars, see as war wages!"

With a clap of thunder, a team of raging black stallions broke through the side of the house, scattering battle dust and crumbled drywall throughout the room. The magnificent beasts pulled a gigantic, glorious, quadriga chariot – fiery red and adorned with golden wolves, which seemed to prowl the footboard.

A large, imposing figure stood in that chariot, and, when the dust settled, the residents of the room saw who it was: none other than the powerful and horrifying God of War himself, Mars *Senior.*

He was a near giant, towering and muscular, white-skinned and black-haired all over. He wore little, his bareness displaying a powerful physique of raw strength. What little Roman armor he wore was caked thick with blood. A buckler and javelin propped up inside his chariot were fouled with more than blood. As the fallen angels looked into the god's wide, wild, black eyes, they realized

terror already had them in its exquisite embrace and was whispering into their ears enchanting tales of their certain death.

Mars Junior knew better than to reproach *his father's* traditional entrance, even though he knew for a fact that The Commander preferred his red Ferrari to his old chariot. But rather than say anything, Junior dealt another blow to Jarel to make the old man proud.

Cornelius and Tommy knelt so fast that you could hear their knees crack against the hardwood floor. Tamara's dress prevented a modest genuflection; she instead curtsied deeply and remained bowed, which would surely get tiring. Jarel scrambled around Mars Junior on both knees to position himself before The God of War, then lowered his head to the floor in the deepest obeisance yet: he *had* been fighting the god's son just now, who was *also* a god.

Mars Junior merely nodded to acknowledge his dad.

Senior slowly lowered the golden reins and stepped out of his chariot. He walked forward and slapped one of his steeds on its hindquarters. The team snorted fire, and the flaming jet set Cornelius' hair ablaze.

Corny leapt to his feet, screaming. He yanked his red shirt over his head to muffle the flames before they devoured his entire fluffy mane.

Mars Senior chortled. That fire was a gift from his brother Vulcan – *the same brother,* thought Junior, *who's*

married to Venus, dad's mistress. Go figure.

The horses obediently backed out of the gaping hole they'd just made in the wall. After they'd positioned themselves to the greatest convenience of their master, they lowered their massive heads, letting him know they awaited his subsequent commands.

Mars Senior stomped over to his son and spoke far more loudly than the tiny room required, "You called me because you've come to blows?! And what of it?! Do you seek approval? I say it's long since time you showed some backbone!" The Bellicose Being slapped the back of the bowed Jarel, who shook in terror. "This jiggling, trembling, groveling mouse is your formidable contender? You summoned me to help against *him?*"

"Um, no, Dad – sir," Junior quickly corrected himself, suddenly as insecure around the old man as ever. "Actually, it's, um," he scavenged his brain for the right words. The God of War cast a pretty big and boisterous shadow, and Mars Junior dared not sound like a mama's boy asking for daddy's help, even though that was exactly the case. Junior stuck out his chest and put on a brave face. "It's Pluto with whom I intend to battle."

"Bah!" Senior boomed in his stentorian voice. "The mouse must have struck a good blow to the head! What audacity to assault a god!"

Jarel shook to the point of damaging his insides, but Mars Senior merely lowered his face toward Jarel and

whispered in a voice that could have nonetheless been heard next door, "I would smash you under my heel if your fearlessness or foolishness didn't inspire me to enlist you into my army. Tell me, Jupiter's Angel, do you prefer spreading love or would you like to try your days dispensing war?"

Mars Junior realized he was losing the thread of this conversation, a typical risk when engaging the scatterbrained elder deities. Junior was also heftily offended at having to interrupt a job interview that might conclude with his father hiring an angel who was bashing his son.

"Commander Mars, sir!" barked Junior in his deepest, loudest voice, which nonetheless sounded anemic following his father's mere whisper. "I haven't been hit on the head. I've received intelligence, sir, that our Commander in Chief, your step-father, Jupiter, is being undermined by Pluto. It's a plot, sir, to destroy the love that Jupiter commands – and possibly to dethrone the king himself!" Junior kept his eyes steady even knowing the last bit of what he'd said may not be entirely true, but it was likely. *Any threat to Jupiter's power,* Junior reasoned, *was a threat to the kingdom.*

"Bah!" Senior boomed again, straightening himself out to his full height and finally taking notice of Tamara, who strained in her continued half-curtsy. "Pluto is always coming up with schemes to take over the world. It's sibling rivalry, nothing else. If you'd had a brother, you might have

found the value in a rivalry that ends with broken bones. Builds character!

"My dear," his voice suddenly softened, and he offered a hand to Tamara to help her out of her curtsy.

As if she needs help, thought Junior with a visible sneer.

"IS THAT LOOK RESERVED FOR ME, SON?!" challenged his dad in a voice that could make steel crack. Cornelius slammed his charred head to the ground and prostrated himself, shaking. Tommy froze and looked like he might never move again.

"No, sir," droned Junior, embarrassed that this conversation might turn into a public berating to mimic the worst of times growing up.

Senior growled a slight acceptance and turned back to face Tamara, who was by now standing and smiling demurely.

Typical, fumed Junior. *Girls always love a bad boy. Or a big boy. And dad's both. Grrr…*

Anxious to keep the conversation moving before the old man ran off with the only double-X chromosome in the room, Junior tried a different tact.

"Sir, they may have fought since time immemorial, but Pluto now threatens the domain of your occasional consort – my mother – and me. He is a misanthrope, sir, and, as such, I must stop his plan. I seek your help, sir, the counsel of the wisest militarist to ever roam the earth

and skies."

Senior kissed Tamara's hand – Junior didn't like it – and led her gently to a window. The elder Mars released her hand softly to let it rest at her side, and then he gently clapped his hands together. From them sprung a nubilous mass, which grew and formed itself into an ornate, curvy divan. Mars Senior recaptured Tamara's hand to help her sit on it. She smiled her thanks and looked dreamily out the window. When Mars Senior was assured of her comfort, he turned away from her and walked over to Junior to address his complaint.

"Don't be a kiss-ass, son!" he roared, snapping back into his normal brutish and combative ways. "If you're warmongering, just man up and call for war. But I warn you, you'll lose your head in a battle against Pluto."

"Perhaps my battle doesn't have to be with Pluto himself, sir," answered Junior, still not liking the dreamy look in Tamara's eyes but needing to focus now. "If I can defeat the leader of the fallen love angels here on earth who does Pluto's bidding and remove the temptation of others to take his place, I can probably defeat Pluto's plan without directly challenging him. And if I can prove that the new Cupid is in cahoots with Pluto, I'm sure to recapture my throne."

"Aha!" hooted The War Hawk Hero. "Now we've come to the thrust of it! It's your own skin you're looking after!"

Junior shifted his eyes to see who was judging this conversation and was happy to find everyone in the room too terrified or beguiled to watch. "Dad, I, uh … I mean to say, sir, that, um…"

"Don't hem and haw, son! It's perfectly alright to want back your own damned throne. And if that means a fight, all the better! If you win, you'll have fewer dogs nipping at your heels!"

Junior remembered his father once saying, "No better way to rid yourself of a bully than to beat him up." *Easy for him to say when he was born to fight.* Junior was confounded – and not for the first time – that his father and mother ever saw anything to like in each other. They were absolutely dissimilar. She spread Peace and Goodwill, and he spread Blood 'n Guts. They had no hobbies or interests in common. Their lifestyles were only comparable in their transiency. *Guess that's why they never made a 'permanent alliance', as Dad would say. They more 'encamped' together. Opposites attract.*

Mars Senior slapped his hands together again and clouds sprung forward to form a hard, rough-edged bench that could not have made more of a contrast to the soft, wavy divan he'd made earlier. Senior dropped onto it and waved his hand in a fancy flourish. A lime-green mojito popped into existence, and Senior took a deep pull. He spread his knees as king of his domain and prepared to school his son in the art of war.

"So, son," he said, smacking his lips in satisfaction. "*Who* is your enemy? That's the first thing you must understand. Get to know his habits, his mindset, his weaknesses. Then strike a blow with … *whatever* strengths you might possess."

The note of doubt that he might possess strengths stung, but Junior ignored it, deciding he needed the advice of a war-hardened strategist more than he needed to argue with one.

"Mom says my aptitude lies in love and that love conquers all."

Senior's eyes showed internal struggle. "Well, if that's the best weapon you've got…" He didn't finish his sentence, and the insinuation was clear.

"But how can love help in a battle against the heartless?" Junior asked, addressing the million-dollar question.

"That's for you to figure out, son, as general of your own army. Use your strengths where your enemy has none."

His drink drained and his counsel apparently exhausted – or, more likely, his interest waning – Senior rose and walked to take Tamara's hand. Her person rose at the invitation, and it was clear that they meant to go away together.

"Dad!" interjected Junior. "I mean, sir! She's part of my army. You can't take her!"

Tamara opened her mouth to object, but Senior raised her hand to his mouth to impart a good-bye kiss.

She accepted his warm attention long enough to hear his parting words, "I love a woman with moxie. I'll return at the end of battle to hear your tale of victory."

She smiled at his presumption of triumph, and Junior huffed over it *(Dad didn't assume success for me.).* Still, he could tell she intended to fight. That was good. And maybe Senior wasn't the only one who liked a girl with moxie. Maybe he wasn't the only god interested.

The elder Mars turned and walked through the gaping hole in the wall, completely ignoring the three male angels still prostrating in painful positions. He mounted his chariot, grabbed the reins, and roared for his team to fly. More red fire erupted from the stallions' nostrils, and the clatter of hooves filled the room. In an instant, they were gone.

The three vassals cried out and tipped to their sides. They groaned in relief and massaged their aching kneecaps.

Mars Junior didn't give them another moment's rest. "Up! Up!" He pulled on Jarel's arms to help him rise. "Time to prepare for battle!"

Chapter 15

DIVIDE AND CONQUER

OR

ABOVE AND BELOW GROUND

Mars *could* have ripped some more feathers off Jarel to call his old driver because Mars needed a lift and maybe Jarel wasn't busy just then, but Mars *had* just picked a fight with Jarel and *had* just brought his dad into the fray, and Mars *was* trying to build an army, and he *would* need Jarel as an ambassador to The Fallen, so Mars refrained from another physical assault.

"Jarel," he said seriously. "I need you to give me something."

"Ya jes', yuh, almost got me killt by yer dad!" Jarel sputtered. "I'll give you something!" And he pushed Mars hard in the chest.

"Pandora's box!" protested Mars, smarting. "Stop it! I want *a feather*. To summon my driver."

Jarel pointed to the down still on the ground.

"No, a full regime."

Jarel glared in answer.

Mars rubbed his pec. "O-o-o-or you can take me yourself – right to the middle of wherever The Fallen dwell."

Tommy shot Cornelius a worried look and whispered, "He's mad."

"Um, sir? *Did* you hit your head?" Corny asked. "We had our heads down, so we wouldn't have noticed. If you did get concussed, please remember that it's Jarel's fault for laying hands on you – twice in the past hour."

Jarel frowned at him before turning to Mars and warning, "M.J., goin' t' da rest of The Fallen is the wors' idea in the history o' yo' bad ideas. We already tol' ya that ya got no friends dere and, yuh, yull lose another precious one right in dis room if ya touch my wings again."

It took nearly all of Mars' scant discipline to not immediately do so.

"Da Fallen," Jarel continued, "uh'd jes as soon stab ya in da heart with dey leaden arrow as t', yuh, help ya get ridda dey arrows. Da Fallen, dey working. Dey doin' som'n other'n sittin' around an' dyin' a starvation. Ain't nobody dere, yuh, wanna risk nothin' fer ya."

"I'll take the risk of an unfriendly welcome, Jarel. They can't really want this existence, and I really am the only one who could change it. My dad said to use my strengths. Love is my strength, and helping people out of misery is one way to show love. I could get them rehired were I back in power, doing the work they were meant to do, and I promise that to you if you help me."

The Fallen Four looked at each other, tempted.

"We need to meet," Mars continued. "I'll need to convince them to fight with me – with *us* – against Pluto should it come to that. I hope it won't. If Pluto sees that

he's lost the bulk of his support, he might just give up this latest scheme on his own."

Jarel shook his head, the first to question their new alliance.

"You don't have to show yourself if you don't want," Mars assured him, seeing a potential crack in his armor. "But I'd sure appreciate the help of my newest general."

Jarel's head shaking stopped. Mars took advantage of the silence to add, "I'd like the help of all four of you."

"As generals?" asked Tommy, clasping his hands. He seemed in awe of Mars once more.

"Sure," answered their new leader.

Tamara buffed her nails on her silky dress and cooed, "Mmmmmm. Not. Interested."

Mars sighed, expecting that complication. He'd pegged her as a particularly prickly female and hadn't really expected to win her over with mere authority over an army. He pulled the lapel of his hideous overcoat, hoping to straighten it. No way. It was a wrinkled mess.

"I see," he said. "Perhaps you'd prefer a more hands-on role, something more suited to your obvious talents. Hmmm." He paused to rub his chin, more for theatrics' sake than to settle an itch. "Yes, how does 'Chief Spy' suit you? There's enough danger and intrigue and adventure for even the most desperate thrill-seeker, and you'll be vital to the mission. If I'm to know my enemies, I'll need to learn their methods, their associations. We're

going to infiltrate both heaven and hell."

Tamara broke into a slow, snide smile that revealed she'd revel in the assignment. Mars felt relief that she'd gone over to his side.

He reached into his oversized pants and fumbled around in his diaper. The Fallen Four watched with plain disgust. Mars pulled out something golden, grabbed Tamara's hand, and slapped it into her open palm. Tamara's expression was a mixture of revulsion and surprise until she looked down to see what was in her hand: a golden obol. Her expression changed to wonderment. Such coins were exceedingly rare and precious, minted especially as an offering to the gods. Tamara grinned. "What else do you have down there?" she asked.

"Wouldn't you like to know?" he replied saucily. "Opportunities lost and all that. But here's a great opportunity to prove your resourcefulness. He touched the coin, which glowed under his godly touch. The four had never seen an obol, much less one in such perfect condition.

"It was a gift from my father ages ago after he'd spent time in Sparta, a city very appreciative of his skills. Common silver coins were minted for the populace, but the king cast two elaborate, golden obols to honor their favorite god. My father kept one and gave this one to me. It will help you, Tamara, to pay Charon, the rower of The River Styx, who'll ferry you over into Pluto's realm."

Tamara was transfixed on Mars' every word. He

went on.

"You'll need to find lots of the sweetest pancakes you can to feed the three-headed dog that guards the place. He's a glutton – usually of meat, but also of sweets, it's not widely known – and then you'll go into The Netherworld itself. Don't accept food or drink. Just find out what you can about Pluto's operation: how the god of The Underworld is getting enough ambrosia to feed an entire army and how he's delivering it without Olympus learning about his scheme.

"As soon as you know, get out. Mortals can't escape The Underworld alive, and even *im*mortals are severely weakened there, so don't linger. It's a dangerous job, but you seem … daring. Aaaaaand you possess a certain … *fascination* that I think will help. In fact, I think you'd be the most successful of all of us." *Including me,* he thought to himself.

Tommy shook his head, worried.

Tamara stood silent, considering the task. She frowned nervously.

"You won't be without means of escape," Mars added to soothe her concerns. Without hesitation, Mars extended his left wing and ripped out one of his few remaining flight feathers.

"What?!" Jarel barked. "You'd rip out yer own feather for *her* but you'd, yuh, rip out one of mine otherwise?"

"Yuh huh," he answered and then continued

addressing Tamara. "My driver would go to Hell and back for me, and I know he'd crash right into Pluto's bathroom if he had to get me. If you can't get out on your own, toss up the feather and get ready for a fast and messy getaway. Tyrone'll think he's coming for me, as it'll be my feather sending the message. Don't stand there explaining. Just say "love hunts" and he'll know we've talked. Then get out – quickly – because crashing Pluto's pad will anger him to no end, and Pluto won't genteelly let anyone depart his realm unscathed. Better to be a good spy and leave undetected, alright?"

Tamara nodded and turned to the gaping hole in the wall. She spread her strong, shapely wings. They were golden with tiny red sparkles that seemed to exude a faint scent of strawberry. Mars was momentarily stunned. She leapt up and flew to start her mission. Mars stood staring at the place she'd been. He thought her takeoff was the most beautiful thing he'd ever seen. And now she was gone from him. He regained his composure in time to run out and shout his well-wishes.

The Libertine Lord then returned to the three left in the house and found Tommy shaking his head.

"Don' seem right sendin' Tamara to … to … da bad place while we goin' t' da nice place."

"I think she'll do better there than any of us would," Mars responded. "Women can often get into places where men would be seen as a threat – *as if* women can't be

conniving. Ha! But the ferryman won't care if she belongs so long as she's got a coin. And the dog will be appeased by the food she carries. And if Pluto catches her, he'd be a lot gentler on her than us. Not a lot of live females show up there. She could probably sweet-talk her way into inheriting half his kingdom before he'd realize he was being played. Anyway, Tommy, you called her capable and smart, and she obviously is, as she's taken my side in the rebellion."

Jarel rolled his eyes. "And what about us?"

"You can't just drop in to a group of hostiles, sir," Cornelius said, directing his answer to Mars, "and expect to convert them."

Mars sighed. Cornelius was seriously raining on his parade.

"Nope," affirmed Jarel with certainty. "Only, yuh, one ting works on da masses."

"And dat's a whole 'nother problem," added Tommy.

"The suspense is killing me," answered Mars sarcastically.

"No need to be flippant, sir," chided Cornelius.

Mars tried to draw patience from within. Civility to underlings would take some getting used to. He cleared his throat, then said forcefully, "You were saying?"

"We're talking about *ambrosia*, sir," Corny answered, apparently satisfied with Mars' feeble, throat-clearing non-apology. "The same thing Pluto uses to garner his

army. The crowd will be a lot easier to talk to and maybe even convince if they're fed. You know the saying: Everyone wants a free lunch. If you feed the masses, you'll have their attention long enough to perhaps win their sympathies."

Mars looked down his nose at the three angels before him and wondered whether they hadn't hit *their* heads. "Perhaps I've missed something here but you three said you work for 'Da Boss' to get your share of ambrosia. How are we to get ahold of any ourselves – much less a store that's big enough to feed a small army?"

Jarel laughed and fell into coughing. When he was done, he answered as if speaking to a child. "Well, yuh, you da one dat said we'd havta go ta Heaven an' Hell before dis was all ov'r. Yuh, s'lookin' like we gonna have da job a goin' t' heaven."

"I was talking about spying on that counterfeit cupid!" Mars retorted. "Or else stalking Jupiter to tell him face to face. Warn him. Sound the alarm."

"And start a war wid a huge, hostile force, M.J.? asked Jarel. "Ya gotta win soma da fallen ov'r firs'. 'N wid da way that cherub spoke ta ya, ain't nobody gonna letchoo see Jupiter alone. Ya gotta get some 'brosia, man, ta get anyone ta listen."

"But I don't know where the ambrosia is. It's always been simply *supplied* to me. I've never questioned how."

Jarel slapped a hand to his forehead.

"And even if I *can* find out where it's stored," Mars went on, perplexed, "how will we get into Heaven and get a huge cache of ambrosia, and, see, I'm pretty sure no one will just give it to us, and I don't know about you, but I sure don't know of any secret passageways into Olympus."

"None exists, sir," confirmed Cornelius. "Mankind has been searching since the dawn of its existence for a shortcut into Heaven."

"Well, how do you propose we get in then?" Mars inquired.

The three stooges stared at him with deadpanned severity.

"What?!" Mars demanded.

"See?" Jarel asked his companions. "He ain't that bright. You, yuh, can see why I didn' believe he was a god."

"True dat," agreed Tommy.

"Whhhhat?!" intoned their clueless leader.

"You don't *need* to sneak in, sir," answered Cornelius sagely. "You are not *personae non gratae* like we are. We're outsiders now. We cannot enter, and, even if we could, we would attract unwanted attention. You, on the other hand, are still familiar."

Mars blanched.

"You could go in," Cornelius went on, "and smuggle some out – and quite a bit of it, sir, to feed all of Cacciari's confederates."

Mars wanted to keep his distress hidden but

couldn't help sucking in a deep, steadying breath. He started to sit back on the bench his father conjured, but it had already vaporized. Mars tumbled onto the floor.

"M.J., I, yuh, know whatchoo thinkin'," Jarel warned, eyeing him but not offering a hand up. "You 'spect us ta go up dere and take care o' dis, but you can't delegate ev'rythin'. You gonna have ta do it yerself. You jes' gonna hafta git over it. You was da big shot once, yuh, but no mo', and ya can't keep hidin' from people, no. I doubt Jupiter exiled ya. More likely *you*, yuh, don' wanna go back ta work under da new Cupid an' don' wanna be seen up dere, disgraced."

Mars sucked in another breath. He *didn't* want to show up in Olympus before he'd regained his rightful position. He wanted to parade into Heaven with his upper half sticking out of his limo, waving at adoring and repentant crowds, being begged for kisses by scores of angelettes whose very hearts were restored full at his sights. He wanted to strut up the walk to his castle and come out with the fullest quiver of arrows he'd ever carried and spread love so magnificently that the story of his comeback would be told for millennia.

"M.J., pride can be a terrible thing," added Jarel. "It can prevent ya from doin' the very thing you, yuh, need to do to get ta where ya wanna be. But ya gotta let go that pride, M.J. Our pride was buried long ago. You, yuh, wanna turn tings aroun', you, yuh, git yer butt into Olympus and git some ambrosia. If ya don't – if ya let

yer pride win – you, yuh, might as well join Pluto because I'd go so far as t' say pride is, yuh, prolly one of his mos' powerful weapons."

The words wounded. Mars lifted his eyes to look into Jarel's and decided there was no way in Saturnian Sanctity that he'd have anything to do with Pluto's sins. He got to his feet and set his stance.

"Let it be known," Mars announced, "that the son of Mars is no coward." (Never mind that there was no proof of any bravery exhibited by him throughout all recorded history.) He went on, "I'll go to Heaven and get the ambrosia we need."

Mars walked behind Tommy and placed both of his hands on Tommy's shoulders. "No offense to you, Jarel, but it's time for fresh wings. Tommy, let's go."

Tommy grinned widely, as if he'd just received a flattering invitation. He stepped away to bow and then motioned to step outside. Mars followed. Tommy spread his wings, which were much more robust than Jarel's – blue at the base and tinting purple at the tips. Mars grabbed hold for the aerial piggy back ride, and the two shot upward, Mars somewhat distractedly, wondering how he could possibly face the task ahead.

How can I show my face? Mars asked himself. *And steal ambrosia? No, not steal. I'll be* borrowing *it,* Mars decided because he didn't want to *think* of offending Jupiter by stealing from his realm, even if it was in the name of

defeating a threat to the kingdom.

I'm really going to take on Pluto's forces. He felt sick.

"Tighten yo grip," shouted Tommy over his shoulder. "Gotta lotta hot air up ahead. S'looking like we in fo' a bumpy ride."

As if lately I've had anything but that, Mars thought. He tightened his grip and hung on for dear life.

Chapter 16

FATE INTERVENES
OR
THREAD THREATENED

The four conspirators reached the edges of The Cloudy Mist just as Apollo was settling his horses. Mars would have greeted his uncle, but the end of day was never the time to do so. Apollo's normally elegant and robust creatures were, after their daily dash across the sky, lathered and exhausted. They'd sleep well that night, as they did every night. The result of their labors was not only the golden dawn with its hope of new beginnings. It was more even than the bright day with the warmth and security that only the gods could bring. No. The steeds' labors also brought the crimson, soothing kiss of a beautiful dusk that bathed the world's lovers in reds and oranges and purples. The Cloudy Mist was as grateful for the attention as the Earth below, and it reached out for the streaks of color as readily as a beautiful woman reached to pluck flowers for her hair.

Mars ignored all that, though. The dusk only made him realize that everyone in Olympus had now clocked a day and a half of gossip about his dethroning – at least he assumed he'd be the main topic of conversation, that pompous, egocentric, disheveled ground-walker.

It so happened that he *wasn't* the talk of the town after the first day because something more interesting had piqued the fickle celestial attentions *du jour*, and that was the great number of arrows the new Cupid had shot off on only his second day on the job. Some were saying it was a record, but Mars hadn't heard anything about it yet – and that was a good thing, too, or it might have distracted him from his mission.

"Go on," urged Tommy, settling into The Cloudy Mist, the outermost edges of heaven. "I can't hold ya ferever. Yer heavy."

Mars frowned but didn't argue. Instead, he put a tentative foot onto The Mist. It was somewhat like an elephant stepping onto a cobweb and hoping the gossamer thread would support its bulk. Mars knew from eons of experience that even a single molecule of water vapor was enough to keep him comfortably aloft, as if in a hammock, but in his new, tenuous position as demoted god, he wasn't so sure.

"You'll catch me if I fall right through, won't you?" Mars asked with a hint of panic.

"Well, a brick falls faster'n a feather, M.J.," answered Jarel, "but I'll do ma best."

Mars decided to concentrate on The Mist rather than insults and chanted to himself: The Mist is solid and will hold. *The Mist is solid and will hold.*

He shifted his entire weight onto the foot

enshrouded in cloud. His foot wobbled tentatively but didn't plunge through. Mars was thrilled that it held. He was solidly on Olympic ground. *So I* am *still welcome here.*

"Okay, now dat dat nonsense is over, why, yuh, dontcha git on wit it?" Jarel prodded. "We'll be, yuh, waitin' fer ya right here at da edge a' Da Mist. Dis's da closest we can git, yuh, inta Heaven righ' now. Yall havta walk in from here."

Mars looked deep into The Mist and caught sight of a twinkling, honeyed light: the glow of The Gates of Heaven. Simply approaching it was enough to bring mortals to tears, as well it should; this kingdom belonged to gods, angels, and only the most compassionate of mortals.

Mars suddenly felt … odd … as if something pricked his heart. It was a brand new feeling, unlike anything he'd ever felt before. The twinkling light was sublime. Precious. His palms grew damp with anticipation, and he was temporarily overwhelmed with the most intense sense of .. of … what was it? … *gratitude* that he'd ever felt in his oh-so-long-and-privileged life. He suddenly felt so … *overjoyed* to be there … so … amazed at his luck at being not only still welcome into Heaven but once deemed one of its most prominent citizens.

"Yes, sir," spoke Cornelius in a tone of great respect. "I get the same feeling every time I see The Gate. I always have. We were honored to have been allowed past it once, and you're blessed to still be."

To prove the point, he stopped fluttering his wings, and his body dropped immediately through the clouds, like a child jumping below a water's surface. When Cornelius popped back up, he was just as wet as that child would be, his brown and bushy wings soaked flat, but his face showed none of the joy of a child frolicking at the pool. No, Cornelius' face scrunched in agonizing sadness. He turned away, and Mars could see his wings beating hard to keep him where he was. The Mist would not hold him; thus, The Gate would never let him pass.

Mars didn't know what to say about that heart-breaking display, and he didn't know quite how to react to the new feeling in his heart. *Gratitude,* he decided, *makes a person feel as mushy as love.* He suddenly wondered whether the two might be somehow linked.

"We'll be waitin', M.J.," Jarel repeated. "Don' forgit about us once" – he stared hard into Mars' eyes – "once yer back in da comfort 'a Heaven. We already, yuh, been abandoned by Jupiter an' Habandash. Dey, yuh, don' wanna think about unpleasantries, I suppose."

"But Tamara means da world ta me," added Tommy. "And she's on a mission for ya, and we're countin' on ya."

"And if the rest of The Fallen hear that you used us to get back into Heaven, sir," said Cornelius, "to return to the lap of luxury, and then you became cozy and spaced out and left us, sir, well, you can imagine their reaction. The Fallen will despise you anew with a fever that might

shock Pluto himself."

"Dere won' be anywhere on Earth, yuh, dat ya could fire off an arrow without The Fallen stalkin' ya ta hand ya over ta Pluto. They'll love fer him to decide yer fate."

Mars looked at the three and registered that he really needed to work on his team's sense of trust. "I *will* be back," Mars promised before turning back toward the twinkling lights of Heaven's Gate.

He badly wanted to return to Heaven. He walked, then ran until he was close enough to see the giant, ancient, brass key set in its keyhole. He had almost reached it when three forms popped up from The Mist, blocking his path and forcing him to skid to a halt.

The forms were of three elderly women. They were slightly hunched and wore muted red robes. The first held an unruly mass of shorn wool in one hand, which she deftly spun into thread. The second woman stretched the newly formed thread from one outstretched hand to the other and repeated the act several times, measuring out a particularly long length. The third woman held the longest and sharpest scissors that Mars ever had the displeasure of seeing – so sharp, in fact, that the mere sight of them elicited haunting chills.

"Well you should shake, Son of Venus," croaked the hag with the wicked shears. "'Tis your fate we touch."

Mars gulped. The Fates. Measurers of lifespans. Conductors of the preordained. Older and likely stronger

than the reigning Olympians – and guardians of Heaven's Gate. These ancient goddesses together have, since the dawn of time, woven the thread of life, measured lifespans in each thread's length, and cut the thread at life's end; in fact, the cutting ended a mortal life.

Mars watched the second hag's hands slow in her measuring. She looked deep into his eyes, and Mars had the distinct impression that he was in danger. While The Fates could not cut the thread of a god, Mars knew he was not as strong as one in his current state, nor as weak as a mortal – yet. He'd have to listen to what they had to say, which must be the purpose of stopping him, and hope they'd allow passage into the heavenly realm.

Thinking quickly, Mars did the thing he knew best – besides shooting off arrows – in the hopes of greasing his path. He smiled his most charming smile and honeyed up, "Lovely, wise, and powerful Fates! You three look faaaaabulous!" He stepped forward and reached out oh-so-slowly, as if mesmerized, but, in actuality, to avoid any sudden movements that might cause an accidental cutting of life thread. When his hands had nearly reached the white straw hair of Nona, the first Fate, he asked, in his most heartbroken and begging tone, "May I?" Without waiting for her answer, he touched his forefinger to a frayed lock and gently, reverently, trailed its length. He finally lifted the split ends as if setting aloft a beautiful and fragile butterfly that chanced to land upon his finger. "You are

even more enchanting than the last time you graced me with your presence."

Mars remembered that last encounter well. The Fates had knocked on his castle door about a hundred years ago blathering something about a change of fate and generally irritating him by interrupting his dinner. At the time, he'd thought them overzealous fans. Looking back now, he wondered, *Had they tried to warn me?* Wondering if they might now have more advice for him – advice that this time he'd heed – he continued his flattering serenade, oozing affection that did not exist.

"You three, who are the first of time's beauties, your words are wisdom. Do you wish to speak to me – or ask a service? My time and energies belong to you." The Sycophantic Scoundrel bowed deeply, his face nearly in The Mist and thought, *Gods, Dad would have puked if he'd heard that. But you catch more cherubs with sugar than with vinegar, as the saying goes.*

Mars counted to five. The move would show respect and submission. When he lifted his head, he found the three ladies staring him down with a dull, golden thread stretched taut between them. Morta, Miss Scissors, had her shears ready and looked like she was just *dying* to cut it.

"Nay, Son of Venus," Morta croaked. "Such niceties and sweet words were absent from our last union. You had no lovely words then, even there at your famed Love Nest." Her disdain stung. Mars watched her fingers tense

in the scissors' rings, eager to cut. The thread looked less golden and more grey by the second.

"I was young and foolish," Mars cried, not wrong on either count. The Fates looked at one another. "I would like today to hear your words and do what I may to make things right." Mars decided to flatter them again; appealing to vanities was always the ace up his sleeve. "You Fates see all. You know what's happening and why I must return!"

Decima, the Apportioner and second Fate, was the only one who looked capable of pity. She spoke in a high, frail voice that creaked like old shutters in a windstorm. "It seems a shame to measure so many years and see them wasted when they could still serve Fate."

Morta scalded her sister with a look. "Nay! Vanity and desperation sway your judgment!"

"And lust of death sways yours!" accused Nona, the first Fate who went through an unappreciatedly large amount of work weaving lives and destinies only to see her sharp-bladed sister become more feared and honored by humanity. "You see the future as well as we," she went on in the dry voice of old age. "Whether he employ false or true sentiments to *us* is of no consequence. It is best he know."

"Know what?!" interjected Mars.

"You will again enter Cupid's Castle," Nona whispered.

Mars might have jumped for joy had the morbid

Morta not iced his happiness.

"But, vain and foolish creature, you are no longer Cupid," she hissed with perverse satisfaction, "and you shall not enter as Jupiter's Chosen One. Oh, larcenist of affections, continue in your craft just as the new purloiner Mandre plunders yours. And as your sights grow, beware the smallest sights below."

Mars stood still, hoping one of the other Fates might explain that last bit. *It sounded like a warning,* he thought, but it could as well have been a recipe for ambrosia latte. Nervewrackingly for him, neither Fate helped clue him in. The Fates were notoriously ambiguous; they couldn't directly advise someone, lest they alter the very Fate they help mold, but they could nudge. Obscurely. Frustratingly so. Apparently they banked on him to sift meaning out of their cryptic counsel.

The Fates began descending back into the darkening Mist.

"Wait!" Mars urged. The Fates stayed themselves. "I'm going to re-enter my castle but not as the reinstated Cupid? What does that mean? If I'm not the new Cupid, who would I be?" He gasped as a terrible thought and an image of Tyrone entered his head. "Not the help! I'm not going to become Mandre's servant, am I?!"

The Fates stared into his eyes and sunk into The Mist, disappearing from view and leaving Mars distraught.

Chapter 17

A LOVELY THEFT

OR

SANDCASTLES

The crimson dusk fled, and black night rushed to take its place. As Mars stood panicking, The Cloudy Mist rose like a bear to its hind legs and pounced, swallowing him and the tiny spark of light from the gate's ancient key.

He was blinded, obnubilated. Degrading images assailed him as if from a dream:

He wore a French Maid's outfit and stood perched on a stepladder, methodically dusting his – but now *Mandre's* – chandeliers. He cleared motes and wondered why anyone with anything useful to do could possibly care whether a chandelier had dust. As he worked, Mandre sauntered in and smacked him across the rear, hooting, "Nice work, Sugarbutt!"

Mars toppled, The Mist swirled, and the scene changed. He next found himself in a black-and-white striped jail jumpsuit. He was hauling *his* old belongings to the trash while *Mandre* ordered him around. Mars saw himself toss his rose-stemmed ERP onto a trash heap while Mandre's new ERP was delivered; it too showcased flowers, only the stems turned into snakes at its base. The snakes hissed and struck at Mars' feet. Mars bobbed from

foot to foot to avoid them while Mandre howled with laughter. "Dance, monkey! Dance!"

The last vision, though, was the worst: Mars' nightmare. He watched in horror as he polished Mandre's arrows, the very same leaden arrows that the villain employed to destroy Mars' legacy. And while the outcast cupid was polishing, Mandre and Cacciari cackled about how, next, Mars was to lead them through Olympus tossing flowers at their feet. In a tutu. Wearing a tiara.

"YAAAAAAAAAHHHH!" Mars screamed, breaking free of his waking nightmare. He heard faint laughter and spun, looking for its source. He couldn't see them, but he was sure The Fates were there. *Did they bewitch me?* he wondered. The Fates were so powerful that no one wanted to be in their crosshairs.

Best to leave.

Mars hurried the last few steps to the gate, fumbled with the ancient key, and turned it in its keyhole. It grated and scraped like the oldest metal in all creation. It probably was, short of godly weapons. Old but solid. No way the key guarding heaven would be fragile.

When the lock clicked, Mars plunged forward, breaking into a blind run. Anything to get away from The Fates. It was a good hundred meters before The Mist cleared and he could see the stars once more. Realizing he could see *them,* Mars quickly looked around for anyone watching *him.* No one. Mars crouched and hunched from

one hiding spot to another.

He was desperate to avoid detection. He couldn't simply saunter into his castle asking for ambrosia, and he also couldn't ask just anyone he came across where it was made without people asking legitimate questions in return. He surely couldn't risk bumping into Habandash because his old boss would undoubtedly demand his return to work as a lesser angel. No, he decided he'd have to sneak in and out undetected and steal from his own stash – well, Mandre's stash – and hope his heist went undetected.

Does the ambrosia replenish itself? Mars wondered. He was amazed at just how out of touch he had to be to not know anything about his food. *How does Tyrone get it? Would he notice if some went missing?* The moral dilemma of the God of Love stealing heavenly gifts began to cook his noodle past al dente, but he didn't have the luxury of time to contemplate impractical ethos. He had to take advantage of the cover of night.

And I can always ask for forgiveness later, he reasoned to himself. *If Pluto gets his way and all of humanity is left bereft of love, well, that's a much bigger problem than me feeding a few thousand Fallen Angels.*

Mars crept into Paradise Plaza. There was no one around, which wasn't always the case; it was a meeting place. But not tonight. Thank Jupiter, Mars thought. The accursed platform where he'd been dethroned stood abandoned and mocking him. He grimaced at it but moved on,

scurrying from hiding spot to hiding spot and jumping at every sound. His nerves were stretched tighter than the leather of his mom's skirts.

When he finally reached his castle gate, he was breathless and jittery. Mars was glad that that horrible little hovering insect, Pimple, was nowhere to be seen. His faithful driver wasn't around, either, apparently. No light illuminated any room, not even the flickering candlelight from a romantic night in. *Huh. Guess Mandre doesn't enjoy entertaining the ladies,* thought Mars smugly. Then he frowned and realized, *Or maybe he's at their place right now. Grrr.*

Mars decided not to think about that anymore. He pressed his face between the gilded stanchions and gazed at the beautiful building beyond. It really was a most gorgeous gift from the Council of the Gods. It was his home, and he missed it. The graceful arches were just his style. The marble columns were elegant and classy. It had been a long time since he'd really looked at it.

He decided not to think about that anymore, either. *Onward,* he told himself and pushed on the heavy and impressive entryway. It swung open easily, and Mars smiled. This gate, like all the others in Heaven, stood perpetually *un*locked. They were never really meant to bar entry; after all, everyone in Heaven belonged there. But a heavy portal still had its uses; it gave its possessor the illusion of privacy, implying separation and exclusion. It

acted as an unwritten sign: "This is a place where you need a reason to be and permission to enter." Mars had neither, but he wasn't going to stand on ceremony.

He tiptoed forward through his magnificent rose gardens and stifled more than one curse for their many thorns. *Argh! Stupid pointy things!* Mars exclaimed to himself. He decided that, while the roses were handy for bestowing upon guests, nearly nothing justified wading through that sea of pain.

The thorns continued cutting his legs and spilling his godly blood. Unlike the blood of mortals, his was ichor, the golden, ethereal, ambrosia-infused fluid of the gods and the bringer of death for man and plant alike. Mars couldn't spare ambrosia, so he was wasn't exactly sorry to see that each scratching thorn paid the price with its life, shriveling on contact.

He rubbed his calves to stem the flow. Then he generously acknowledged that it wasn't the poor flowers' fault. He liked his roses, and it dawned on him that they were way more effective at keeping out undesirables than any door. He promised himself that, if he ever got possession of this place again, he'd definitely expand his garden.

Past the florid field, Mars finally reached the castle's side steps. Spotting no one inside or out, he pushed on the light birch door and tiptoed through. Two steps in, he stopped short. Even in darkness, he was shocked by the opulence and beauty of his former abode. Compared

to the dilapidated, old Safe House, this mansion was … *heavenly*. The walls were marble, not rotting, greyed wood. The furniture was abundant and plush, not non-existent. And the sense of well-being here, well, this was a *home* rather than a shack for the post-abducted. This place was magnificent, and Mars never wanted to leave.

More sad and homesick than he'd ever felt before, Mars retched. Nothing but air escaped his lips, nothing to soil the place, but Mars still felt woozy and faint. He stumbled back outside just in case and collapsed at the bank of his koi pond. Memories flooded his mind. He'd created that pond, digging out the space in the cloud himself and even selecting each fish that inhabited it. The fish knew him and stopped their usual aimless swimming to gather to him. He smiled and then puked all over them. They scattered. Pizza going up is just as bad as pizza going down, he thought sadly, wiping his face with the back of his hand and regretting having polluted the pond.

How could I have been forced out of such a fantastic place? he cried to himself, dismayed and confused. *How could Heaven allow a scoundrel like Mandre to live as a king?* He buried his face into the bank's clouds and cried bitter tears. The Love Lord's heart was broken.

Several painful minutes passed. Mars tried desperately to forget his problems, to lose himself in the soft feel of clouds on his face. He wished it were daylight so he could see his castle in its full splendor, but, then again,

he was glad he couldn't. The moonlight was enough. He lifted his head and sat upright, feeling the cushy clouds puff up around his legs, taking his form. He dragged a finger through the vapor and watched a thin trail form behind it, like the contrail stream behind a high-flying jet. Mars snagged the strip, bent it, grabbed some more cloud and shaped it, like a child building a sandcastle. He smiled, pleased at this peaceful pastime that reminded him of better days. He built a miniature palace just like his own, then a small car, just a tad shorter than his trusty limousine. His hands worked by themselves, and he idled. He roused only when he noticed that he'd created a mini stage like the one from which he'd been deposed. He stared, confused and upset until he heard a quiet *tsk*-ing behind him. He tensed and rolled to find its source.

An eidolon of a beautiful young woman was lying on her side, watching him. Mars stared, but she didn't say anything, so he looked her over. She was of Indian descent and had lovely, dark skin and long, straight black hair. Her eyes were such dark and flawless pools of liquid that he wanted to swim in them. Further down, swaths of nearly see-through fabric swept across her exotic form. He looked back into her eyes, and she spoke.

"You have never been one for self-control," the beauty stated with a hint of pity, "but you mustn't stray from your task. You must face this challenge. You've been days away and weakened, weak though you already were,

but you must not be induced to stay. Choose now to rise."

Aw, phooey, Mars thought. *She's all business.*

Choosing to temporarily ignore her advice, he asked, "Who are you?"

"Does the message gain validity because of its messenger? What does it matter who I am if my words are true?"

Mars considered her question. How many times had he discounted people if those people weren't "important enough" to him or couldn't give him something? He shook his head and decided, "You're right. It doesn't matter who you are." He pressed his palms onto the clouds and pushed to stand. The eidolon laughed like a tinkling bell and began to rise as well. As she did so, her laugh turned dry and her form blurred. When it reorganized itself, she had become Decima, the Apportioner. Mars resisted the urge to step back only because The Second Fate still held pity in her eyes.

"You are learning, Mars," she croaked, "but I believed it prudent to present my words through a pleasing form so that you would lend your full attention."

Mars opened his mouth to protest but thought better of it; it would be lunacy to claim he didn't pay close attention to beautiful women. But here he had a very wise goddess who'd provided two warnings; the first one by Heaven's Gate he hadn't understood, but this one he did: Get back to work. *Right. Work. Here I go.*

"Thank you, Decima," Mars said.

She nodded and faded entirely.

Mars shook the water vapor from his smelly trench coat and strode into the castle again. This time, he didn't linger to pine over his old life. He marched straight to the kitchen and pulled open cupboards until he spotted the silver tray upon which his ambrosia was always served.

Maybe it'll float to the stockpile, he thought and pulled it out, but, as soon as he had both hands on the handles, four *petit four* squares of ambrosia materialized onto it. Mars would have dropped the tray in surprise if he weren't so agog over that splendid little meal. They were lovely squares, as swirly as cirrus clouds and as pink as cotton candy, with a dark blue arrow design that swept across the top. They smelled ever so slightly sweet. Mars snatched the epicurean dainties and gobbled them as greedily as a pig in slop.

The fairy-light food was sumptuous and sooo badly needed. He felt his courage grow and could have eaten another four, but he decided he had to keep looking for the source before anyone returned.

He continued opening cabinets and spotted another tray, this time porcelain. He held it in his hands. *Tyrone's tray?* he asked himself. Before he could ponder it further, another four squares of ambrosia appeared, the same style as the last.

Mars delighted – but then paused. *Why are they*

the same?

He lay down the tray, and the delicacies disappeared. He walked back over to his silver tray and put both hands on *its* handles. The same four squares reappeared.

Hmmmm.

He picked up his tray and walked it back over to the porcelain one. Putting one hand on a silver handle and another on a porcelain one, his suspicions were confirmed. Two treats on each tray.

So the tray delivers the ambrosia that it decides is needed or wanted at that moment by the person handling it.

I want a million squares! he thought loudly.

The four squares that were already there disappeared.

Oops. Too greedy. Okay. I'd like a thousand squares, he thought less loudly.

Nothing.

Mars was getting worried; he'd need a lot to feed a small army. *Okay,* he thought steadily and calmly. *How about a hundred?*

Nope. No change at all.

Mars became unsettled. "Four?" he said aloud.

Four reappeared, and he sighed in gratitude. He cautiously lifted them from his tray and popped them into his mouth. "Thank you," he offered gladly. The tray didn't shake or spin or acknowledge him in any way. *Of course it wouldn't. Idiot,* he chided himself.

Hmm. He decided on a test.

"Four more?" he asked aloud. None appeared, and he hadn't expected them to. He didn't need more, being satiated.

Okay, he thought, clapping his hands together. *So I can't get more from the trays than what I legitimately need. Or perhaps I can't get more than what I'm supposed to get, as determined by whomever enchanted these trays. So where's the source?*

Just then a door at the front of the house clicked open, and light from a front hallway peered its way around the closed kitchen door. Mars jolted and spun in circles trying to find a hiding place.

"Be right there, Mr. Mandre, sir!" Tyrone shouted. "Just need to take out this trash, sir! Can't have you dealing with this terrible stink, sir!" And then his long-time driver entered the kitchen, closing the door behind him with one hand and waving Mars still with the other.

"Tyrone!" Mars whispered urgently.

Tyrone didn't answer. Instead, he grabbed Mars by the collar and lowered his former boss' head to whisper directly into his ear, "You smell like a Titan's toilet, sir, but I knew it must be you because who else would dare to enter smelling as conspicuous as you? Why are you here?!"

Mars knew his jacket was musty, but he didn't realize he was quite that offensive. Still, too much time on Earth had a way of sullying people.

"T., I need to know where our ambrosia comes

from. I need … a lot."

"Take the tray, sir. Mandre's got his own, this porcelain one, so yours won't be missed, and you'll have a constant supply."

"No, T.," Mars hissed. "I mean, thank you, but I need way more. Where does it all come from?"

Mars could tell that Tyrone had a million questions, but his most prominent expression just then was incredulity.

"Sir," Tyrone answered cautiously. "It all comes from Jupiter. His palace chefs make it. Everyone knows that."

Everyone but out-of-the-loop, deposed gods, thought the Match-Making Machiavelli. *So now I know what to do.* His plans set, he pulled his silver ambrosia tray toward him and meant to quietly tuck it into his back waistband. Instead, it hit the porcelain tray and sent it crashing to the ground. It shattered into a hundred pieces. The noise was deafening.

"My gods, driver!" roared Mandre from the other room. "What are you doing in there?!"

Tyrone scrambled to pick up a broom and dustpan. He ran through the door with them, shouting, "Just a little accident, sir! Cleaning up now!"

"Well, move it, you! And then fumigate this place -- or are you *trying* to infuriate me?!"

"Oh, no, sir. No, sir. Right away, sir. Just make yourself comfortable, sir. I'll be right with you."

With that, Tyrone re-entered the kitchen, foul-faced, and whispered. "You better get back to living here soon because that guy's a tyrant."

"I'm trying," Mars answered simply. "Thanks for covering for me, T." Then the Castoff Casanova remembered Tamara. "T, if a feather of mine goes up, don't waste a second getting to it, alright? Not a second."

"Have I ever?" Tyrone countered smartly. "What do you expect to happen?"

Mars never got to explain. He and Tyrone heard footsteps and knew Mandre was approaching. Mars waved goodbye, dashed out the side door, and sprinted across the garden, heedless of the damage the thorns reaped on his legs and making slightly less noise than a sphinx crashing through brush.

Once off the grounds, Mars kept on moving. He crouched and dodged and maneuvered his way to Jupiter Heights and was immediately worried again. The palace's famous glow would reveal his approach, he was sure of it, but there was nothing he could do to prevent that. He pulled up his collar to hide his face, dashed to the giant, pearl door, and pushed. It was heavy, like the doors to all the classiest places. He cracked this door open just enough to slip inside.

The first thing Mars noticed was the magnificent, glowing staircase that so enchanted him every time he saw it. Remembering its effect, Mars slapped his hands

over his ears and spun away from it. Facing the door, he could still see the staircase's reflected glow, but its direct power was gone. In this way, it was just a source of light.

Mars glanced left and right, his hands still covering his ears. There was no other light spilling into the hallway; even the communication room was dark. *So Habbi takes nights off.*

Mars shuffled to his left along the wall, still facing it and circumventing the staircase until he was behind it, near the back of the house. He stopped at another entryway, this one featuring two intricately carved, dark walnut swinging doors. Each featured a rectangular, eye-level viewing window, the better to see comings and goings. The kitchen, Mars concluded. He pushed where they met and was astounded by his first view of Jupiter's enormous industrial-style kitchen.

It was easily the size of a soccer field – and Mars had traveled enough on Earth to recognize a soccer field. The floor, walls, and ceiling were silver-toned cirrus cloud, and silver pots hung from silver hooks within. Below the pots spanned rows of long, stainless steel tables.

Along the side walls, steel shelving units bore empty silver trays. Between the shelves hung scores of slate bulletin boards with recipes and notes written in chalk. Finally, at the back wall and claiming all its height sat the biggest, most impressive masonry oven that Mars had ever seen. This room was surely the busiest, most

hustle-bustle place in the palace. Mars imagined dozens of white-hatted chefs working here, rolling the ambrosia, decorating it after it was cooked. *Yum!*

But Mars wasn't there to daydream about food. He was there on business. He walked toward a table – it took a bit to get there, the place was so big -- but it turned out to be clean. Not a scratch.

He walked over to a shelf and peered at a tray resting there. Nothing. Not a crumb. Not even one teeny, tiny clue. These were the cleanest pastry chefs ever, Mars decided. He was sure that every spot in that kitchen would be just as tidy.

He read one of the bulletin boards and noticed that they all had different names on them, organized alphabetically. This one read: "Mars, Jr, est. 15, Mars Sr, est. 25."

Mars pondered this a moment and guessed, *This must be the estimate for tomorrow's needs, sort of an advanced menu so the chefs know approximately how many squares to make in a day.* Mars walked down the row of signs, not knowing what he was looking for until he'd spotted it: a board that had room for many more lines had only one. "Pluto, est. 30,000."

Mars gasped. *Jupiter's chefs are feeding Pluto?* Mars asked himself. But his shock quickly dissipated. Of course his chefs fed the gods and all the immortals, he now knew. *But with enough ambrosia to feed an army?* Mars shook his head. He didn't understand. Then he didn't want to

believe it. He couldn't accept it – until he had no other choice. It was there, reality in stark letters. *Jupiter was feeding the revolt.*

But Jupiter can't understand what he's doing! reasoned Mars. *He must not understand what's being done with all that ambrosia because no king would ever purposely undermine his kingdom! Does he even know that the number is so high?*

Mars wondered whether the chefs paid close attention to these lists. Of course they *looked* at the numbers daily to fill the demand, but did they pay so much *attention* that they'd notice a change? Would they simply make as many as demanded without heed to whom they went? There was only one way to find out, and Mars knew that his dad would be proud of him for *this* move.

Mars pulled the grubby sleeve of his trench coat over his hand and rubbed out the four zeroes after the three. Tomorrow Pluto would have to survive on three squares, not even enough for him alone. Mars then walked back to his own sign, erased the 15, and wrote 30,000. *Who's in control of the army now then?*

Mars turned and headed back to the main door. There was one other thing he wanted to do: try to see Jupiter. No one was there to stop him. Mars could tell him about Mandre's plot with the leaden arrows and about Pluto's army and then he'd plead his case for reinstatement. He would ask why Jupiter was feeding Pluto – without

mentioning his own planned takeover of the army, of course. *No sense in laying down arms before the war is definitely over,* Mars thought. It was worth a try, he figured, and it was now or never.

Mars stepped out of the kitchen and circled right around to the base of the staircase. Its glow and music gently called him, and he was eager to let it help him along. He put a foot on the first step and was amused that it felt springy, like a mini-trampoline. *Fun,* he thought with a foolish grin. He bounced up ten steps before all the fun came to a crashing end.

"Intruder!" someone shrieked. "Sound the alarm!"

Mars jumped but had the presence of mind to pull up his collar before whipping around to see who was screaming.

It was Pip, wearing a long, red nightcap with a white puff at the end of it but not looking happily elfin. Pip slammed his hand down on the curl of wood at the end of the railing and the stairs slanted. Mars fell on his bottom and slid down the super fun happy slide – or what would have been at any other time.

Mars crashed into Pip and rolled a few feet from the palace door.

"Stop, you! Identify yourself!" ordered the undersized security guard.

Mars was deeply grateful that his ugly coat had such a huge, pointy collar. He kept it up to hide his face

as he scrambled to his feet and bolted out the door. It was hard to run with both arms at his ears holding up his trench coat, but there was no way he was going to drop his cover.

He was halfway across the grounds when he heard several pairs of large angel wings flap in the darkness overhead, barreling down on Jupiter Heights. The Royal Security Force. This was probably the first actual emergency in generations. No doubt they were scrambling. Mars would have to not only get away from the palace; he'd have to leave Olympus. His unsightly, smelly trench coat was too distinguishing.

Mars ran and ran through the night, fighting his twisted desire to get caught for a chance to explain it all to Jupiter. But if Mars never got to see Jupiter when he was one of Heaven's first citizens, how would he be allowed to see him when he was gate crashing? And stealing? *Thank the gods I didn't lose my ambrosia tray.*

Mars burst through Heaven's Gate and ran to the very edge of The Cloudy Mist. At first, he didn't see his Fallen comrades. He sprinted back and forth, thinking they were hovering just under The Mist to prevent being seen and simply had to see it moving above them. No such luck. He frantically called out. They burst up through The Mist and were clearly surprised to see him.

"Yeah, you didn't expect me to come back, but here I am, and we've gotta go!" He ran at Cornelius, hooked his arm around his neck, and swung himself onto Cornelius'

back like a cowboy leaping onto his horse. "Pip spotted me and called The Royal Security Force! Let's disappoint them!"

The Four plunged through The Mist and skies, and only as they plummeted away from his home did Mars realize something. He slapped his forehead and groaned. "*As your sights grow, beware the smallest sights below!*" *PIP! The Fates had warned me – despite hating me!*

Mars vowed to treat them better the next go-around – if he ever got that chance.

Chapter 18

HELL ITSELF

OR

MMMM, PANCAKES...

The Safe House never looked so good. Coming in for a landing, Mars, Jarel, Cornelius, and Tommy saw it as their refuge. They burst in through the back door and spilled into the bare living room, huffing and puffing. They quickly flattened themselves against the walls, hiding from a feared pursuit.

None came.

As the seconds spent waiting turned to minutes and dawn began to break, they caught their breath and realized they were probably safe from being dragged back to the scene of their crime. They sagged in relief.

"Wha' happen, M.J.?" demanded Jarel. "Ya ain't, yuh, got no ambrosia on ya, so, yuh, whatcha bein' chased fo'?"

Mars didn't answer but instead turned an icy stare his way and held it just long enough to let him know he'd heard him.

Tommy squirmed uncomfortably. "Wha's da problem? You mad or som'n?"

Mars turned to stare at Tommy, equally silent.

Cornelius was the first to catch on. "Ah," he

announced to his companions. "I believe he'd like an apology, and I'd say he deserves it. We're sorry, sir – or at least I am – for doubting you and speaking so harshly. By the escape we just executed, I'd say you were caught in an act most un-celestial. Will you now be banned like the rest of us, sir?"

Mars broke his stare to properly address Corny. "I accept your apology, Cornelius, and no, I won't be banned. Pip didn't recognize me and probably doesn't know I was in the kitchen, so I doubt they'll check the boards."

Cornelius tilted his head in silent question, a silence that was immediately broken by a terrific crash outside that made them nearly jump out of their skin.

They reached the curtainless window just as Tamara pushed through the door. Tires squealed outside, and Mars recognized the sound as the same wheels that had nearly run him over the previous day. He looked down the street in time to see his old limo turn the corner. Metal garbage cans rolled in the street.

Good old Tyrone, Mars thought. *Dependable.*

All eyes turned to Tamara, who looked as black as if she'd rolled in coal ash. Her hair was matted by what appeared to be strings of black tar, and her wings were equally coated in goop. It all looked dangerously toxic. She coughed, and a small puff of dark smoke escaped her black lips.

Mars' heart turned over. He was overcome.

"Tamara! My TamTam!" sobbed Tommy with heartache. He rushed to her and, pinching her feathers between his fingers, tried to squeegee the bog off her wings. That only transferred the stickiness to *his* hands. Seeing it, she waved for him to stop.

"I got pulled into The River Styx on my way out. That water – if that's what you'd call it – is thick as syrup! It pulls you down! I was lucky to have tucked your feather in my hair, Mars, and to keep my head above water because that kept the feather dry enough to flutter in the air when I tossed it."

Mars froze imagining the danger she'd been in.

"Your driver was there before my next breath. The limo came swooping out of the sky, and he opened his car door and stuck out his hand. I caught it – or maybe *he* caught *me*, I don't know – and he almost veered into the river, but he hit the gas, and that sucked me right out of there."

Mars let out pent-in air that he hadn't realized he'd been holding.

"Your driver is very dedicated. When I finally got myself situated in the car, I must have kissed him a hundred times for saving my life, and I would have kept going except that I was covering him in this filth." She shook her arms and tar flew.

"Oh, I'll kiss him, too, if I ever meet him," Tommy vowed.

Mars noted the familial concern and looked down at the black tar pooling at Tamara's feet. *She'd kissed Tyrone?* He frowned not just about the kiss but that it bothered him so. *But those were just thankful pecks*, he decided, tilting his head. *And surely they're rarely given?*

Mars felt a ping deep down. Uneasily, he realized that he wished Tamara's kisses had gone to him and not been bestowed on another. And then with sickening understanding, Mars realized. He was jealous. Of his driver.

That was almost worse than being a servant.

He looked at Tamara and saw Tommy struggling to brush the goo off her face. Mars remembered that the last time *he'd* touched her face was when he'd kissed her and she'd fainted. *Would she ever react the same way again – or just for Dad showing off in his hot-rod chariot?*

Mars' countenance clouded.

"That won't work," Cornelius announced to Tommy. "She needs a bath. We don't have any soap and towels around here, do we?"

"Nope," answered Jarel, coughing hard again. "But I'll, yuh, run out and get some. I, yuh, gotta report to Cacciari anyway. He was 'specting me awhile ago. You good, TamTam?"

She nodded.

"'K. Won't be but, yuh, 20 minutes." He walked to the front door, and everyone heard his tiny wings ruffle,

the sound as anemic as a sparrow taking flight.

Mars removed his trench coat and slipped it around Tamara's shoulders. "To keep you warm," he whispered softly. He was left bare chested, cold, and rather humiliated at his mutilated wings. Still, she was looking, so he slowly and inconspicuously swelled out his chest and brought in his gut. No harm trying.

Tamara tightened the coat around her. Her sclera were the only white spots on her filth-covered face. Mars casually swung his hands behind his back as if he planned to rest them at the small of his back. Instead, he pushed his ambrosia tray further down his waistband, all the way down, until it was hidden from view.

"I'm so glad to be back here," Tamara said quietly. "Back on Earth. The Underworld is a horrible place. Dark and dirty and smoky and dead. No trees or grass or anything that looks alive and thriving. No bright sky." She looked up to the dingy ceiling, and Mars would have flown right through it, blasted a hole for her comfort, if he'd had the wings to do it.

"I got to there through the portal at Cape Matapan. No problems there. And going *in* was easier than going *out*, let me tell you, as I'm sure the few people who ever got out would agree. I reached The River Styx and offered the ferryman your coin, Mars, which seemed to really please him. He actually nodded, which I don't think he does for everyone because his movements seemed jerky and I'm

sure I heard his neck bones crack.

Well, he got to work, and it was a scary ride across. I'd see movement in the water, and then something would touch the surface just lightly enough to send little ripples out and catch your attention. And then when you'd lean a bit over the side of the boat for a closer look, the things would stay just low enough to make it hard to see them, but their bodies gave off little sparks of light, probably to draw you in, and that light was just enough for me to see thin bodies that couldn't be anything but serpents, and they held something in their coils deep in the water. They held … *people* … I think … just low enough that I couldn't be sure. I think they wanted me to lean closer to the water to see, but I wouldn't fall under their trance. I looked to the shore instead, but even that was confusing. There were times that it seemed to move further away rather than closer, and then the ferryman began to hum a dirge, so I covered my whole head with my wings so I wouldn't see the dead or hear their songs."

Tommy had been wiping her hair with the sleeve of Mars' trench coat still wrapped around her, but he stopped to glare at Mars for putting her in such danger. Mars felt the same way. In penitence, he joined Tommy's hopeless attempt to wipe the muck out of her hair. She was sticky and no longer smelled like strawberries; instead, she smelled of swamp.

"When the ferryman finally finished rowing across,

I hopped out and whistled for the dog."

Cornelius' eyebrows shot up, and Tamara explained, "Well, I didn't want him to smell the food and sneak up on me. There are a lot of columns and ruins and corners to hide around before pouncing on someone. Anyway, he seemed to really like being called because he came bounding around a rock face with all three heads bouncing and all three tongues out and his huge tail wagging all over the place and knocking over dead trees. It was so sad. I'm sure everyone runs from him."

It wouldn't be a bad idea to kill him, Mars thought.

"But I put down the pancakes for him and then sat down."

"You what?!" asked Mars and Tommy simultaneously.

"You were supposed to use the food as a diversion, not as an appetizer before it eats *you*," exclaimed Cornelius.

Tamara sighed. "I've seen neglect before, and that poor dog was a vision of neglect. I hoped that after I'd called him and fed him, he'd be easy to befriend. He was. Cerberus is such a loving dog, and the poor baby's in Hell."

Mars knew that some pet owners were blinded to the smell, bad behavior, and wild nature of their animals, but seeing such oblivion applied to *that* beast was something new. Still, she showed compassion, which he doubted any of the males would have shown, much to the detriment of the mission. Mars wanted to hear more and coaxed, "I'm sure he makes a fierce guard dog against

everyone but you, what with your charms. I'm glad to see you weren't hurt." He gently stroked a lock of her hair.

"Ow!" she cried.

Mars flinched. He looked at his hand and was mortified to see that he'd pulled out a chunk. "Oh, wow. Sorry, Tamara." He shook his hand and the black clump plopped flat onto the wooden floor. It looked like a squashed tarantula. "I'll – I'll stop touching your hair. Uh, please go on with your story."

She stared at her buggy hair, blinking, but must have decided that it was accidental – or at least not Mars' fault entirely. She looked at her hands covered in goop.

"The dog, Tamara," Mars cued, wanting desperately for her to forget the faux pas. "You fed him."

"Right," she replied, remembering the thread of her tale. "I fed him, and we became fast friends. I hopped on his back, asked him to please take me to Pluto's place, and he trotted right on over that horrible land, miles and miles of black, burnt expanse, full of monsters tormenting broken souls. I lay on my stomach and buried myself in Cerberus' fur and only poked my head out occasionally to see where we were going so that I could make my way back if we got separated, but each glimpse of that place was nearly unbearable. When it got to be too much, I reburied my face into Cerberus' back, and his warm fur covered me, and he smelled sweet from the pancakes I'd just given him. When he stopped, I looked up again, and we were

entering the back courtyard of a castle. It could only be Pluto's: the walls were made of volcanic rock swimming in glowing lava."

Mars wondered if the sight of Pluto's castle might have sent him packing.

"A blood-covered chef came out swinging a gory ax at Cerberus, I suppose to shoo him away, but my dear pooch stood his ground and growled from all three jaws. Cerberus must've wanted to protect me, although I'm sure the brute of a chef didn't see me. That man was smart enough, though, to back off and return with three moldy, butchered carcasses – I couldn't even tell what kind of animals they were. When he went back inside, that's when I saw it, Mars. Pluto's tray. And it was dispensing a constant stream of food."

She looked him straight in the eye to prepare him, but Mars joined her in saying: "Jupiter's feeding Pluto's army."

"What?!" asked Tommy and Cornelius together.

"You knew?!" Tamara accused, looking mutinous.

"I just found out myself in Olympus. I haven't told my story yet, but your adventure is far more important. As are you. Go on, my brave Tamara."

The Fallen in the room looked as shocked by Mars' civility as if they'd been caught in a Siren's song – and they didn't even have the benefit of centuries of experience to judge the depths of Mars' conceit. Even Mars looked

surprised by his breakthrough – and not necessarily happy by it. *What was* that?! he asked himself, as if his traitorous mouth offered insight to a guarded mind.

Tamara's eyes squinted in suspicion, but she went on. "Well, uh, yeah. Jupiter's been sending Pluto hundreds, maybe thousands of squares of ambrosia a day, easily enough to feed The Fallen. The squares just kept appearing on Pluto's tray while the chef kept removing them – with his disgusting, bloody hands, I might add. Yuck."

"What did his tray look like?" Mars asked, demonstrating his occasional godly tendency toward distraction. "In case I have to steal *it*, too."

"Wait. You stole something?" Tamara asked.

"Did I ever!" teased Mars. "But don't rush your story, Tamara. We only want to hear from you."

Cornelius looked back and forth between them as if he'd missed something. Mars was thinking the same thing.

"Welllll," Tamara went on, a bit confused. "The tray was round, about the size of a manhole cover, just as black, and even more covered in foulness." She paused as if dredging up a bad memory. "It was made from men's bones, Mars, and they *weren't* boiled clean for the sake of His Eminence. Bigger bones made up the bottom, bound by whatever sinew and rotting flesh not claimed by the grave. Smaller bones, probably fingers, curled to form the handles on either side."

"Ah," answered Mars simply, trying not to gag at the mere description. He hated himself for making her see the real thing.

"His ambrosia was black, too, with red slashes across them as if animals inside were trying to tear their way out. They looked poisonous."

A noise outside made them start. Mars, Tommy, and Cornelius simultaneously grabbed Tamara to yank her back. Still wrapped in the trench coat and covered in tar, she stumbled and fell to the ground behind them, while they stood their ground facing the door, ready to defend her. A figure moved past the window. The door creaked, and in walked Jarel.

"I, yuh, got da towels and da las' box of soap. Yall won't believe wha's happening at Da Boss' place." Jarel dropped a cardboard box about the size of a cubic foot onto the floor and looked around at the tense figures staring him down. Tamara's tar-covered palms and feet were giving her enough traction to rise.

"Wha's goin' on? Why's, yuh, TamTam on da floor?" He reached down to help her up, then wiped the resultant muck from his hand onto his girly, bleached jeans. "Here, we'll get ya cleaned up." He threw two large, fluffy towels at Tommy, one pink, the other teal. Mars wondered where Jarel got them – *perhaps he's shoplifting from the same place over and over* – and why Jarel didn't trust *him* to escort Tamara to her bath.

Duh, he answered himself a half second later.

"Man, there was so much movement, yuh, over at Cacci's," Jarel told the room at large while getting to his knees to open the box.

The eye-watering smell of overly perfumed soap infused the room, and Mars was forcefully reminded of the assault he suffered at Cacciari's hideout.

"I was gonna, yuh, report to Da Boss about Mars, ya know, give him a bunch o' bull 'bout how Mars is sufferin' without ambrosia and cryin' over his lost celebrity and all dat," Jarel announced (rather heartlessly, Mars thought), but Cach didn' even wanna see me. He, yuh, waved me off and said he don't wanna hear nothin' about dem spoiled gods. Then he went on mumblin' about gods not caring about they supporters and how, yuh, he was nearly out of some'n and was needin' a shipment, tho he, yuh, didn' say what, but I think it was da soap 'cuz, yuh, dey was only a few boxes lef' and one guy movin' 'em out into da hall. I don' know why, yuh, dey suddenly be lovin' dey soap 'cuz dey ain't usin' it. Ain't none of 'em smellin' all that good." Jarel tore open the box and pulled out a few bars of soap. "So, anyway, I, yuh, figured dey'd be too upset to notice a li'l bit missin', so I snagged this box when, yuh, the guy wa'n't looking, and… and…"

Conversation and movement in the room stopped as all of them, every last divine being in the room, caught the sweet scent of ambrosia delicately wafting above the

offensive smell of that repellent soap. As one, the five immortals leaned in to peer into the unassuming brown cardboard box, finding not one, not two, but ten neat stacks of ambrosia. Jarel tipped one over with a finger, and it collapsed. Ten squares had tumbled. Times ten stacks. One hundred squares per box.

"Wha' da-?" asked Jarel, who'd missed all of Tamara's story and Mars' revelations. "Why's there-?"

"Soap!" interjected Tamara. "That's how he's smuggling it."

"He's hiding the sight of them in boxes and the scent of them with soap," deduced Cornelius.

"Not anymore," Mars teased again. "Last night I stole their lucky star. In a few hours, Cacciari's men will be hungry and willing to listen to anyone."

"You had better hope a lot of them are charmable, like Miss Tamara upon first meeting you, sir," warned Cornelius, "because it will take a lot of skill to convince them of anything."

"Naw," said Mars with a smile. "All it'll take is this," and he triumphantly pulled from his back waistband his shiny, silver ambrosia tray, which glinted in the now vibrant and slanting morning sun.

Chapter 19

INCURSION

OR

SPLASH, SWISH, AND BOOM

How'd ya get an ambrosia tray?!" Jarel asked, astounded.

Tamara gasped. "You stole it! You stole someone's tray when you went to Olympus! They'll starve. That's awful. How could you?!"

Mars turned to look her in the eye and realized he'd have to do a lot of charming for this girl to not see him as a cad.

"It's mine, Tamara," he answered moderately. "I got my tray and rigged it to receive Pluto's allotment."

The gasps and questions and gesticulations and coughing that ensued from his brazen act were supremely gratifying to Mars. His companions were talking over each other so much that he really couldn't answer all their questions at once.

"Whoa. Hold on a second," Mars called with both hands up. "We've got the means now to command the army's stomachs, but we've still got to win their hearts. For now, let's hear the rest of Tamara's story." He was fascinated by it. And her. "We've got a little time – well, at least until Pluto figures out that someone's diverted his supply."

"Oh, Pluto won't figure that out for a while yet," Tamara replied, "because he won't be able to find his tray and not a single one of the poor souls trapped in Pluto's depths will be able to tell him where it is."

Then it was Tamara's turn to silence the crowing. Mars couldn't help but admire her gutsiness, quite unlike any of the other women with which he surrounded himself.

"Well, here's how it happened." She quickly brought Jarel up to speed in her story, to the point of approaching Pluto's kitchen and discovering his tray.

"You know, Tamara," interrupted Mars, "at that point, your mission was complete. You'd found Pluto's source of ambrosia and could have left right then."

"My mission would have been complete had I discovered Pluto somehow brewing his *own* ambrosia or heard plans of or witnessed its theft, but once I saw the tray, anybody's tray, then I knew the source had to be Jupiter. Everyone knows that Jupiter's the only one to make and freely give ambrosia."

Mars couldn't help feeling small; he didn't have a clue how much he didn't know.

"So my next job," continued Tamara, "was to find out how he was smuggling the ambrosia to Earth, so I stayed hidden in Cerberus' fur while that darling dog gnawed on those disgusting carcasses.

"Pluto's chef finally stopped scooping the ambrosia off the tray and moved to the back of the kitchen. There

were fireplaces lining the back wall, and the chef moved toward the middle one, which no one could miss because it had a huge, black cauldron suspended over seriously unnatural green flames. Then the chef reached up for a flex hose hanging from the ceiling, swiveled it over the cauldron, and smacked the side of it. What looked like black sewage spilled out, and, when it made contact with whatever was in the cauldron, a plume of really foul smoke billowed up like a dark mushroom. The more filth from the pipe, the hotter, blacker, and more noxious the gas. It enveloped us.

"I knew the chef's back was still towards me, and I had an impulse to break Pluto's tray or at least disable his supply somehow, so I slipped down Cerberus' neck, and that's when things started to go wrong."

Tommy shot Mars another dirty look. Mars caught it but kept focused on Tamara, who never stopped telling her story.

"One of Cerberus' heads *growled* at me, and, even through that wicked gas, we were close enough that I could see his eyes. He looked like he'd have gnawed on *me*, given the chance!

"It was that terrible, tainted meat, I just knew, that had turned him feral again. Maybe he saw me as a threat – you know the saying, 'Never get between a dog and his meal.' Well, I backed away, and he went back to eating, but I was suddenly very scared of him and angry *at* him,

yet needy *of* him because how was I going to get out of there without his help?"

Tommy's hands balled in fists, and Mars wouldn't have blamed him for any amount of violence as revenge.

"Tamara, I-," Mars began, but she was in the throes of her story and not to be interrupted.

"Well, I decided to worry about that later. I kept going, creeping into the kitchen, not just to be quiet but also because I couldn't see two feet ahead of me. And my feet kept slipping on the cobblestones, like the floor hadn't been mopped *ever*. I felt my way to the table with Pluto's tray and just grabbed it. I don't know how I was planning to break it, but I didn't want to start smashing it against the table right there because the chef would hear me. Well, the tray was heavier than I expected, and I stumbled sideways under its weight, and that's when I saw the glint of a coin to my left. More than just one coin. There were a bunch of coins, a pile of them sandwiched between two canvas sacks, which, by the way, were seeping blood onto that already vile floor. Well, I suddenly realized that I couldn't count on the ferryman taking me back across again on the strength of the first coin that I'd already surrendered, pristine though it was, so, as opportunity knocked, I reached between the sacks and snagged a new coin." She laughed. "It was like grabbing an Oreo cookie. I only wanted the middle stuff."

Tommy and Mars looked at each other, not finding any of this remotely funny. Cornelius and Jarel stood

stone-faced. Tamara was too involved in her story to notice.

"When I took the one coin, though, the whole pile shifted and spilled across the cobblestone. What little sound they made was enough to stop the movements of the chef. He stood still – or at least silent – listening for an intruder. I turned to go back out and I guess I got turned around. I couldn't see anything in that black fog and was getting confused. I couldn't hear Cerberus chewing anymore, so I moved quickly to get out. Unfortunately, I knocked over a chair.

"The chef went nuts cussing for Cerberus to get his noses out of the kitchen. I plunged ahead and crashed right into the side wall. It sent a half dozen pots and pans crashing down and clattering all over the place, and I must have loosened a second hose from the ceiling because it swung outward and dumped at least half a hogshead worth of River Styx at my feet."

She looked distant for a moment. "The splash was the strangest noise I'd ever heard. It wasn't the sound of water; it was more like chunky soup splattering on pavement and then echoing, like the chunks were living things writhing and swimming against the broth rather than spreading out with it." Her gaze returned to the present, where her audience had become still as statues. Tommy was turning purple from holding his breath.

"But the broth did spread, and it put out the green fire, which completely unhinged the chef. He cursed in

ways I'd never heard before, and I saw his outline coming toward me swishing his ax and no doubt thinking I was Cerberus. The sound of that ax swishing through the air – *brrrr.*" She shivered.

"I ran out, ready to hop on Cerberus' back, but my lovely puppy was now dusted over in that black soot, and he growled like a hellhound."

"Which he is," Mars reminded her.

"Then I remembered. The River Styx is The River Fear, and it grows with human distress. It's what feeds Pluto emotionally. It recharges him. The problem is that Pluto has figured out a way to use it as a weapon." She looked intently at Mars, willing him to understand.

"Oh, dear," Cornelius said. "If the King of The Underworld burns The River Fear, the black smoke rising will infest Earth with fear. Everyone will panic. It's world-wide chemical warfare."

"And that will undermine Jupiter's dominion even more," Mars continued the reasoning. "The fear will feed Pluto alone." Mars couldn't help but think that his war-hardened dad would be impressed by Pluto's move. It was hateful strategy but nonetheless effective.

Jarel's face suddenly lit with understanding.

"Dis cough! Didn't, yuh, always have it until recently. And flyin's been terrible lately. All dat hot air an', yuh, turbulence, and all da angry people 'round lately, M.J." Mars suddenly remembered being laid flat by the angry

young man on the sidewalk and the fearful looks from neighbors peering past curtains. "It's all Pluto's doing!"

The immortals looked at each other with deep concern etched in their angelic faces.

"We, yuh, gotta stop him!" announced Jarel. "We Fallen may work fer him to not starve to death, but dat don't mean we support him!"

Mars couldn't help but think of all the wars throughout history started by ambitious despots whose followers didn't really embrace their ideologies. Deep need, he thought, such as the angels' need for ambrosia, can turn even the most moral beings into unwilling villains.

"Well, Pluto can't feed us anymore," Tamara assured Jarel, continuing her tale. "Remember, I was running toward Cerberus. I still had Pluto's tray with me, so I slapped the tray's base, and it coughed up a square."

"No, Tamara!" Mars interjected. "You didn't!"

Her jaw dropped. "No! Of course not! I couldn't have escaped if I'd eaten anything from The Underworld, now could I? Persephone taught us all that. You can't eat in The Underworld without then permanently belonging there – even if the food comes from Jupiter."

All four males sighed in relief.

"But, remember, Cerberus was growling at me!" She put her fists on her hips and frowned. "Aren't you four listening?"

"We are! We are!" Mars assured her. "We just – I

just – I was only thinking about you, not the dog. I forgot about the dog." He was shaking his head, trying not to offend her sensibilities regarding her newfound friend. "Please go on. Poor Cerberus," he feigned.

"To clarify," she said deliberately and with a huff, "the ambrosia was to soothe Cerberus." She shook her head but quickly regained her story-telling demeanor. "The ambrosia still looked horrible, but I knew it wasn't toxic; after all, it did come from Jupiter's kitchen to Pluto's tray. So I tossed the square toward Cerberus while I was still running towards him.

"Oh, my gods," whispered Tommy, horrified that his darling friend ran *toward* a hungry and enraged three-headed hell beast.

"Don't worry," she turned to pat him on the back, leaving dabs of Styx gunk on his shirt. "Cerberus chose the ambrosia over me. He snapped at it and caught it right in his lovely black chops. I scrambled one-handed up one of his collars because my other hand held the tray, and then I hid in his fur. I knew the chef was close behind.

"Well, the ambrosia did the trick to re-befriend Cerberus and me – or maybe it broke the spell of that nightmarish fog. Either way, Cerberus turned on the chef and triple snapped so ferociously that that horrible butcher fell back, turned, and crawled back to the kitchen faster than one of your arrows can fly, Mars."

Cornelius gasped, realizing that such a comparison

could insult a god to the point of annihilation. Mars was pleased that at least *Corny* recognized the slight. Mars remembered the mortal weaver Arachne, who certainly learned the hard way the cost of disrespecting immortals. The Goddess Minerva transformed Arachne into a spider as punishment for her arrogant boasts of superior weaving skills; now the girl is doomed to weave spider webs for all eternity. And the Greek city of Argos regretted comparing its princess' beauty to that of Venus. *But Mom* was *always easily offended. I'm much less vain*, Mars thought, kidding himself. That Deluded Lothario. Still, he let the slight pass.

"Then, get this," Tamara added. "The chef, now at his safe distance, started shouting at Cerberus for putting out the fire and causing the brew to fill the kitchen. Actually, the brew had long since spilled well beyond the kitchen and into the courtyard, and the smoke had certainly spread throughout The Underworld. I'm sure no one was seeing anything well. And yet the chef raged on about how he'd have to find a match to relight the fire."

Cornelius gasped again, and Tamara smiled, happy that he was keeping up. "Yeah, you can imagine," she said. "Naturally, I whispered to Cerberus that it was really, really time to go. I put out my hand with another square, and my dear puppy licked it off and sprinted fast as the winds to the ruins, faster than I'd have ever guessed he could run."

Tommy gulped but squeaked out, "Good stealth job."

"Thanks, T-Bone," she answered. "The smoke was everywhere. I couldn't see a thing, but Cerberus could. He took me right to the shore of The River Styx, and I flung the coin out into the abyss for the ferryman."

"Couple of thieves, we are," intoned Mars with a crooked grin. Tamara returned a genuine smile.

"Well, you've guessed by now that I heard an explosion behind me-"

Mars hadn't guessed. Cornelius nodded, confirming that he'd predicted it. *Figures.*

"-far off in the distance. Soon shouts broke out, and I knew that the chef's match, that spark, lit up all that muck and probably blew up half of Pluto's castle. All hell was breaking loose."

Jarel chuckled.

"*If* they chased down anyone, assuming the chef survived to talk, and I don't see how he could have, they would chase Cerberus and me, which is silly because it wouldn't even have been his fault, were I there or not, and, as it stood, no one knew I was there except the ferryman, and Charon speaks to no one.

"Regardless, I preferred that we both be hard to find, so I slid down Cerberus' neck and whispered to him to hide for a looooong time, which I knew would leave me alone and exposed and, worse, would separate us from each other. He looked so sad, my poor, lonely, darling, little baby."

Yup, she's the affectionate type, thought Mars, *even if*

her affection could go toward grander beings – like me!

"So Cerberus kissed me goodbye. Three big, wet, sloppy, doggie kisses, one from each head, up my whole upper half! It was so sweet."

It sounds revolting, thought Mars.

"I heard the heavy flap-flap of really big, bat-like wings and knew we'd run out of time, so I told Cerberus to hurry, and he ran into the ruins.

"The ferryman appeared out of the fog, but he was still a good eight feet from shore. The wing-beats got louder, and the fog wasn't going to hide me forever, so I took a few steps back, hugged the tray to my chest, ran, and leapt for the boat." Tamara paused as if hoping the telling of the tale would purge the memory. No one else spoke.

"It was horrible. While I was soaring through the air, black, murky hands came out of the water and grabbed for me. The water below me churned, and I knew I'd never get away from them if they reached me. I couldn't even flap my own wings to help because I knew they'd touch the water. Thank Jupiter that I'd jumped hard enough because my feet just made the very end of the boat! I tumbled forward and rolled right onto the ferryman's feet, and he turned his faceless, cowled head toward me, and, if it's possible to be scared to death, I was nearly there. And if he had delivered me to Pluto," she whispered with a shudder, "Pluto would have probably imprisoned me for eternity."

Mars put his arms around her to comfort her. "No

way he could keep you forever," he assured her. "I'd destroy any prison he'd ever make to free you."

She didn't shrug him away but also put a hand on Tommy's shoulder to share the affection. She went on.

"The ferryman stared awhile, warning me silently but very effectively to never touch him again. Believe me, I didn't need the warning. He ignored the tray and finally lifted his head to get to the business of rowing. He steered the boat back around and started across."

"But wait," said Jarel. "How'd you, yuh, get all dirty if he ferried you?"

She shrugged in resignation. "We only got about half way through that thick, goopy, black morass when we heard – I'm sure all of The Underworld heard – a high pitched, screaming whistle. It could only have been Pluto calling his minions for a rescue party, probably less of a rescue for his chef than for his tray and coins, which no doubt flew all over the place.

"The whistle made the ferryman start to turn the ferry. Well, I couldn't go back! I just couldn't! I'd get caught! And even if I didn't, how would I get another coin to cross again once the coast was clear? So I opened my wings to fly and jumped for the sky, but I ended up falling right into the river. I guess we can't fly in Pluto's province."

"And that's why the coin's needed in the first place," said Mars gently. "Only the inhabitants of The Underworld can fly or those, like Tyrone, conducting godly transport,

in his case, the limo."

"Yeah, well, logic escaped me just then," Tamara answered with a hint of irritation. "So I jumped – and fell right into the river. The murk tried to pull me down, and I felt hands on me, and I only had one hand to tread water, and I wasn't going to release the tray because the river would just give it right back to Pluto, and the boat had disappeared. I only had one way out."

Tears rolled down Tommy's cheeks, and Mars squirmed. He wanted to flagellate himself for her suffering.

"I pulled your feather from my hair, Mars, and tossed it up. That's when Tyrone came tearing out of the sky like a knight. I screamed 'Love hunts!' like you told me, and he didn't question. He threw open his side door, stuck out his hand, and pulled me from certain death. I owe you both my life."

There was a sudden movement. Mars turned in time to see Jarel catch Tommy, who'd just launched himself at Mars, all limbs flailing. Mars wouldn't have denied him his right, but, before being struck, Mars decided to look Tamara in the eyes.

"What you owe Tyrone and me," he said clearly, "is nothing. What I owe you is an eternity of gratitude and apology." He sighed. "I'm sorry you're down here on Earth. I'm sorry you're having to work your way out of here. I'm sorry for getting you involved in my problems. And I'm sorry for asking you to take on this mission. I knew you

could handle spying, but I didn't think it'd turn into this. It was too much to ask of anyone, especially to help the supposed god of love. Pfft. No one who loves should ask so much of another."

Tamara's eyes softened as she registered what he'd said, but she didn't respond otherwise.

Mars turned to face the others. "I'm sorry to all of you, too, for everything that I've put you through. Please release him, Jarel." Jarel did so, to no immediate violence. It appeared that that which satisfied Tamara also satisfied Tommy.

The silence and tension in the room was broken a few moments later by Cornelius, who said, "Tamara, we are so very grateful that you're okay. But there's still something you haven't explained. If you refused to let it go, where's Pluto's tray?"

"Thanks, Cornelius," she answered. "The tray's in the bushes outside. I just didn't want to hold it any longer. It's got … powers. It gives off … dread. I almost wish I had left it in the kitchen. Maybe it would have blown up."

"No, it wouldn't have," Mars said definitively. "But don't worry about it anymore. I'll bring it in. It won't affect me as much. Right now, Tamara, you should bathe. Your clothes must be burned, along with my trench coat and Tommy's shirt and anything else that's got The River Styx on it."

"Why?!" protested Jarel. "Dats, yuh, alotta clothes

I'll haveta, yuh, um, replace when we can jes' wash it."

"The River has powers, too, Jarel," answered Mars. "Do you remember Achilles? The River gave that demigod invincibility except on his heel, where his mother held him while dunking him."

"So Tamara'll be invincible?" asked Jarel, opening his arms to hug her and coat himself in the stuff.

"It kills mortals and has various effects on the *immortals* and *children* of immortals who've managed to touch it and escape The Underworld, who aren't many, I can assure you. There are *im*mortals languishing under the surface of that river as surely as there are imprisoned mortals."

The group shivered.

"I don't think it'll do anything to us here on Earth, Tommy. We're outside Pluto's lands, so it'll just be swamp water or some other foul liquid. But Tyrone and Tamara? They touched it where its power lies. We'll have to wait and see what comes from her dip in The Styx. There's no hurry to bathe, Tamara," he said as she furiously rubbed her hands up and down her arms to remove the goop. "If anything were to happen, it already did. But I'm sure you're sticky and uncomfortable. Once you're clean, I'll tell you what happened in Olympus, and then you can choose to rest or join us. By day's end, we'll fly to meet Cacciari's forces."

Chapter 20

SECRET ADMIRER

OR

ANY SHOE WILL DO

Tamara took a long time in the bathroom. More than once, Mars wanted to knock on the door and offer his help, you know, because cleaning oily gunk off of wings is hard work, but he knew no one there would judge the offer as innocent.

Again I'm a victim of my reputation, thought Mars. Then, upon reflection, he accepted that he probably *couldn't* be trusted to keep the offer innocent; she was beautiful and would be naked, and he was the god of desire with a growing admiration for her daring and passion. He looked down and realized he could really use that trench coat.

Jarel had already run off to fetch some clothes. Mars hoped he'd come back with something really loose and frumpy for Tamara so that he could concentrate on the mission. Convincing Cacciari's thugs that they should abandon their "deliverer in time of need" wouldn't be easy, and it'd be harder if his attention was elsewhere.

Restless, Mars went outside and brought in Pluto's tray. It was just as foul and loathsome as Tamara had described. It also smelled like a fresh grave, although Mars doubted that she could have distinguished that odor

amongst the many equally putrid smells of Hell. The tray had to come in, though, lest it attract animals.

Mars put it under the kitchen sink next to a pair of mousetraps and a half empty bottle of dishwashing liquid. He was borrowing a page from Cacci's book to hope that soap might mask adjacent scents. With a laugh, Mars wondered why there'd be dishwashing liquid in a house with no dishes.

When he stood from his crouch, Tamara walked in looking as fresh as spring's first dawn. Her cheeks were rosy from the scrubbing, her wings and hair still damp. Worse, her dark purple, short-sleeved dress was a perfect fit. Mars closed his eyes and inwardly groaned. He was falling for her.

No. Impossible! Mars chastised himself. *Cupid falls for no one. I'm a rolling stone. No strings. No attachments. All yen.* But when The Concupiscence Kid reopened his eyes and took in that dress again, he couldn't stifle an inward growl and tart observation: *Jarel must "shop" for her often.*

"Whew! That tray smells terrible!" she said, holding out three bars of soap. "I had some extra, but I doubt a hundred bars could clean the stink off that thing."

"We won't bother trying," replied Mars, who nonetheless took two of the bars and put them alongside the tray. They didn't help.

He took the third bar of soap and washed his hands with it, hoping to extinguish the stench. It helped

to take the death off a bit; well, it added the scent of flowers. Still, it was better than nothing. Then he wiped his hands on his pants rather than risk touching Tamara and getting her wet again – or perhaps wanting to touch her a lot more.

Jarel swept into the kitchen, chattering about clothes.

None too soon, thought Mars, who didn't know what else to say to Tamara. The Love God enjoyed ages, lifetimes even, of analyzing love and inspiring romantic odes and lais, yet, in front of Tamara, he was blanking badly.

Jarel wore desert camouflaged fatigue pants rather than the bleached teeny-bop jeans he'd worn earlier. It was a great improvement. He tossed Mars an oversized, hot pink polo shirt. Mars' jaw dropped.

"Sorry, but not really," apologized Jarel, shaking his head. "I, yuh, got wha' I could. Tommy spotted me firs' and, yuh, got dibs on da black workout shirt. Ya get whacha get."

Jarel turned toward Tamara. "Your dress looks great, TamTam. A' course, you look good in anything." He pecked her on the cheek and walked out, calling, "We's all waitin' on ya, M.J. Stop flirtin' wit' da girl and come on out."

Mars smirked at Tamara. She shook her head and laughed. When they reached the living room, Tommy was cracking open a window, and Cornelius was wiping the last of The Styx muck off the floor. He tossed his filthy rag into a small metal drum that Jarel must have borrowed

from a hobo camp. The flames within eagerly leapt for their next meal.

Too bad Cornelius' clothes didn't need burning, Mars thought, again eyeballing Corny's purple pants and red shirt. He'd have to help that man get his fashion sense together. Then Mars remembered what *he* was wearing and determinedly stamped down his braggadocio.

When they'd settled around the fire with its perfectly normal, light grey smoke venting easily out the window, Mars quickly recounted his adventures in Heaven, which seemed very *un*adventurous and tame after Tamara's story. He wondered if she'd see it that way, too.

"Well, that was very risky, Mars," she assessed.

He didn't see why and sent her a quizzical look.

"If Jupiter had caught you," she explained, "he might've seriously punished you for daring to take a god's allotment of food. And he might even've banished you forever from Olympus so you could never step foot there again. That'd be horrible for you."

Mars couldn't believe what he was hearing. "That's no more than what you're suffering now."

"And it's terrible," she replied with a sigh. Her gaze dropped to her feet. "Entrance into Heaven is not something to risk, Mars." Her eyes returned to him. "I think any one of us Fallen would do anything to get back. I hope you're never found out to have done what you've done."

"And you," Mars answered. "Pluto wouldn't be as

forgiving as Jupiter might be." Mars rested his eyes on Tamara for some time after speaking. He lingered on her eyes – dark brown, nearly black as her hair. He admired again her high, strong cheeks and beautiful nose. And, oh, those lips.

"So, yuh, what's da plan now?" asked Jarel's muffled voice from somewhere in the distance.

Mars, our Knave of Nooky, turned slowly to face the noise's source. It was one of the three males around him, and he realized he was becoming lost in Tamara, maybe already was lost as he drank deeply from her beauty and worried over her concerns. *Not now,* he told himself. He shook off the enchantment of her – with effort – and then realigned his thoughts toward his generals.

"We have," he said, holding up his shiny tray with all its promise, "the means now to garner the attention of The Fallen, and we'll use it when they've had a little more time to work up an appetite. But first, my dad's advice was to learn more about my enemy. So I've thought that through, and decided that Jarel and I are going to do just that. Now don't get angry," he added, seeing multiple eyebrows rise. "I can't have a big group or we'll be seen. No worries. We'll only be gone a few minutes. In the meantime, have a snack."

Mars touched the tray's handle, and thirty-something squares of ambrosia appeared, all with his signature blue arrow. The crowd *ooh*-ed in delight. He selected two

squares and offered them gingerly to Tamara.

"Have some, Honey."

She smiled as he put them into her outstretched hand.

He plucked another square off the tray with one hand and grabbed Jarel's shirt with the other and pulled him outside. Then he dropped the square into Jarel's hand and said quietly, because the window was still open, "Time to go back to see Rachel."

Jarel popped the ambrosia into his mouth and said around it, way more loudly than necessary, "I can' believe you, yuh, wanna see dat girl agin!"

Mars waved both hands frantically, trying to get Jarel to stifle. He noted that the contented chatter floating through the window abruptly stopped, so he answered loudly, "Cacciari warned me away from her. Naturally I've got to know why. She must be important to him."

"Oh! So Rachel's da girl you two was arguin' 'bout?"

"Jarel!" Mars shot his hands up and then let them slap against the side of his thighs in annoyance. "Why do you think I went earlier to see that girl?!"

"'Cuz you was horny. You's, yuh, always horny, ain'tchya?"

The silence emanating from the house was deafening.

Mars didn't know how to diplomatically answer that. Recently he would have bragged *yes!*, and the truth

of the matter is that, as the Prophet of Passion, *yep*, he was sorta focused on it, but – he shook his head clear – that had nothing to do with the current situation. "My love life is none of your business."

Jarel laughed. "Your love life is everybody's business, and, yuh, dere ain' a person alive, immortal or not, dat, yuh, ain' heard 'bout yer escapades. If ya ain' makin' others fall in love wid each otha, you, yuh, makin' off wid them yerself. Yer ma's da same way, from what I hear. 'S why nobody trusts you two within a mile o' dey loved ones. Not dat all da other gods is all that faithful, neither. Yo papa got how many kids?"

Our Trysts Titleholder frowned, angry at this line of questioning. Realizing Tamara was listening, he said, "I'm often falsely accused of causing trouble where the seeds of infidelity were already sown. And let's not forget that plenty of people fall for the wrong person. Happens all the time. They realize it later and want to move on."

"You jes help 'em find another to move onto."

This is not how this was supposed to go, thought Mars. "Most people don't need help fanning their lust. I only find them another lover *if* it's their time – and then I find them the *right* person. My arrows spark true love."

"Ha! Yer the world's most renowned lover! Don't try dat phony speech wid me! Yer too full of cupidity fer dat."

Mars never liked that word attributed to him. He

was growing impatient, and the window was still open, so he raised his voice to finish this conversation. "Affection and true love are two separate things, and I feel neither for Rachel." He stepped back to look through the window to his newest and strongest female interest and found her looking through it, too. When their eyes met, she turned away. Mars added, "True love is not something to take for granted."

Jarel rolled his eyes. "Whatever. Hop on."

A few minutes later, they landed in the alley across the street from The Red Flag Gentleman's Club. Strong morning light blanketed the front of the building. There'd be no patrons inside, no dancing, Mars knew, but he hoped he'd get lucky and see Rachel, maybe ask a few more questions about her mysterious relationship with Cacciari. *If they're a couple, is their bond really so fragile that Cacciari fears my presence?* he wondered. He remembered Jarel's comment about no one wanting him around their loved ones, and he distinctly recalled plotting to steal her away out of spite. Mars rubbed his aching head. He was learning a lot lately about himself and what others thought of him.

Rolling his neck for relief, Mars spotted a speck in the sky. It was coming closer. He pulled Jarel behind a dumpster and poked his head out just enough to see, and what he saw amazed him.

Cacciari landed softly right in front of the nightclub's entrance looking, well, not like the Cacciari that

Mars had seen before. This Cacciari was … dapper. He wore an elegant, well-fitted tan suit with a baby-blue shirt and coordinating tie. His hair was slicked and combed back. He carried a giant bouquet of white lilies, purple pansies, and pink bleeding-hearts (also known as *Venus' Car*, thought Mars smugly). Struggling with the unwieldy assemblage, Cacciari managed to press the buzzer for one of the apartments above the bar. Then he quickly straightened his tie.

A sleepy voice cracked across the intercom, which must have been set to its highest volume because Mars heard it clear across the street – probably a necessity considering the business below. "Mmmm … hello?"

Cacciari cleared his throat and spoke equally loudly into the aging intercom. "Hello, Miss Rachel." He sounded nervous. "It's Vilnius. I've brought your daily bouquet. Take pity on them, darling, for they can never be as beautiful as you."

Mars heard the sudden crack and swoosh of a window opening. He looked up from Cacciari to see Rachel poke her whole pajamaed upper half out of the building. She looked down toward the intercom but made no obvious motion of recognition. No wave. No smile. Instead she looked perplexed.

"How do you do that?!" she yelled into the street. "Every day you talk into the buzzer and answer me like you're standing right there, yet you're *never* there! You

send me flowers and love letters, yet never show your face. When will I get to see you, Vilnius? Are you even real … or," she said sadly, almost to herself, "am I losing my mind?"

Cacciari rubbed a frustrated hand through his slicked hair, messing it up. He put down the flowers at the door, sighed, and called up to her, "Someday you'll see me. Until then, please accept my gifts as small tokens of my affection."

"Ah," whispered Mars with a grimace. Jarel nodded but said nothing, and Mars couldn't help but think, *So Jarel* can *be quiet when it suits him. Wish he'd've been that way outside the window of The Safe House!*

Cacciari stepped back from the building, yanked angrily at his tie, and shot upward, taking a furious bank to the left. As soon as he was far enough away, Jarel and Mars took off, too, back to The Safe House. They entered through the back door, calling out to announce their presence.

"Learn anything?" called Tamara from the front room.

"Just that Cacciari has the same weakness as most men," answered Mars on his way to her. "He's in love." He reached her and smiled. "I can eventually use that to my advantage."

Tamara stiffened and asked, "Love is a weakness? You're the god of love. How could you say that? And what do you mean, 'use that to your advantage?'"

Mars froze. He had intended to redirect Rachel's attentions to knock Cacciari to his knees. It would have been his father's move. But that would definitely not impress Tamara.

Jarel stood behind her, smirking, dying to see how Mars would answer.

"Just, uh," Mars hedged, "just that it's my area of expertise. And, no, love definitely isn't a weakness. It can just make you … change your priorities. Maybe he won't be so keen on destroying love if he himself is in love. He might be, uh, moldable."

"Ah," she answered noncommittally.

Time to change the subject. "Jarel and I are going to try something!" With that, Mars yanked him into the kitchen and said hurriedly, "Jarel, I need your shoe."

His lead general balked. "Naw, you don'," he replied. "You, yuh, got yer own."

"But I don't want to get mine wet."

Jarel frowned. "I don' wan' my shoe wet, neither, yuh, whatev'r you got planned. I'm tired and don't want no wet shoe on my foot." He crossed his arms resolutely, and Mars realized this was probably a battle not worth fighting.

Fine. He stuck out his right foot and look pointedly at his commander. More squinty eyes. Another standstill.

"My shoe, Jarel. If you won't give me yours, I'll need my own."

"An' you got it. On yer foot."

Mars sighed. *Not this again.* "Look, Jarel, I'll learn my laces later. Let's just get this done now."

"And agin, you, yuh, know wha' I want." Jarel just couldn't be convinced to fan Mars' royal ego.

Another sigh. Another notch knocked off his pride.

"Please, Jarel. Please take off my shoe."

Jarel bent down and removed a single wrestling shoe. Leather exterior, rubber sole. It'd work nicely for the task ahead.

Mars took it to the sink and placed it under the faucet, filling it with cold water. Carrying it ahead of him and into the living room, Mars watched as the water sloshed over its side in fat dollops. The resultant deep-colored splatters made the wood underneath look almost salvageable.

"Ugh! Not thirsty, thanks," joked Tommy upon seeing the odd water jug.

Mars chuckled and put the sopping shoe on the floor. A dark puddle soon grew under it. Reaching for his tray, he popped two ambrosia squares in his mouth and felt instantly stronger. He pointed for Jarel to help himself. Cornelius already had. Snagging two more squares, Mars dropped them into the water in his shoe – *plop, plop.* He inserted his index finger and swirled.

"We've tried that, sir," said Cornelius, courteously covering his mouth in case food remained. "In our loneliest

and saddest moments, we've all tried to glimpse Olympus again."

Mars was distressed to hear of their desperation but also heartened by a rare instance of superior knowledge. "Only the gods can create Earthly Reflecting Pools, although we can bestow ERPs to others, if we wish."

"Cupid! Thank the gods!" the water shouted. Everyone crowded over the tiny shoe ERP, hoping to see who was inside. It was Tyrone.

"I've been waiting for you to construct an ERP!" he chided. "Mandre brought in his own, a temporary one from Jupiter, and wanted me to disintegrate yours, but I managed to sneak it into *my* room. I had to destroy the water nymph fountain statue, though, so he'd see some debris. I'm sorry, sir. I know you liked animating her."

Tamara looked up at Mars, who failed to have the decency to look sufficiently ashamed.

"Never mind the fountain, T. What's wrong?"

"The feather, sir. What happened there?"

"Oh, well, that's a long story, but I'm glad you were quick to get there."

"And I'm glad to see the young miss is fine. Hello," he said with a nod her way.

Tamara smiled broadly. "Hello, Tyrone. Thank you again."

"You're very welcome, Miss." He shifted his eyes to Mars, which Mars was sure would be a very disappointing

change of view – it would have been for him. "I've been waiting for you to show up here because I've got to tell you something. When I returned from retrieving Miss Tamara, Mandre seized upon me and asked me a lot of questions. Then he went to his own ERP, and I overheard him set up a meeting with someone on Earth. When I casually asked later when we'd be leaving for the day's work, he said he wouldn't need me to drive today – AND he sent away the ladies at the door. It's suspicious, sir."

"Very suspicious!" agreed Mars.

"You have ladies at your door?" asked Tamara with a sour look that worried Mars.

"Um, yeah," he hedged. "They're fans. They want to meet me."

Tamara schooled her face to indifference. Mars chose to leave it alone. Tyrone rescued them.

"The meeting was set for 8 a.m. in Death Valley, Devil's Golf Course."

"Devil's Golf Course?" repeated Tommy.

"Hmmm," hummed Mars, ignoring Tommy. "That can only mean a meeting with Pluto."

"I thought the same since plucking Miss from The Styx. Why was she there?"

"It's still a long story, T.," he said but then looked at Tamara and sensed … disappointment, perhaps? "Uh," he added quickly. "Let's just say she's a heroine who penetrated The Underworld and figured out Pluto's game."

Tamara's face changed somehow, subtly, and Mars sensed he'd done right by acknowledging her work rather than glossing over it.

"Congratulations, Miss," Tyrone offered sincerely before returning his attention to Mars. "You'd just have time to make it, sir, if you left now, what with the time change heading west. It's best if I stay here."

"Right, seeing as you're not supposed to know about this meeting," agreed Mars. "Thanks, T. We'll let you know what we find out. Bye."

Mars picked up the shoe, walked with it out the front door, and dumped its contents where Pluto's tray had been. The soil turned instantly black and fertile, the stench of The Underworld gone. Mars inserted his foot back into the shoe with an audible squish.

Jarel walked out the door, too, and reaching his side, loudly exclaimed, "M.J.! Yer leavin' a mess!" He then bent down in a show of fixing the undergrowth but instead covertly retied Mars' shoe. Mars' eyes widened, but, not one to refuse service, he also bent down, ostensibly to help with the foliage but really to thank Jarel. It was good to have someone watching out for him again.

The pair returned to the room, and Mars tucked his tray into his back waistband.

"Cornelius, maybe it's your time to fly me. Let's slip into Dante's View on the north side of Coffin Peak so that we can see the golf course below. We'll see what

Mandre and Pluto are up to."

"Yes, sir," Cornelius answered. "And, Tommy? The Devil's Golf Course is a bumpy salt pan in Death Valley, California, so named because a human describing it once jested that 'only the devil could play golf there'. Human ears hear the noise of tees being hit and attribute the sound to the salt crystals cracking in the heat."

"And da salt do crack, right?" asked a nervous Tommy.

"No. The sound is Pluto torturing golfers for all eternity," answered Mars matter-of-factly.

He walked to the door and pointedly held it open in a rare show of courtesy that should have tipped them off; he was either changing the subject or distracting them from what lay ahead. The perceived smartest in the room, Cornelius, walked through that door, however, and the rest filed along, too. Unquestioningly.

Chapter 21

TEEING OFF

OR

THE DRIVER

Stepping outside, the first thing the group heard was the muffle of heated arguments issuing through closed doors all along the dirty and dilapidated street. Doors slammed. Dogs growled from back yards. Babies cried. Tamara shuddered.

"Wha' da – ?" asked Jarel.

"The Styx Smoke," answered Cornelius. "It's working. It's taking over love's goodwill."

Tamara looked at Mars with an expression he was sure was rare. It was the look of fear. And fear run rampant was the problem here. It was infesting the Earth, and, once it took hold, it would be hard to reverse. The smoke may not have affected her as strongly in Hell, perhaps because the smoke hadn't ripened or because her body surged with adrenaline or she felt protected by Cerberus or perhaps she could fight it for a bit, but now it was becoming overwhelming. Whatever the case, the smoke was affecting her more quickly now.

There was only one thing to do, and, by the gods, if Mars wasn't glad to do it. He turned, took Tamara's panicked face in his hands, and drew her in. She closed

her eyes, giving Mars the consent he so desperately desired, and Mars kissed her, deeply, passionately, with a longing and fervor he'd never given or felt before.

Fireworks. Flashes. Choirs. Strawberries. Mars wondered if this was what it was like being struck by one of his arrows.

Her lips were softer than he'd ever imagined, her breath sweet with ambrosia, her tenderness intoxicating. Given time and explicit permission, he'd have lingered for ages to savor her more thoroughly. Instead, he gently pulled away and licked his lips for one last taste of her.

She breathed deeply and opened her eyes.

"Don't fear, Tamara. Love."

She said nothing, but the fear and panic that had nearly overwhelmed her moments before were gone from her face. She instead looked calm. At peace.

"And we won' be having no more a dat," Tommy announced, killing the romance. "Ya coulda jes' as wella given her a knife to help her feel protected and safe against Da Smoke and da angry people. She got jes' as much ta fear from you as she do da dirty air."

Jarel stepped between them and put a hand on each's chest. "Yuh, let's not let Da Fear make us suspect *each other* and, yuh, fight amongst ourselves." He shook his head. "We, yuh, gots ta stay together in dis."

Mars and Tommy looked at each other not with outright hostility but guarded territoriality, each trying to

determine the other's intentions. A few moments passed before their eyes called a truce.

"How're we, yuh, gonna keep from fighting fer da long run wit' dis poisonous air all aroun' us?" Jarel asked Mars.

"I'll think loving thoughts," answered Mars.

Jarel spit out a laugh.

"No, seriously," he replied. "I'm the god of love, remember? If I think loving thoughts, those thoughts are strong around me. Thoughts have a way of affecting how we behave and the way others behave toward us."

Even though Jarel was a love angel, he looked doubtful that the god's mere thoughts could affect those proximate. Still, he extended his paltry appendages, and, the cue thus given, everyone did the same to extend their wings, save Mars, who held onto Cornelius for takeoff. The flight was long and bumpy, but they arrived at the hot, rocky stretch of land known as Death Valley unharmed. They touched down at Dante's View and looked far northwest.

"There they are!" exclaimed Mars, pointing. "Mandre and The God of the Dead. Aaaaand some of The Damned."

Mandre looked his normal, dashing self, this time in a sparkling white tuxedo. Pluto was taller than Mars expected and gaunt and intimidating in flowing, black robes that seemed to dematerialize at the edges, as if he were caught between two worlds. The Damned would

have been transparent had they not been coated in fine ash dust from The Underworld and their ankles shackled with balls and chains.

The Fallen Four leaned forward, squinting their eyes and turning their heads to better see and hear the specks in the distance. Too far for the non-gods to see. Too far to hear.

Mars lifted his arms to the sky. There was little moisture on that barren land, but atmosphere everywhere contains some, and it came to him. Mars closed his eyes in silent relief; air vapor hadn't come to him earlier in Cacciari's hideout, but now it did. Perhaps the ambrosia was making him stronger or perhaps his confidence was growing. Either way, when a cloud of moisture gathered in his cupped his hands, he brought the mass to his chest and rubbed it as if shaping a snowball. Instead, what appeared in his opened palm moments later was a glass-like lens, a spyglass, which he handed to Tamara. She took it. He let his fingers drag against her palm as she pulled away. She noticed it, caught his gaze, but otherwise did not respond.

He made three more lenses, offering one each to Jarel and Tommy, and keeping one for himself. Mars could see well, but he knew there was no harm in seeing even better. Cornelius, being proper and polite, did not mention the omission of a lens for him.

"Oh! This works great!" exclaimed Tamara. "I can see them really well. Oooooh, is that angel in white

Mandre?"

Mars did not like the way she *ooh*-ed. "Yes. He's the impostor," he replied, hoping to remind her of Mandre's infamy.

"But, yuh, we can't hear nothin'," Jarel uttered.

In answer, Mars raised his arms again. Before their eyes, water droplets from the air gathered at his fingertips. He swirled his fingers, pulling the miniature clouds down. As they swirled, they formed long, curved funnels, the tips tiny but the open ends as wide as their heads.

"Let's listen in, shall we?" suggested Mars, handing over two cloud funnels and raising his hands to make two more. "Water is an excellent conductor of sound, and there are water droplets all along the way leading to these ear horns. We'll be able to pick up quite a bit of what they say so long as they're not whispering, but I don't expect to hear everything. That's why I'd like you, Cornelius, to get closer."

Corny blanched.

"A lot closer," added Mars. "I'd like you to play the part of a tourist who obviously can't see or hear Pluto or Mandre or The Damned but is just there to take in the sites. Fall down a lot on the crags. Talk to yourself, like so many humans do when they think they're alone. Get close enough to listen in but not so close to get caught because, if you do, I don't know how I could get you out of there; I couldn't even fly to you, and those who can, even

Tyrone in the limo, are no match for Pluto.

Cornelius looked very concerned. His worried eyes searched everyone for a way out. Nothing. He opened his mouth, seemingly overwhelmed with questions but settling on one. "And how am I to get there?"

"Yuh, borrow a human car," suggested Jarel. "They's a bunch in the parking lot we passed."

Cornelius frowned. "I can't say that I remember how to drive. It has been some time since I traveled the earth as a mortal."

"Dat's okay," answered Jarel. "From what I seen, yuh, most humans don't know how to drive neither. Lotsa, yuh, crashes and near misses all ov'r da place."

"It looks far by road travel," Cornelius contested.

"I'll drop a square of ambrosia into the gas tank," Mars offered. "You'll get there in no time, just a few minutes, I'd gather, but you better slow down before pulling up to Mandre and Pluto, or they'll notice the unnatural speed."

"Oh, and, yuh, grab a car wit' some golf clubs in it or jes take the clubs outta any car and take da car a yer choice. Ya can't show up widdout clubs."

Mars looked at Jarel, now convinced that, yes, this love angel was also a thief.

"Well, he gotta make it look aut'entic."

Tommy shook his head in amusement, then turned to put an encouraging hand on Cornelius' shoulder. "Ready, Corndog?"

Mars stepped up and put his hand on Corny's other shoulder. It's good to have friends in time of need. "You'll do well, Cornelius. Have another square for courage." And he handed over two squares, one for his friend and the other for the car's engine.

Cornelius grimaced at his turn for danger but took flight toward the parking lot. It was only a few minutes later that Mars saw an old, brown Honda Accord on the main road going at a tremendous rate of speed. It was the sort of car he saw a lot of around the same time as Rubik's Cubes. Mars remembered arrowing up a few teens who had their faces pointed into their laps working the cube, much like teens do today with their cell phones; and he remembered hitting a black-haired Latina traveling in that same kind of car. Everywhere there were memories.

Mars watched the car slow just before the salt pan. He, Jarel, Tommy, and Tamara immediately brought the water lenses to their eyes and the funnels to their ears. Mandre and Pluto joined in watching the vehicle skid to a halt. *Ay. He* really *is out of driving practice,* Mars silently agreed.

Cornelius stepped out. He'd secured, probably from inside the vehicle, a red baseball cap that clashed horribly with his fluffy, brown hair and that pushed the puffs of curls out to the side, like a monk's haircut. *Cornelius, the red-capped monk.* But the costume was convincing as a prudent precaution for a tourist concerned with sunburn,

which such a fair-skinned lad would surely be. The cap had the added benefit of hiding his face.

Cornelius walked around to the trunk, pulled out clubs, and dumped them onto the ground. A driver spilled out of the bag.

"Cornelius!" whispered Tamara, as if he could hear her. "Golfers treat their clubs well!"

"Unless dey angry at dey golfing," added Tommy.

"Shhhh!" admonished Jarel. "We gotta hear dis."

Mars turned his ear horn left and right like a human turning rabbit ear antennae. He heard a lot of wind before catching some broken conversation.

"And where – *crrrch* – Styx – *crrrch* – from?"

Static interrupted the transmission, and Mars didn't know whether that static came from the heat of the Death Valley floor or from The Styx Smoke or even from Pluto himself, who was talking again.

Mars looked to his cohorts for interpretation.

"I think he asked where to fly sticks from," said Tommy.

"Naw. He asked where to, yuh, fly fish from." corrected Jarel.

"No!" refuted Tamara. "Pluto asked where did the fragments of The Styx come from."

They all hastened to readjust their ear horns.

"*Crrrch* – Jupiter – *crrrch* – forces – *crrrch* – thought it – *crrrch* – you."

"Confound this!" admonished Mars, slapping his ear horn on its side as if it could behave any better. The others lowered theirs, too. "I can't catch whole sentences!"

"And that's why you sent Cornelius," reminded Tamara. "There! He's getting closer!"

They raised their eyepieces to see Cornelius purposely stumble across the jagged terrain. He took pains to catch his foot on points of rock. Mars saw his mouth moving tirelessly and hoped he was muttering, complaining about the serrated surface.

Mars saw several dozen of The Damned tee up around Cornelius. They swung back, Pluto waved his arms, sending all the golf balls falling off their tees, and the Damned, every last one, missed the shot. They moaned in woe.

"We're witnessing a torture," whispered Tamara.

Mars held up his ear horn again and heard that maligning Mandre laugh and ask, "Why – *crrrch?*"

"*Crrrch,*" answered Pluto. "And worse as the heat rises."

More laughter. Mars shook his head at watching Pluto torture former golfers with the worst terrain in the highest heat. Probably every day. Diabolical. Sure to drive them mad. Mars hoped Cornelius would know enough to not bump into anyone out there and get himself found out.

"If it wasn't you – *crrrch* – who?" asked Mandre.

Pluto turned his evanescible form to pace. He

went in Cornelius' direction. Corny had his head down looking for his ball.

"Cornelius!" whispered Tommy. "Look up! Get outta dere!"

"No! Don't!" urged Tamara, looking to Tommy. "He can't see Pluto, remember? He's supposed to be mortal. He just needs to back away, coincidentally."

Mars held the eyepiece and saw Corny do just that, "accidentally" trip and toss a ball the opposite direction and go after it. He even had the authenticity to grandly scratch his rear end in the withdrawal.

"Ha!" Mars laughed. "He's doing great!" He lifted his ear horn just as Pluto stopped dead in his tracks. Well, Pluto always stops dead, being the Lord of the Dead. Anyway.

"I smell" – and Pluto's eyes alighted on Cornelius – "ambrosia!"

Cornelius moved suddenly faster to retrieve the ball, and Tommy dropped the lens from his eye, readying for flight, but Mars stayed him as he saw Mandre pull out something from an inside pocket.

"That's me," Mandre answered. "Haven't had breakfast – *crrrch* –."

"Nor I," interjected Pluto, turning to snatch the item from his companion. Mandre didn't stop him, although he looked chagrined.

Everyone sighed in relief except Mars, who calmly

explained, "Cornelius smells more like Earth than anybody down there. He and his clothes have been here a long time. The rest of them either smell like Heaven or Hell. But maybe I shouldn't have given him that second square of ambrosia. Ambrosia's so … amazing-smelling, and that smell's indiffusible."

Mars raised his ear horn and eyepiece again. Frustrated damned golfers putted over jagged "greens" that wouldn't have easily allowed water to flow, much less golf balls. Pluto's lips split into a depraved smile before answering Mandre's earlier question.

"Perhaps it was that sleazy Vil-*crrrch*," said Pluto. "*Someone* was in my realm. There are … *things* … missing, and the dog, well. Cerberus hasn't been the same since the explosion. He keeps sniffing around the kitchen and not guarding the river; someone has taken his loyalty. Perhaps this someone plans to defect."

"To join who?" asked Mandre.

"Cupid perhaps?" asked Pluto, ignoring that he was standing before the newly appointed Cupid. Mars smiled at the continued acknowledgment. "Perhaps Cupid convinced – *crrrch* – to flip sides and – *crrrch* – that driver of yours."

"Tyrone?" asked Mandre. Mars and Tamara dropped their eyepieces and looked at each other. Concern deeply etched both faces.

"Bring him to me!" demanded Pluto before turning

again toward Cornelius. "This human takes 20 swings when most take one, simply to vainly say they've done it. And yet he lingers."

"Stupid golf!" Cornelius shouted as if on cue. "I'm out!" He hustled toward his car even as The Lord of the Dead floated in approach.

"Hurry, Corndog! Hurry!" urged Tommy.

"My lord," asked Mandre, staying Pluto and undoubtedly saving Corny's twisted bogey in the process; Corny didn't stop moving. Mars kept listening.

"Where would you like him delivered?"

"If your driver had The Styx on him, I say he'd like to go back into the river. Permanently."

Hearing that, Tamara opened her wings and shot down the far side of the mountain, no doubt gaining distance before rocketing up to Heaven to save her new favorite chauffeur.

"Go after her, Jarel!" urged Mars. "Tyrone can't fly! I'll tell him to jump, but she'll need help catching him or he'll end up dead and in Pluto's clutches before we can scrape him off the sidewalk. Go!"

Jarel's little wings opened and flapped quicker than Mars had ever seen them go.

Tommy was about to take off, too, but Mars grabbed him. "We stay here for Cornelius." Mars looked through the eyepiece to see Corny drive away at human speed, his eyes darting back and forth. Surely his heart

was racing, too – faster than the RPMs of that vehicle. Neither Pluto nor Mandre was in pursuit. Cornelius was escaping unharmed.

Mars let go of Tommy's arm to take his hands. He formed them into a cup and then retrieved out of the dirt both Tamara's and Jarel's abandoned eyepieces. Dropping the lenses into Tommy's hands, Mars poked them. They broke apart into liquid water. Mars pulled out his tray, thought up a square, and dropped it into Tommy's hands, which were leaking despite his best efforts. Tyrone's face immediately swam into view.

"Tyrone! Get out of there!" demanded Mars. "Mandre's going to take you to Pluto!"

Tyrone's eyes widened in terror. "What? Why? Where do I go?"

"Out of Olympus. Don't take the limo. They'll trace it."

"I can't fly, Mars!"

"Just run to The Mist and jump. We're coming!"

The last drops of water seeped through Tommy's fingers and were gone, which suited Mars fine. *Less talking. More moving.*

Cornelius was a safe distance and picking up speed.

"Now, while we're alone and have a second, tell me, what's the story between you and Tamara?"

Tommy gave him a disbelieving look. "I can't believe you askin' me dat wit' all da danger aroun' us right

now."

"Yeah, well. I need to know, more than I've needed to know about anyone." And while it was the blurted truth, just saying it made Mars uneasy.

"Ya can't treat her like jus' any other girl – use her and dispose a' her. She ain' jes' any other girl."

"I'm seeing that for myself, Tommy. Are you two a thing?"

He jerked his head back in surprise. "Naw, we ain' no thang, but I care fer her like family. She brought me backta life afta we was all kicked outta Olympus, altho' I didn' know her at the time.

"I'd been eatin' mortal food to survive. I didn' know about Cacciari and his band. I was wanderin' around, starvin' fer almost two weeks, it turns out, losin' strength every day. I fell down, an', the next thing I know, I wake up in a sof' bed, an' this beautiful angel's hoverin' ov'r me, pettin' my face to wake me an' feedin' me her share a ambrosia. It took a week 'a her sharin' her allotmen' with me, a week 'a her growing weaker to make me stronger, bu' she did it. She brought me back ta life and brought me ta her friends, who ended up bein' the bes' angels a person could ever hope to know.

"I'd do anything fer TamTam," – and here his eyes bore into Mars' – "including take on a god. There ain' no one could hurt her as lon' as I'm livin'. They'd havta kill me firs'."

It all suddenly made sense to Mars, why Tommy would "let" her go off on her own adventure without any claim of proprietary interest yet want to beat Mars for encouraging the danger. And here she was off to catch an angel that, in Pluto's eyes, was now his property. And still Tommy didn't stop her and was poised to take off in pursuit.

"I have no intention of hurting her, Tommy," Mars tried to assure him.

"Yeah, well, then exactly what are yer intentions?"

Chapter 22

CONSPIRACY
OR
A LEAP OF FAITH

Mars had no intention of stating his intentions because he intended to have no intentions, intentionally or not. He'd never had to explain his plans to a protective father, mother, or loved one because he'd never actively pursued someone who hadn't chased him first – or at least made themselves *awfully* available.

But this was different. Not only was Tamara keeping her feelings to herself, she wasn't letting her body language do *any* talking the way so many of Mars' previous acquaintances had. Mars would have loved to have left the idea alone, but Tommy was waiting for an answer, and Tommy was obviously going to be an obstacle if he weren't placated, and Mars still needed Tommy's help from a purely military standpoint, so Mars answered as truthfully yet briefly as he could.

"My intentions are to get to know her better – better than I do most girls."

Tommy raised his brow.

"Not like that, Tommy." *Well, maybe like that,* he admitted to himself with a sly grin, *but more.* "She's special."

Tommy pursed his lips but otherwise said nothing.

A car revving in the parking lot brought them back to the situation at hand. A few moments later, Cornelius fluttered up the path, purple-faced and sweating.

"Hiya, Cornelius!" greeted Mars with a little too much enthusiasm. Nerves, you know.

"Oh, sir! Thank Juno that I managed to escape."

Mars grinned. His grandma, Juno, who was also queen of the gods, would appreciate credit for the escape, especially as she did no work to earn it. Mars hadn't asked her help because he knew from experience that she was too lazy to actually *do* anything. She was sort of crazy that way.

"Actually, you can thank Mandre," stated Tommy, eliciting a frown from Mars, who'd never want to credit Mandre with anything helpful and knew that grandma wouldn't want credit once given to her to later be bestowed upon another. "Mandre's da one dat got Pluto's nose off'n ya."

"We've got to help your driver, sir! Pluto has ordered Mandre to bring him to him."

Mars explained that the situation was well in hand and asked Cornelius to fill them in on the conversation on the valley floor.

"Well, sir," he began. "I'd have to think this through to decide whether it's a turn of events in our favor, but Pluto suspects a plot. He knows someone entered his dominion, and he believes it to be either Tyrone or Cacciari, the latter of whom he suspects may be in league with *you,*

sir, to foil Pluto's plans and help you regain your throne."

Tommy balked. "Whoa. We did *not* git all dat from dese water-logged earpieces." He waved dismissively at his ear horn.

Mars frowned again. He inwardly agreed that the ear pieces were feeble but didn't appreciate the scorn. "That's why I sent *him*, remember?" reminded Mars while pointing to Cornelius. "An ear horn used miles away won't receive sound as well as a person standing right next to the talker."

"Good t'ing he was dere, too, 'cuz all we heard was a command to retrieve Tyrone and complaints 'bout Cerberus."

"Right," continued Cornelius. "Cerberus is not guarding the river, so there's real concern there that the dead may try to leave The Underworld – or that *living* ones might try to rescue them. That's a whole different problem – and one that will likely consume Pluto's time in the very near future. He'll be the one most wanting to control his kingdom, so a crack in the hull will keep him awfully distracted. That's great luck for us."

"And it's all Tamara's doing," praised Mars with a doe-eyed appreciation before he could stop it. *Fool,* he chided himself. He felt color rise in his cheeks.

Tommy said nothing, apparently letting the subject of courtship rest. Cornelius merely nodded in agreement, oblivious to the conversation that had taken place in his

absence.

"Yes, well, that move of hers will prove to be huge for us, I'm sure. Pluto will spend a lot of energy posting guards at the entrances to and exits from his land and retraining Cerberus, but he was here today, sir, so that means he must feel confident that few know of the breach and there won't be an immediate exodus. But he *does* want to know who caused it."

"Mandre mentioned Jupiter," prompted Mars.

"Yes, sir. Mandre asked Pluto if he was the intruder at Jupiter Heights because, apparently, Mandre spotted The Styx mud on Tyrone, and your driver said he'd tackled someone during the break-in while assisting Jupiter's Special Forces. Mandre assumed the intruder had to be Pluto. Well, sir, Pluto nearly accused Mandre of being a double agent on his way to reporting to Jupiter."

"So Pluto don' trust no one den," assessed Tommy.

"Would you expect him to?" asked Mars. "He'd love espionage on others but then turn around and not trust his own spies."

"Correct, sir. He doesn't trust Mandre nor Cacciari nor Tyrone, so he has commanded Mandre to produce Tyrone for questioning, and he's called a meeting at noon in The Underworld."

Mars paused and gazed at his still-wet right shoe.

"I believe you're contemplating espionage for that meeting as well, sir, and I'd advise against it. After the

now-known infiltration into his realm, Pluto will surely implement tightened security. Plus, sir, any intelligence gleaned from such congress would be minimal. They'll likely toss around guesses about the latest events while we already know what's happening. I suggest we reconnoiter; use their absences to propagandize our new troops, sir."

"What in da constellations did ya jes' say?" asked Tommy, throwing his hands in the air.

"He said we should join back up and use the time that Pluto's gone to flip Cacciari's men our way," Mars clarified.

Tommy grudgingly nodded in thanks.

"And that sounds like a good plan from an intelligent strategist." Mars slapped Cornelius on the back before then hitching on for a ride back to The Safe House.

The flight was bumpier than any before. Mars' hands, arms, and shoulders ached from holding on so tightly. He wasn't used to using those muscles for much more than shooting arrows. Once on solid ground, Mars stretched his joints and swung his arms in huge circles. Following the arc, Mars looked up in time to see Tamara and Jarel descending, Tyrone sandwiched between them. He had one arm over each one's shoulder and was pedaling his legs as if they could challenge gravity.

Mars, that Grief Giver, decided right then and there that he'd had enough of Tyrone's fear of flying. *If I've got to learn to tie my own shoes, then Tyrone's got to learn to fly.*

The three landed, and Tyrone bear-hugged both his companions and Mars. It was awkward for The Macho Master.

"Thank you, sir," gushed Tyrone, "for letting me know! And you two for catching me! You have no idea what it's like to jump into open sky without any hope of stopping yourself. I leapt, felt my stomach lurched up to my throat, and just lost all control."

"Yeah," Jarel confirmed, rubbing his cheeks. "He was, yuh, thrashin' like Hercules' hydra. I tried gittin' my hands around his wais', but wid all that lashin' out, I, yuh, got smacked in da face a coupla times."

Good, thought Mars, still miffed about having to wear a pink polo shirt. Meanwhile, Tamara stood as a bastion of beauty, straightening her purple dress.

"*You* weren't hurt, were you, Tamara?" he asked.

"No," she said with a little laugh. "As soon as I said his name, Tyrone relaxed and spread out his arms. Jarel and I moved in together to catch him. No sweat."

Tyrone shuddered at talk of his free fall and then exclaimed, "Imagine! The newly appointed god of love in league with Pluto! I'm thankful beyond words you all freed me from that tyrant and his ilk."

This was the third time Mars had heard Tyrone speak ill of Mandre – first just outside the lingerie shop, then in the castle kitchen, and now here. He'd never heard him speak badly of anyone before. *I can't imagine being*

so awful that people say horrible things about me all the time, he thought. That Amnesiac Egotist.

Mars looked to the sky and again saw Apollo on his daily ride. He wasn't quite a quarter of the way across the sky, which made sense; Pluto met Mandre at 8 a.m., and that meeting had lasted about an hour, so it was mid-morning. It was hard to believe that only three days had passed since Mars had been dethroned, but he couldn't let Olympus settle in with a new love god, neither for the sake of his legacy nor his chances of a comeback. Mars also couldn't let Mandre and Pluto plot against the kingdom. Pluto was meeting Cacciari at noon. They had little time to prepare.

"Let's go inside," Mars said to the group at large. "It'll probably be our last time in this place because once Pluto talks to Cacciari and confirms his allegiance, and once Cacciari confirms that Pluto hasn't cut off his ambrosia supply on purpose, and once Mandre convinces both that he wasn't involved with either thing, if they believe each other, they'll turn to the next logical culprit. Me. And you all, too, because they'll realize how long I've supposedly gone without ambrosia, and they'll add one plus one and get five traitors."

"We really in it, den, ain't we?" asked Jarel. "We's fugitives agin, firs' from Heaven, den from Hell. Who else can we tick off?"

They laughed nervously. Not wanting to stay

outside a second longer, Mars walked ahead of the others to the door and opened it, not out of courtesy, as it appeared, but to air out what he knew was coming. A dense funk of death rolled out the door in a palpable wave. The house reeked like an overflowing sepulchre. A chorus of complaints told Mars that no one *wanted* to enter, but there was still work to be done, so Mars led the way in ahead of his grudging companions.

There'd be no question to anyone arriving later that Pluto's tray had been there. *In a couple of hours,* Mars reasoned, *Pluto, Mandre, and Cacciari would figure out everything. The war's begun.*

Chapter 23

TEACHING OLD ANGELS NEW TRICKS

OR

MOLD AND MADNESS

Cornelius?" began Mars, turning to the angel in this company who would both know the answer and be the most polite in answering. "When do The Fallen usually meet to get their ambrosia?"

"Midday once a week, sir, in Rome. Today's the day, and it's nearly time. Some will be arriving already to socialize and gossip or attempt to cozen off with an extra portion. Mr. Cacciari typically presents himself around noon to grandstand; well, I should say he walks around the tables while his associates distribute food, but I believe the purpose is to remind us all from whom we receive our allotment, lest we question our allegiance.

"This week, however, Mr. Cacciari will be detained due to Pluto's summons. The Fallen awaiting will be very hungry and testy, sir. It will be risky approaching then but undoubtedly our best opportunity. If they don't commit angelicide on us, they'll at least have their ears open while they're gormandizing your ambrosia."

"The latter would be better," answered Mars in a nervous tone. He cleared his throat. "Okay, so tell me where exactly in Rome they meet, and I can have Tommy

drop me off."

Tamara shifted her weight and looked at her friends. Jarel crossed his arms.

"So, yuh, all dat stuff abou' bein' generals in yer army was all, yuh, bupkis, wuz it? Ya ain' never had no intention a includin' us?"

Mars opened his mouth, but Cornelius spoke first.

"Sir, you're not suggesting leaving the rest of us, are you?"

Again Mars opened his mouth to protest, but Cornelius cut him off.

"You'd never make ingress without all of us as a buffer. You *will* require neutral ambassadors, and we are they. I believe we've made clear, through our expeditions and actions, sir, that we are a faction. We challenged Pluto's plan as partners, sir, and we intend to face any fracas or broil as a contingent."

Tommy threw his arms high again and huffed. "What in Vulcan's Lava are ya sayin'?!" He turned to the others. "He ain' makin' no sense."

Tamara turned to answer cooly, "He's telling Mars that we're a team and that we proved it by risking our necks." She turned an angry, steely glare toward Mars. "Cornelius is reminding Mars that we went to Heaven and Hell for him."

The room fell silent, and Mars got his chance to speak.

"I never said I wanted to exclude you or that I don't appreciate the hardships that you went through–"

"Good," piped up Tommy, "because if ya put TamTam in dat much danger—"

"But," Mars interjected, "I know that once The Fallen see my face, you, having brought me there will be in danger, real physical danger. I'm giving you your chance to back out from any more problems, even Tommy, who'd just drop me off. I can't fairly expect you to take on more."

"Well, I, yuh, ain' losin' my title o' general," spat Jarel. "I, yuh, ain' never had no cool title before, and I, yuh, ain' gonna waste it now. I'm goin'!"

"As am I," declared Cornelius. "Standing next to Pluto, witnessing his Utopia in torturing those poor golfers only cements an angel's distrust of his nefarious plans. I want nothing more to do with him, up to the cost of starvation."

Tommy's brow raised at the word 'nefarious', but he must have gotten the gist of the speech. "Yeah, I'm 'ginst Pluto, too," he reassured everyone.

"And I. Am. Going." Tamara avowed this in a way that left no room for argument.

Tyrone nodded his equal intent.

Mars knew that they were immovable, and it irked him a bit. *Shouldn't the lesser classes yield to the god?* But his slowly developing humility spoke up and reminded him: he'd have starved without them, and they'd proven

themselves more courageous and loyal than some of the most celebrated gods, but, if they were going to join him, at least one thing had to change.

"Okay. Fine. You're all aboard. But, Tyrone?" he asked gently. "I've been needing to hitch rides as I can't fly at the moment because my wings were clipped." Tyrone gasped in shock, as Mars knew he would. "Look, Cornelius can explain it all to you later, along with what happened in the meeting between Mongrel and Pluto, but, right now, you need to think about flying."

"I can't fly, Cupid," Tyrone insisted, his eyes widening in fear.

"You *don't* fly, but you're capable of it, Tyrone. You no longer have the limo, so, unless you learn, you're as grounded as I am."

"And I'm okay with that," he answered, taking a step backward.

"But I'm not. I can't have a fully capable member of my army choosing to make himself dependent on another. Someone might not be around to save you."

"But I can't!" protested Tyrone.

"Why can'tchya fly?" asked Jarel, who lifted a hand to absent-mindedly rub his still-stinging cheek.

"I'm, uh." He looked down, ashamed. "I'm afraid of heights."

"But yer an angel!" Jarel answered with a laugh. "Ya live in Olympus – on a floating mountain!"

Tyrone turned, flabbergasted.

"I *know* where I live, but it's solid ground as far as I'm concerned, and when I drive I'm solidly in the limo. I became a driver in part so that I wouldn't *have* to fly like the rest of the love angels. I'd be no good at it."

Tamara stepped up and put her hand on his shoulder. "I think your fear of heights might come from looking down and because you move every part of yourself when you fly. When you jumped out of Olympus, you had your arms swinging and your legs kicking like you were trying to swim. With all that movement, maybe you can't keep your wings in sync." She had a soothing demeanor that allowed her to point out a deficiency without sounding judgmental. All the heads in the room (except Tyrone's) bobbed in agreement.

Tyrone wasn't blinking. He looked petrified, being asked to learn something for which he had a mortal's fear.

"T," added Mars, trying to emulate Tamara's soothing tones. "Try again. We need you to fly. We need all our soldiers ready to go. We're in a room with an eight-foot ceiling. Even if you fall, you'll probably be fine."

Tamara facepalmed herself at the word 'probably'. Tyrone took another step back.

"Okayyyy," Mars quickly added, that Foot-in-Mouth Flimflammer. "Here's the deal. Practice. Flutter around the room, learn to fly, and you'll never have to dress me again."

Tamara's head snapped his way. "He dresses you?"

Jarel barked out a laugh. "Yeah! Ha, ha! He, yuh, got him tyin-"

"Jarel!" shouted Mars bossily. "Why don't you show Tyrone how to float? Isn't that how I met you? You leering over me in a dark alley?!"

Cornelius' eyes swiveled from speaker to speaker.

Mars continued with Tyrone. "All you need to do is keep your wings pumping. Don't let them stop."

"Why would he dress you?" asked Tamara.

Mars normally didn't have any trouble lying to a girl, but he didn't want to start out with Tamara by lying to *her.*

Tyrone, as usual, rescued him. "The God of Love, as a representative of Jupiter, sometimes needs straightening to look his best, Miss. I keep him presentable."

And from going barefoot, thought Mars, grinning appreciatively. He immediately knelt and readjusted his shoe to impress his idea: he would learn to tie his shoe in exchange for Tyrone's learning to fly.

Before Mars' ineptitude could become evident to all, Tyrone lifted Tamara's hand, led her to a corner of the room, and asked, "How can I fly, Miss? Would you please show me?"

She laughed at his gentlemanly behavior and newfound enthusiasm before beginning her lesson. Cornelius and Tommy stepped over to be her living mannequins or

her helper or his catcher, whichever was needed.

Mars grabbed Jarel's hand and yanked him into the kitchen, which smelled horrendously musty, thanks to the festering tray under the sink. Mars turned on him, demanding, "*How* could you almost tell her?!"

"Aw, man. I dunno," Jarel answered with a shrug. "I, yuh, kinda forgot it was a secret. I tell ma' crew ev'rythin'."

Mars scowled but accepted that Jarel had been with The Fallen much longer than he'd known *him*; it's not surprising that Jarel would talk at ease around them.

"Okay, well, how about you tell me how a shoe's tied?"

Jarel's brow raised. Mars knew what that meant.

"Argh! Fine! Please, Jarel. Please teach me to tie my shoe. I made a promise, and it'd be easier to keep if I had help."

And so Jarel showed the patience of an angel in teaching that Loafing Loop-the-Looper how it's done. He needed patience; Mars kept dropping the loop and getting his thumb caught after the roundabout.

After a frustrating half hour in which he heard shouts and thuds coming from the other room, Mars could competently tie a decent enough bow to keep his shoe in place, albeit looser than he liked. When he and Jarel walked out of the kitchen and into the living room, Mars was amazed to see Tyrone zooming back and forth, gliding just under the ceiling, then skimming just over

the floor, stopping to hover, then tilting forward again to zip in another direction like a busy bee buzzing in a field. He looked at ease and smiled broadly after landing in front of Tamara.

She clapped her hands together in delight. "Oh, you're a natural, Tyrone! I *knew* you could do it."

"Thanks to your kind words and patience, Miss, and the help of you two, too," he added, nodding at the gents. "I've always wanted to fly." Tyrone took Tamara's hand again and patted it. "Thank you, Miss."

Mars was overcome with the desire to run off with her. He pictured her in his castle, the embodiment of his firmamental fantasies, padding barefoot to the fireplace to stoke the fire, settling onto the shag carpet before it, and seeming accustomed to the place. He smiled at the image before scowling at it.

No! I'm Cupid!, thought our Hubris Hero. *The universe's most celebrated 'player'! And I don't chase girls! They chase me! And this one's not even interested from what I can tell. So stop the fantasizing already! Stop it!*

Tamara withdrew her hand and hugged Tyrone. "I'm proud of you."

Mars was instantly jealous – and then angry at himself for being so.

Tommy slapped Tyrone on the back in congratulations. Cornelius merely nodded. Mars noticed that they looked disheveled and slightly squashed, like they

had to catch Tyrone more than once. Cornelius' feathers bent at all angles and Tommy's neck sported red welts as if Tyrone had wildly grasped him. Mars couldn't decide who among them had the worst task.

Tyrone looked happier than he had ever before.

Mars shook off his strange, new emotions and clapped appreciatively. "I always knew you had it in you," he said and discreetly tapped his foot, nonchalantly so as to not catch Tamara's attention. Tyrone spotted the move and nodded. Mars' promise had been kept. He turned toward the group and took a deep, steadying breath.

"It's time to go see The Fallen. Just let me grab Pluto's tray."

Mars walked back into the craptacular kitchen with its horrid stench and opened the cabinet below the sink. He was shocked to see big-as-his-head green and black mold spores growing along the inside walls of the cabinet. Crawling between the spores were brown centipedes as long and wide as his finger, black earwigs with needle-sharp pincers, and silvery waterbugs with waving rows of thin, caesious legs.

Mars' eyes found the U-bend of piping and followed it up, above the countertop to the faucet, where strings of slime oozed and grey overgrowth coated the spigot.

Not sure that plumbing will ever work again, he thought.

Kneeling at the under-sink cabinet, Mars took a steadying breath and plunged his hand into the furry decay. He withdrew Pluto's tray, drawing strands of fibrous mildew along behind it. Mars shook them loose, releasing a spray of beetles that scattered and skidded across the kitchen floor before scurrying into crevices between wall and floor.

Maybe the whole house *will never be the same again.*

But he decided that wasn't his problem. Not now, at least, if ever. He stepped back into the living room, and the fetor spread. Everyone backed away.

"Yup," announced Mars. "We'll all smell like death, but maybe it'll be to our advantage, facing The Fallen, I mean. It's got to make us seem tougher than if we smelled like freshly baked cookies."

"What *is* that thing?!" asked Tyrone.

"We'll explain on the way. Let's go."

Everyone headed toward the door except Tyrone. He stood planted.

"Some'n wrong?" asked Tommy.

"I – I – flying in *here* was one thing, but out there? I could fall!"

"Oh, Tyrone," sympathized Tamara. "You've got jitters. We understand. We do."

Mars had difficulty keeping himself from rolling his eyes. He was proud of his driver, but, *honestly, how hard is flying when you have working wings?* And there

wasn't time to lose.

"But you need to know that flying out there," she said, pointing out the curtainless window, "is no different than flying in here. There's wind, sure, and you'll have to flap hard to get lift, but, once you're at altitude, the wind will only make it easier to glide."

"Yeah, Tyrone!" encouraged Tommy. "You'll love soarin'. 'S fun!"

"I'm – I'm not ready for an open-sky, open-water flight. I – I don't want to practice above city streets or shark-infested waters. If I have to escape from something later, I promise I'll try, but right now I'd like to get a ride, too. I – I – I just don't want to do this yet."

Although Mars' ire was rising, Tommy and Jarel didn't skip a beat. They got on either side of Tyrone and walked out with him. Mars followed. Outside, he shook Pluto's tray again to release more entrenched bugs and tucked the infested thing into his back waistband, hoping it wouldn't infect his own tray. More importantly for the moment, he hoped his pants would stay up.

He hoisted up his sagging jeans, remembering that humans could see him now. *Imagine,* he thought to himself. *'Bare-assed angel overhead! Don't look up!'* He chuckled and held onto Cornelius' back.

Tyrone draped an arm over the shoulders of Tommy and Jarel, and everyone took off. Tamara led the group, being the only one of The Fallen Four not carrying

someone.

Peering past Cornelius' shoulder, Mars looked ahead, ostensibly to see where they were headed but in reality to watch Tamara's graceful form.

She flew beautifully. Her strong, golden wings would beat once and hold, beat again and hold. The tiny red sparkles throughout added a blush of color to each powerful stroke. He wanted to be flying next to her, next to this brave and compassionate and inspiring woman. Mars suddenly realized he'd do just about anything she asked, and that's when he came to understand that he was *gone.* No longer his own. He was *in love.*

It took the god of love a lot longer to realize it than anyone else in his company.

Chapter 24

THE SEEING SEA

OR

SUN GLARE

Flying over the Sea of Atlas, or, as humans call it, the Atlantic Ocean, was terrifying – and bumpy. The unusually large, blue waves below may have looked pretty to angels with *intact* feathers and strong flight, but both Mars and Tyrone knew that, falling from their height, the water would be hard as concrete. With each bump of turbulence, Mars saw centipedes and roaches sprinkle out of his pants, and, each time he looked down, Mars could have sworn he saw a shadow trailing them, eyes deep in the depths, perhaps a behemoth hoping for its snack to fall from the sky. Was Neptune following them, he wondered, ready to punish them should they again drop into his domain unannounced?

"Don't look down, don't look down," Tyrone chanted throughout the flight. *Good advice,* thought Mars, who chose to study Tommy and Jarel, who were becoming increasingly sweaty, as if both the exertion and Tyrone's chants were wearing them down.

The continent, when it finally came into view, was a welcome sight. It emerged from the watery horizon as a thin, bumpy line that grew to a mountainous mass lying

supine beneath its empyrean master.

Approaching land, Mars and Tyrone developed new fears, not of falling onto concrete-hard *water* but onto actual concrete.

"Don't look down, don't look down," came the chant. Mars obeyed and turned his gaze to Tamara. Her wings. Beat and hold. Beat and hold.

"Look down!" Cornelius shouted. Mars looked down at the shoreline and saw a mortal beach-comber pointing up at him. His companions lifted their hands to block the sun's glare.

Cornelius, sensing he had mere moments before the fellow's friends confirmed the sighting, shot upward into the clouds. The entire celestial group followed and got soaked as their reward. It wasn't long, though, before Tamara set back her wings and lowered her shoulders for the descent.

"Our commute is long, sir," Corny shouted over his shoulder. "We go clear across the globe to receive our salary, as I suppose you could call it."

"And where in Rome do The Fallen meet?" Mars asked at the very moment that a magnificent building came into view.

"The Colosseum, sir," Corny repeated. "Although the last official *mortal* games were recorded in the sixth century, Pluto never stopped *his* entertainments. We're given our weekly allotment and then forced to watch his

games. Anyone leaving early is deemed…" – he searched for the right word – "uncommitted."

Mars pondered what kind of entertainments Pluto might sponsor, even as the ruins came more clearly into view. He'd flown over the Colosseum hundreds of times but was still amazed by its wonder. The awe-inspiring, iconic colossus stood out in the modern city as a vestige of its past. Elliptical, tall, and huge, most of the nearly two-millenia-old amphitheatre was falling apart, the southern upper tiers having collapsed from earthquakes, the remaining façade intact but ravaged by age and mistreatment. For centuries after the sacking and fall of the Roman Empire, generations of destitute, starving, and homeless humans pilfered its stones to build their little, Dark-Age shacks and live their subsistent, war-torn lives. And so, with the passing of each generation, the Colosseum must have looked more and more like a monument to a greater past, proof to the struggling mortals of the day that their species had *de*volved and fallen into chaos.

And that sense of tragedy would have drawn Pluto like a vulture to carrion, Mars thought.

Even with its exterior walls crumbling, the Colosseum stood 15 stories above the street, remaining majestic and worthy of a god. Inside, the stone seating was chipped in some sections, interrupted in others, or gone altogether. The wooden floor had disappeared to time but was partly rebuilt by historically-minded humans to better help

tourists imagine the scene. The floor was where unfortunate players re-enacted famous battles, gladiators fought for their lives, and the condemned were executed for public amusement. The section lacking flooring allowed visitors to see directly into the hypogeum below; its labyrinth of walls once supported the floor above and separated humans and animals taking part in the great and cruel entertainments. Some of the final sights of those doomed souls were the hypogeum walls as they awaited their fates. Considering the Colosseum's horrid past and its ability to hold some 50,000 spectators, Mars could easily see why The Underworld's Ringleader would want to continue holding games there. They would indulge his penchant for spreading misery.

"Tamara, stop!" Mars shouted. "I – I have to say something before we go in!"

Tamara didn't look back but banked left to a small grouping of trees standing in what locals of that concrete jungle might call a park. She landed gracefully on the top branch of an Italian Stone Pine tree, while all her followers dived in at speed. Mars and Tyrone lowered themselves from their angelic transports, and Mars quickly hid himself in the needles lest keen-eyed humans point him out again.

Mars turned toward the group and took a deep, steadying breath. They looked expectantly at him, their attention quickened, and Mars, for the briefest moment, wished his father were there. *But then again, no,* he thought.

Not Dad himself. What I really need is Dad's flair for fetial words. It won't be long before Cacciari swoops in with orders to hunt me down.

Mars looked up to check the time and was shocked – stunned – to see Apollo himself, the god of the sun and prophesy, looking back at him. Not just looking. Staring. Mars could tell he'd been watching awhile.

Mars offered a feeble wave. He wondered if his uncle had seen him at the edge of The Mist and figured out that it was *he* who'd invaded Jupiter Heights. Or maybe Apollo just wanted to ogle a fallen god as if it were some strange insect under a magnifying glass. Either way, Apollo nodded and returned to his work, shaking the reins – *as if* his horses needed guidance or encouragement. *Odd.*

"Ain't no time for, yuh, sunbathing, M.J.," Jarel scolded and then coughed. "And we don' need no pep talk. Pluto's doin' mo' damage den we can stomach, so, yuh, 's time ta get dis party started." Mars remembered Jarel saying those exact words just before The Fallen Four explained Mars' role in their banishment. *Apparently he likes to call horrible moments a party.*

Mars frowned. "This is probably your last chance, all of you, to step away from this. Look at the skies. There aren't any more angels approaching. That means they're all assembled already. Once we fly into that Colosseum, there'll be no turning back."

Jarel huffed. "Now you, yuh, ain' gonna back outta

dis now. All you, yuh, gots ta do is win da crowd. And, yuh, if ya fail, dis general is ready ta fight!"

Mars appreciated the enthusiasm but perhaps understood the danger better than any of them. A lost fight here might mean an eternal afterlife trapped in The Underworld. This was no joke. Heaven and earth were at stake. He looked into the eyes of each member of his as-yet-tiny army and saw overriding determination in all of them. He eyed Tamara last because he liked lingering on her face. Mars breathed deeply, detecting the faintest smell of strawberries. Tamara's ambiance was strangely comforting and encouraging. "They might go after you," he told her, "perhaps assuming you're with me." And he sorely wished she were with him – in a non-military way.

She smiled and answered sweetly, "Mmmm, I think I'll stay." Mars loved the way she said it and returned her smile.

Then he gathered his courage and stepped back behind Cornelius. "Then let's go. We'll drop in over the tall wall so they don't see us ahead of time. Realize that when we land in the center of the arena, we *will be* surrounded. It's a terrible military position." *Dad would lose his mind with disappointment in me.*

Tamara grinned at him sympathetically before opening her wings to hover at the treetop. Less than a dozen strong wingbeats later, she and the group soared over the highest intact wall of Rome's Great Colosseum.

Chapter 25

WIN THE CROWD

OR

A NEW KIND OF DISCUS

Mars saw thousands of angels' faces – male and female – turn their way. The chatter of their voices died instantly.

Mars and his generals alighted in the center of the Colosseum, atop the vertical, unstable, and poorly defendable hypogeum walls. They fanned out as best they could to see attacks coming their way. The small section of restored wooden flooring was too close to the outer edge for any of them to risk standing there.

Most of The Fallen were seated on rows of wooden benches that were materially absent but magically conjured for the present, immortal audience. Many of the seated angels rose. Some pointed. A few covered their nose and gagged at the newly arrived stench. All stared. They were expecting Cacciari or Pluto, not a despised enemy.

Mars recognized the element of surprise as a gift not to be wasted.

"Angels!" he shouted, raising his hands for attention and feigning bravery.

Among The Fallen, eyebrows turned down, upper lips curled, and teeth were bared, all showing him he'd

been recognized and had no friends there.

Mars' heart raced. He *had* to uphold his reputation as the son of Mars, tough guy god of war. *I can* not *show fear in front of Tamara,* he told himself. *Better to die a gruesome death than live through eternity as the "wet-pants warrior." If I go down, let it be in a blaze of glory!*

And that's when he knew he was petrified: he was channeling his dad.

"*Fellow* angels!" he continued. "I come here to offer you redemption!" *Yeah, that sounds good,* he thought. *Anybody's who's been disgraced would want redemption, right?*

Mars watched something percolate in their eyes and realized too late it was rage.

"It's that two-faced Cupid!" came a shrill female voice to his left.

"The castout's finally come 'round!" taunted a husky voice to his right.

"Begging for our help, is he?" boomed a deep voice from straight ahead.

"Let's make *him* beg for mercy instead!" crowed the angriest voice yet. Voices rose, along with fists, from every direction. The legion took a few threatening steps toward the Colosseum floor.

Jarel raised his arms to the crowd. "Wait! Y'all, yuh, gotta hear what he gotta say!"

"We ain't gotta hear nothing from him! He got us all exiled! We'd be in Olympus right now if it wasn't

for him!"

"And I'll get you back in!" hollered Mars, lifting his hands like a street preacher on crusade.

"And why wouldya?" bellowed a doubter in the crowd.

"He can't!" answered another.

"He's been banished just like us! He's lyin'! We oughta be grindin' him into the Colosseum floor!"

The crowd took another few threatening steps forward. Mars walked as if on a balance beam and grabbed Tamara's wrist. He pulled her over to Tommy, put her hand in his, and ordered, "Don't let her get caught up in anything!"

"Hey! I can handle myself!" she protested at the same time Tommy growled, "You don' needta tell me nothin'! She ain't never been in any danger you didn't bring on her!"

Mars grabbed Tamara's shoulders. "I know you can handle yourself!" he shouted. "But *I* couldn't handle it if you were hurt! I love you!"

She started. Mars froze in shock at the words that had tumbled out of his mouth. The crowd was shouting. The din snapped him back to reality – or at least the murky, possibly murderous reality he'd rather face than possibly read rejection in Tamara's eyes. He quickly turned to face the crowd.

Cornelius raised his hands and spoke louder than

Mars could have imagined. "Gentlemen!" He pointed his index finger to his temple and commanded the crowd, "Think! We are all delivering evil arrows for Pluto. The god of love is promising your return to Heaven. Won't you at least *hear* his offer?"

The crowd roared, some for blood and some for silence.

Mars knew it was time to return to the original plan: *Appeal to their stomachs.* He waved his arms for attention, made a show of lowering them to his waistband, and pulled his tray out for all to see. Then he placed both hands on the handles. Dozens of dainty squares of ambrosia piled up on the tray, swirly pink with blue arrows dissecting their tops. Mars caught sight of some of the angels most near, their eyes glossing over with craving.

"Let me prove my commitment to you first with a meal! I know you're hungry, but Cacciari isn't the only one with food."

Tamara dashed forward and lifted her skirt ever so slightly to form a little hammock at her knees. Then she tipped Mars' tray toward her. The ambrosia fell softly into the gathering. Tamara took tiny, modest-as-possible steps before lifting off the ground. As she flew toward the nearest, lowest wooden benches, she adjusted the skirt-hammock to a one-handed hold and reached in with her other hand to lob squares of ambrosia into the crowd. Like a Roman circuseer tossing bread to the blood-thirsty

masses, so she provided placating sustenance to The Fallen.

She fluttered back to Mars' side and was set to reload her skirt when Tommy gently advised, "Let us dudes with shirts fly above the angry guys. You don' belong servin' nobody." He pulled his shirt hem away from his paunch of a belly to form his own serving basket. He shouted to the crowd, "Some fer everyone! We'll come 'round!"

Mars produced the food and tipped, and away Tommy flew to serve, his protruding jelly belly ahead of him, dropping nourishment into outstretched hands. Cornelius and Jarel flew over for their turns. And so it went, for what seemed a very long time.

Mars couldn't really pay attention to The Fallen's faces or reactions anymore, as he got down to the business of concentrating on ambrosia to produce it, then tipping it, and back again. It was Tamara who gave him occasional updates and eventually took over tipping the squares just to give his cramping fingers a rest from the tray handles. Serving this much food was, after all, more work than The Underemployed Layabout had ever done at once. He'd have never finished the job without her.

"They don't look so angry any more, Mars, and they've all had seconds already," she alerted him.

"And Cacciari could be here any minute," Tyrone warned.

Mars put the tray back into his waistband and raised his hands again for silence. He remembered his

dad's words, to use his strengths where his enemy has noon. *My greatest strength is love,* he told himself, *and love can be shown by offering kindness without expecting it in return. It's now or never, and I better not mess this up.*

He tried to lower his voice to the timbre of his father. "Angels!" he bellowed. *Shyeah.* Didn't work. "For decades, I did not know you existed!"

A growl came from the recently peaceful crowd. Mars lowered his arms and gulped, trying to think of how to *not* re-enrage them.

"And that's due to my arrogance and blindness." He pointed to his chest. "I knew of and encouraged The Deadly Dictator Decree!"

Some of the angels who had been seated stood. Mars realized he was in serious danger of losing the crowd again if he didn't do a better job explaining.

"But I didn't know – or at least didn't think of – the consequences that would come from The Decree. I was ignorant and apathetic and, for that," – here he extended his arms sideways, wide open and vulnerable – "I apologize. I was wrong, and I want to make things right!"

"You jus' playin' us!" someone shouted. "You want yer precious castle!"

Catcalls came from all around, rippling across the stands.

Mars took a fraction of a second to reflect on those words. They weren't wrong. "I *do* want to get back to

Heaven," he admitted loudly, "but I think you all want the same thing!"

A moment's silence. Mars plunged on.

"Shooting Pluto's hate-filled arrows is not what you want! It's not your dream. It's not your destiny! Break free of this horrible prison you've willingly entered! Resist Pluto and Cacciari! Fight with me to break their rule here on Earth, and I'll get you back into Heaven if it takes the rest of my days to do it!" *And if it takes me that long to figure out how,* Mars added silently to himself. Mars' was a sincere pledge, but one that he didn't yet know how he'd honor, seeing as he didn't even know how to get himself reinstated as Cupid. But that second part was a loftier goal, he reasoned, much harder to attain than merely getting The Fallen back to work.

"You want us to turn on Cacciari?!" came an angry outburst from the front row, again to his right. It came from a young, dark-haired love angel whom Mars knew could have his pick of Olympian ladies or those right here in the crowd. Mars felt lucky to have met Tamara before some more handsome angel had won her heart.

"Why should we?" the angel continued. "Cacciari kept us from death's door when no one else would!"

"But Pluto *will accept you at his door* whenever he sees fit to stop feeding you, and Cacciari couldn't save you if he wanted! Ask yourselves!" Mars exhorted. "You work for him because he feeds you, correct?"

A few angels nodded. The rest fidgeted.

"If ambrosia's all that he has to keep you, then leave! I will feed you all!" He held his own shiny, silver tray high and promised. "Fight on the side of love!"

The crowd burst into chatter and motion as thousands of fallen angels turned toward each other, gesticulating and conflicted and disbelieving all at once. Mars heard snippets:

"I am *not* testing Pluto!

"Not with Cupid! He's a weaker god!"

"I hear he still wears diapers!"

"We'd be trading one master for another!"

The Fallen Four and Tyrone tried shouting over them, pleading Mars' case and explaining how *they*, the Fallen, give Pluto power over them, but Mars saw that no one was listening. No hearts were being swayed. Anger started to grow within him. He lowered his tray and slowly ran a finger over its smooth, shiny edges.

The tray had been with him every day since his infancy – with the exception of these few days on Earth. He remembered being bounced on his mother's knee and being offered yummies from that tray. He could picture his young playmates running through the backyard and grabbing snacks off of it to barbecue on the fire. And he remembered in later years offering snacks to his lady guests, but just now he dreamed of offering its bounty solely to the lady standing next to him. He looked to Tamara and was

pleased to see her eyes reflected back at him, albeit with a strange expression on her face, her lower lip trembling, and Mars thought he knew why: *She's given up hope that the crowd will listen.*

Mars petted his tray, perhaps for the last time, and, anger overtaking him, drew it back like a discus. Then, finally showing his mettle, Mars launched his godly tray, sending it soaring toward the throng. It whistled as it spun through the air, and the crowd silenced to watch it. It seemed to glow and catch the sun's light. Finally, hands reached out to it, and its catcher drew the coveted, magical tray to his chest, shocked at what had just transpired.

"I will not be your master!" shouted the enraged son of The God of War. "My men will fight for me because they believe in me! Pluto demands you destroy humanity and offers your enslavement as reward! But I freely offer the very thing that Pluto keeps from you! That tray will feed all of you, and it's in your hands! I give you the power that I could use to control you! I want you to believe in Heaven's work, to believe that you are worthy of returning there, and to spread the power of love once again! Who's with me?!"

The crowd roared. Half the angels raised their hands, the first converts. Some shook fists at Mars, shouting that they'd never forgive him.

Mars noticed a few angels straight ahead in the front row doing neither one. They were looking beyond

him. Past him. With wide eyes.

Chapter 26

WORDS' WEIGHT

OR

TOOLS OF THE TRADE

Mars whipped around to see Cacciari and four huge thugs in black flying over the low wall to the Colosseum. One goon held Mars' bow and quiver. Mars instinctively hooked Tamara by the waist and pulled her behind him. Cacciari noticed.

The horde in the stands silenced. More than half knew they'd been caught in treason.

"Well, well!" Cacciari announced, settling down on the labyrinth wall less than 20 meters ahead of Mars. Cacciari's fine suit was gone. He was back to his Southern street clothes, all black except for rusty red spurs and turquoise beads on his hatband.

"Royalty in our midst!" Cacciari called. "I hardly expected to find you *here!* And trying to turn *my* forces against me!" His voice carried a wicked tone and sent shivers down the spines of many around him. Mars was sure Cacciari hadn't sounded that way the first time they'd met, but "The Boss" had just spent time with Pluto, and Mars knew that entertaining evil, even being in its presence, changes men.

Mars shifted his eyes slightly to watch the faces of

the male and female angels in the stands. He tried to gauge their acceptance of those words. Some looked reticent, as if, no, they'd never consider leaving his side, never think of abandoning the comfort of a benefactor, no matter the spiritual cost. Others, however, glared defiantly, apparently not liking being referred to as *his* forces; those were the ones, Mars knew, who considered themselves their own, not beings belonging to others.

Mars hadn't meant to relinquish the floor, but as he was gauging how many angels he might have in his new army, Cacciari fired the first threat:

"Any angel who assists this betrayer, this outlaw, will face Pluto's wrath!" He turned his eyes to Tamara. "That includes those who harbor him. Pluto wants this ruin of a god caught alive!"

Some of The Fallen launched themselves into the air to be the first one to hand over Mars, but other angels grabbed their feet and pulled them down.

"Pluto commands his capture!" shouted a short little angel trying to free his legs from a much bigger angel's grasp.

"We might never get this chance again!" argued the larger. "A chance to fight with the help of another god!"

"Pluto will rain his forces down on us!" shouted another ensnared angel.

"I can't work like this any more!" answered his captor.

No more time to listen. Mars couldn't risk being grabbed and taken to Pluto – and Pluto himself might show up soon. Mars needed his celestial tools! He pulled from his back waistband the huge, black, foul relic of The Underworld from which Pluto normally got his ambrosia. A millipede as fat as a cigar wriggled over the rim. Mars held the tray high, and the arthropod dangled.

Gasps and shouts confirmed that even though likely none of them had seen Pluto's tray before, they recognized it when they saw it.

"Aahhh," crowed Cacciari. "I see The God of Love has become The Prince of Thieves!"

Mars wasn't going to get caught up chatting, not with half the army holding back the other and a whole lot of movement all around him. "Trade! The tray for my bow and arrows!"

Cacciari laughed. "The Lord Pluto is delayed securing his borders, but, when he arrives, I'm sure he'll be pleased to find that I've secured both his tray and his burglar."

Mars would never correct Cacciari's – or Pluto's – mistaken assumption that he was the thief. *Better they hate* me *than Tamara for the devastation wreaked on The Underworld.*

Cacciari waved his goons forward. The big one holding Mars' gadgets handed them off to The Boss. Then the hoodlums advanced as a group, shakily balancing atop

the masonry walls.

Mars quickly lowered the tray to eye level and looked again at its curved bones with their protruding joints and the dried, hard fibers of muscle and sinew forming jagged little peaks along every inch of its surface. He closed his eyes and steeled himself. What was it his mother said? *The mere scratch of thine arrow changeth worlds.* His strongest power, potent, life-changing love, could change all. It was time for him to show love – love to the Fallen that he'd maligned – and be prepared to sacrifice himself to fix the mistake. He thought hard about Tamara and true love. Then he opened his eyes before dragging his left wrist across the sharp-edged lip of Pluto's tray. The dried filth of The Underworld cut deeply into his skin and stung his flesh. Mars suddenly felt queasy and weak. He watched his godly blood drip onto the tray and smoke upon contact.

The scoundrels stopped in their tracks.

Mars held Cacciari's stare and slid his finger across the spilt ichor, pulling a scorching, hissing path across the tray's base.

The gorillas didn't move.

Mars then wrapped his bloody hand around the tray's handle. The stem snapped off, and the handle landed at Mars' feet. It disintegrated like the natural biological matter it was before Pluto's loathsome enchantment.

"It will only take more a few more drops of my

blood to destroy this tray. Now, Boss," mocked Mars, silently swallowing to hide the effects of blood loss, "*your* boss will not like hearing that you refused to trade his implement for mine." Mars held out his unbloodied hand and waved his fingers impatiently. "My bow and quiver."

"See? He ain't so wimpy!" said someone from behind.

"That's his strategy?! To bleed hisself out?!"

"No, Stupid! He's got 'em!"

The crowd tussled while Cacciari's men looked back and forth between their boss and Mars. One of the meatheads shifted glances so fast that he lost his footing. His arms circled, he gave a shout, and he fell backward, down into the labyrinth. A thud and a fast puff of dirty air told everyone the fool had forgotten that he could fly.

Cacciari ignored him and nodded brusquely for another man to return to him for Mars' tools, which the angel did. The messenger carefully flew over and set them atop the wall on which Mars stood, about two meters ahead of him, and then returned to Cacciari's side. Jarel flew over and retrieved the gadgets, handing them to Mars while drawing a scathing look from his former employer.

"Ah. The turncoat," hissed Da Boss.

"Half yo' army's flipped sides," asserted Jarel. "You, yuh, can't ask love angels to kill love fo'eva, and ya can't ask 'em to stand by an, yuh, watch ya mutilate dey own kind."

Mars appreciated Jarel's rebuttal, but he didn't want

Jarel taking any blame if this little rebellion didn't work out, so Mars turned the attention back on himself. He unceremoniously chucked Pluto's tray over toward Cacci. *The tray's useless anyway,* Mars told himself, *except for inducing dread. Let it work that magic on* them *for awhile.* The foul thing landed on the top of the wall and started tipping over; Cacciari stuck out a foot to spare it from falling into the catacombs below.

Mars felt an urgent tug on his sleeve and looked down to see Tamara's frightened face, her eyes staring off past the walls.

"They're here!" she said urgently. "Pluto and Mandre are about to come out of the clouds!"

Mars looked up, saw nothing. "How do you know?"

"I can hear their thoughts."

"What?!"

She gasped. "He's going to attack! Move!"

The Fallen Four took off toward the stands. Tyrone ran, but Mars stupidly stayed where he was, watching their escape. As soon as they were clear, The Grounded God looked up to see a huge fireball rocketing down from the sky. He couldn't move fast enough. The mass took over his field of vision and was upon him. It hit the wall he was standing on and exploded in reds and ballast and noise. Mars was thrown backward into the stands. His bow skittered across his chest; his arrows clattered as they rained upon him.

When the smoke cleared, Mars saw Pluto hovering above the smoking labyrinth. His shadowy robes billowed in a nonexistent wind. Mars caught himself thinking, *Whoa! Pluto is even worse up close than through an eye piece! Corny must've crapped himself.* Behind Pluto lingered Mandre, looking puny.

Pluto clapped his hands together, and the strike boomed like thunder. It conjured the remainder of the wooden arena floor. Mars looked where Tyrone had just been. He wasn't there anymore nor was he in the stands. Mars realized he'd likely fallen into the labyrinth like Cacciari's man and was equally trapped.

Pluto flipped his hands ahead of him as if shaking a towel. A wave of sand jetted forward and sprayed across the wood, making the arena appear as it had during its nearly four hundred years of gladiatorial games. Pluto settled to the arena's center as he no doubt did every time he arrived. Dust devils swirled at his feet. He sneered haughtily, comfortable in this terrestrial house of horrors.

Half of The Fallen, those that'd flipped to Mars' side, stood gorgonized at the sight of Pluto, motionless in terror. The other half, those on Pluto's side, bowed their heads, terrified. They probably meant it in honor, but Mars thought it made them look guilty, like they were the defectors instead of the ones standing paralyzed in their true guilt.

The mongrel Mandre wafted to Pluto's side as if

he'd had something to do with his master's impressive display of power. Pluto would have none of that. He raised his hands to his army, allowing his robe to slap Mandre in the face, and turned slowly on the spot so that his troops might soak in his fearful aura. Absolute dismay rolled off of him. Pluto's men – and Mars – became woozy in it.

With the stands still, The King of Darkness lifted his grim face to sniff the air. The smell of rot came to him, and Pluto turned to spot Cacciari, who'd been thrown into the ruins even further than Mars. Pluto extended his bony, right hand, and his tray flew to it.

The Dark Lord was not pleased. He turned the relic over and over in his hands, noting the damage and perhaps sensing changes in its abilities. He grimaced angrily, tossed it into the air, and it disappeared.

"My lo-o-o-o-oyal legion," Pluto proclaimed as loudly as the pealing of cannon fire, lingering long on *loyal*. "You've witnessed my weekly games. As you know, most of our … entertainers" – he chuckled at the choice of word – "come from my dominion. The Damned fight for a week's reprieve from their tortures, and the losers are revived from their grave injuries to serve the tortures of the victor as well as their own." He chuckled again. "My denizens have strong incentive to enter the fight – and a stronger incentive to win.

"Today, however, we shall have a *new* gladiator. The Damned who lined up to fight each other will instead

destroy your enemy and mine, that loathsome Cupid!"

Half the crowd roared in anticipation; the other half roared that their new leader was already set upon.

Mars vigorously shook his head, desperately trying to clear the confusion Pluto had caused in it, and moved his feet underneath him to stand. Even in his less godly state, Mars registered that Pluto had again called him *Cupid*, despite the new Cupid standing right next to him, looking pouty. Mars grinned stupidly before stumbling back onto his rump.

"And after you fall on *this* floor, Cupid," Pluto went on, "I will continue your torture in Tartus, my special prison. And," he added with a deep laugh, "no one will even notice you're gone."

Mars noted that Pluto's warnings were very different than Cacciari. Cacciari preferred action to talk; it appeared that Pluto liked both torture *and* long speeches, which might be the same thing.

"Love fails worldwide, Cupid, and soon it will be a distant memory. Already my servant Mandre has broken several of your detestable records and is receiving insipid praise from those dull-eyed cows in Heaven who idolize him for doing the opposite of his task. He spreads *my* hate instead of *your* love and is remarkably adored by the easily fooled.

"And it was so effortless, too, to convince my gullible brother to give a second try to his fallen angel!" Pluto's

tone turned mocking as he imitated the conversation: "O, Jupiter! Your love angel, Mandre, despite your banishment, strikes such powerful love in mortals that their radiance threatens my kingdom! The Underworld can barely hold them! You were mistaken to banish him! Your actions were unwise!"

Pluto returned to his silky-voiced vitriol. "Habandash warned my vain, foolish brother to keep you, but greed twisted Jupiter's wisdom! How often we heed the words of our enemies before that of friends! How much more weight we give to criticism than praise!" His laugh sounded like a snarl.

Mars didn't hear much after the bit about his records being broken. He pictured the huge plaque outside Paradise Plaza with his name etched allllll down the column of records. Now that long line would be interrupted, he imagined, with little pieces of parchment inscribed with Mandre's name. Mandre, the new record holder. *What blasphemy!*

But Mars couldn't wallow. He had to shake off Pluto's buzz to reclaim the floor. If there was one thing he'd learned about Pluto while growing up, it was that you didn't want to get caught up in a conversation with him. Pluto is evil, and evil is persuasive. You shouldn't allow evil a chance to burrow into your thoughts.

Mars pushed *Peace and Love* hard – it was like the worst constipation ever – and it cleared his head, if not

his bowels. Mars gathered his arrows into his quiver and slung it, along with his bow, over his shoulder. Then he scrambled to his feet and leapt down onto the arena floor. It was a move he never would have expected of himself, but apparently there was more to Mars that what he thought there was.

"Good!" cheered The Death Dealer with a grey-toothed grin. "You're ready for my games!"

Hegmata dropped open all around Mars. The hinged platforms led to the labyrinth below, and from them leapt 50 members of The Damned, dressed in ghastly, ancient gladiatorial gear.

Chapter 27

THE FOG OF WAR
OR
CRAB AND BEEF

The cadaverous Damned were hideous in gore-covered leather and ancient armor. They brandished swords and spears, maces and hammers, spiked shields, and every weapon of bodily destruction known to man's morbidity. They quickly turned toward each other, ready to face off.

"Much as you look forward to peeling the flesh off one another," announced The Deity of Demise and Departure, "your new target is the pink pansy you see before you. Bring me his head for a month's liberation from your well-deserved punishment!"

The Damned screeched their unearthly answer and shuffled forward on long-dead legs. These pitiable creatures were different than the nearly-transparent Damned in Death Valley. Mars wondered if, by their promise to fight, Pluto gave their physiques more substance, the better to fight with.

Mars glanced up to see if Tamara was still safely out of harm's way. Instead, his eyes caught on a group of mortal tourists just entering the stands. The group consisted of a family of four, a trio of college girls, an elderly couple, and a guide, who was walking backward

while leading them and detailing the Colosseum's history. When his group stopped short, the guide turned around to see why. He and his charges spotted Mars – and Mars alone – standing on *nothing*. To them, he was poised on thin air between two hypogeum walls. They couldn't see Pluto's magically conjured floor, Pluto himself, his Damned gladiators, nor the battle about to break.

"Ehi! Cosa stai facendo lì?!" shouted the dark-haired, 20-something guide.

Mars, being fluent in the language of love, which is spoken worldwide and supersedes all mortal tongues, understood the Italian, and decided he didn't have time to explain what he was doing there. The mortals would get hurt if they didn't leave, so Mars concentrated hard and shouted, "SEEEEEEEEEE!"

The mortals gasped. The little girl in the family of four screamed, "Ghosts, Daddy! Gladamator – glabatator – glabaramer ghosts!"

Her father shook his bald head in disbelief. He wanted to correct his daughter on the folly of an afterlife but couldn't reconcile that with what he was seeing. He must have decided that this exact moment wasn't the time for a lesson on religion because he and the entire group turned and fled.

Mars realized that the mortals would report what they'd seen. *They'll get security scrambling,* he thought. *What if the Colosseum goes on lockdown and SWAT teams barge in*

and see me battling nobody – unless I let them *see everything, too?* But he reasoned it was better for armed men to swoop in in half an hour than for those little kids to have stayed in immediate danger a second longer.

Mars returned his attention to The Damned. They swung silver sickles and snapped studded whips while slowly encircling him. Mars quickly raised his palms in a silent command to The Fallen Four to hold their place. Almost of all the angels in the stands still tussled and argued, but a few did stop to see how The Shah of Smoochy Woochy would fare in battle.

Mars swirled his hands. *This will work,* he told himself. He'd eaten ambrosia. He felt strong. And he was right.

Immediately the air around him condensed into fog. Mars pulled both hands behind his right ear and then thrust them outward.

The fog converted to water and crashed into The Damned all around him, sending them and their weapons rolling onto the arena sand.

The move shocked The Fallen into momentarily stillness until those who'd flipped to Mars' side cheered. Those backing Pluto looked back at forth at each other. They'd never seen Mars' powers and wondered if they'd underestimated him. The still-undecideds looked confused.

No more of this, Mars thought. Spotting Tamara still perched atop the high wall, Mars stuck out his chest

and opted for valor. "Pluto!" he called. "I demand you release these angels from servitude. You will leave this place and take your impostor cupid with you!"

Pluto laughed heartily. "Oh, how I shake at your commands, Chief of Cherubs!"

Mars ignored the snub. *This isn't about me,* he reminded himself. "The defectors of your army demand freedom as much as I demand their release!"

Pluto's eyes turned to slits. "You do not lead my army." Turning toward the stands, The Tomb Tycoon leveled a single, hateful glance, which froze many. "It seems my soldiers agree, as none lift a finger against me."

It was true, Mars thought. So far, his own supporters had prevented Pluto's loyals from capturing him, but not much else.

As Mars struggled to think of a reply, a figure dropped down next to him and shouted, "I intervene!"

Mars was horrified to see that it was Tamara who'd landed beside him.

"I will never shoot another arrow for you!" she continued. Mars grabbed a fistful of the back of her dress and tried to pull back, but she stepped forward, out of his grip. "I am a *love* angel! From now on, I will shoot love arrows or nothing at all! Mars will return to his rightful place as Love God! He has my allegiance and that of half the angels here!"

Pluto glared at her, his anger rising.

Mars hustled forward and stepped in front of her.

"Half my army defects?" asked Pluto. "Let's see if you're right – and how badly the *defectors* want their escape!" Pluto lifted his arms to the sky, and his cloak draped like the webbing of a bat's wing.

Mars took several slow steps back, forcing Tamara back, too.

Pluto's robe's began to billow in rising waves of power. The air around him quivered, as did his image within it, until, from beneath his feet erupted the choking, black fog of The River Styx.

The Fallen, like their human brothers, may have been able to withstand increased exposure to The Fog, but they were not infallible; they were not endowed with the strength of a god like Mars. The Fallen, all of them, were immediately overcome with hate and fear and misunderstanding. Angry at the other side and each other, they accused their brethren:

"Traitors!"

"Devils!"

Mars knew this would escalate quickly and violently. He scanned the crowd and saw Jarel hop onto a wooden bench to stand above the others.

"I got dis, M.J.!" Jarel waved his hands to organize the undisciplined army.

"Soldiers of Cupid!" he shouted. Every face turned his way. "I, yuh, mean, soldiers of Mars, da real Cupid!"

Half the faces turned angry. He addressed the rest. "If you a defender o' love, it's time! If ya fight fer yer freedom, 's time! If ya fight agains' dem dat'd enslave ya, 's time!" He pointed to an angel to his left. "Javier, yuh, flank left!" Then straight ahead, he shouted, "Lola, create a company and go right!"

Most angels moved. To those few still standing perplexed, Mars extended his tattered, battered wings and bellowed, "Decide now! Decide and fight!"

Pandemonium burst like dynamite. Angels in the stands fought with their bare hands. Mars watched Cornelius soar out of the stands and dive through an opening to the underground hypogeum. Tommy, looking confused, followed behind.

Mars turned from the in-fighting in the stands and saw Pluto's face changing expression by the second. First his furrowed brows and slits for eyes screamed fury over his fractured forces. Then a small grin spread across his cheeks until it had grown to a wide sneer.

"Ah, how sweet is the aroma of Fear and Loathing," he purred to no one in particular. "And so man and angel alike fight tonight!"

Mars looked around. The Damned returned to their feet and, powered by The Evil Fog, challenged anyone within reach, including those angels still on Pluto's side. Those on Mars' side were well organized by Jarel but needed weapons.

Mars scanned the ground and saw Cornelius and Tommy soar out of the hypogeum, their arms laden with axes, lances, halberds, pointed helmets, and jagged shields. Behind them scrambled Tyrone, screaming that he'd found more; the arsenal had undoubtedly been conjured by Pluto for The Games. Mars stepped closer to Tamara, keeping her safely tucked behind him. For once, she didn't object.

Pluto grinned wickedly. "Son of Mars, while our forces battle all around, let us make use of the precious arena floor. It should have animals as in times past, don't you think?" Pluto shot his arms out to the side, his long, bony fingers splayed wide. "Let's see, Mars, how you battle the Creatures of Hell!"

Out of the hegmata climbed horrible, hellish creatures: winged wraiths and giant, grey crocodiles; monstrous fire-red crabs and minotaurs with horns as fat as conch shells; blue serpents as long as trees and, finally, the dead from The Styx, limping and dripping tar.

Tommy and Cornelius dropped alongside Mars, who shook his head in desperation.

"Tommy! Get Tamara out of here!"

"Why you think I'm here?!"

"But," she began, "we can fight with y-"

"Look out!" Cornelius shouted.

Mars whipped around to see a giant crab's claw swinging toward him. Before he could move, two small arms shoved their way under his armpits and hoisted him

into the air, just out of the monster's reach. His legs were within a half meter of the extended claw. Tamara struggled to keep Mars' bulk aloft – until Tommy swung over and pulled up on Mars' collar.

Mars felt ridiculous and angry. He was about to kick his way free when a sudden jolt sent him airbound. He dropped onto the crab's hard back and quickly flattened himself against it. The creature swung its claws wildly and snapped at the air above. Mars was thrilled to discover the animal couldn't reach him. He looked up to find Tamara struggling with Tommy. For some reason, she had her arms scooped under his now and was shouting for him to hold on.

He wasn't holding on. In fact, Tommy was limp with the shaft and fletching of an arrow sticking out of his side. Red blood oozed from the wound, and Tommy was visibly greying. Mars recognized the dull gold arrow with its distinctive black feathers. It was Mandre's and had surely been touched by Pluto.

Rage exploded within Mars – no doubt aided by The Fog but sparked by such a ruthless act. *That assassin Mandre launched a* deadly *arrow! Was it meant for me or for Tommy – or,* he shuddered, *did Tommy take it to protect Tamara?*

Mars leapt to his feet atop the giant crab and reached over his shoulder for an arrow. The crab's massive claw snapped at him. Mars leaped to escape. Mid-air,

he set his arrow to his bow, stretched the string, and fired. As he fell toward the arena floor, he saw his arrow split Mandre's cleanly down the center. Tommy twitched in Tamara's embrace. He was still alive – a moment's relief. Mars landed hard and off balance. He tumbled onto the arena floor, kicking up sand and dust. In his peripheral vision, he caught sight of a massive coil from a blue serpent and barely dodged it.

Mars looked back at Tommy, whose color had returned. In the same instant, Cornelius dived in to help Tamara pull him away.

There was so much going on, Mars was having trouble knowing where to look. He turned again and spotted a bull-headed, man-bodied minotaur bearing down on him. Slobber flew from its mouth, and its beefy fists were balled like huge hammers. The beast looked crazed.

Mars wished he could just *fly* again. Instead, he was forced to turn tail and run. A few meters ahead, he spotted another snake. It writhed to push down a huge bump behind its head. Bare feet stuck out of its jaw, and Mars knew it was the body of one of The Damned.

In full sprint, Mars leaned down to slap the serpent on the back. He ducked and rolled, cloaking himself behind the kicked-up dust. The viper lifted its horned head, saw only the approaching minotaur, and struck. In an instant, its fangs were deep into the minotaur's chest. The bullman flailed its arms in defense, but too late. The

snake positioned its jaws around the bull horns to take in its next meal.

With a moment's reprieve from beasts, Mars looked around and spotted Cornelius and Tamara settling Tommy into a quiet vomitorium. Just seeing Tamara again, his Tamara, whom he'd nearly lost to Mandre's poisoned arrow, made up his mind. No matter the cost, Mars would stop those arrows from flying again. He reached back for another arrow of his own.

Mars' standard arrows did only Good, bestowing love on its targets, but an arrow supercharged with his essence would prove too much for nearly anyone. Mars took the arrow and dragged its head across the wound still open at his wrist. He coated it in his godly ichor. Mars felt ill from the blood loss, but turned on the spot and fired the toxic dart.

Mars watched it fly as if in slow motion. It hummed as it split the air. That scum Mandre either saw it or heard it coming. His eyes grew wide and he shifted out of its path. Bad minion that he was, though, by moving, Mandre exposed Pluto.

The arrow sunk into Pluto's chest and soared out his back to the stone wall behind him, then drilled itself into the masonry, finally stopping with just the nock left to be seen.

Pluto gasped and lurched forward. He dropped to one knee, clutching his heart like a mortal suffering heart

failure. Only this wasn't heart *failure.* It was heart *revival* – the awakening of a dead heart infused by the blood of The God of Love. His heart was forced to beat again, perhaps for the first time in centuries. His heart would be *assaulted* by the memory of centuries of evil. Hell's Grim Tyrant moaned in agony.

Chapter 28

CORNY'S CHARGE

OR

MARS MANAGES TO GET HIS SHIRT OFF AGAIN

Mandre stepped in front of his master and drew an arrow. Slowly, with challenge in his eyes, he turned to tap it on Pluto's shoulder, drawing unconsented, precious power from Pluto's dwindling supply. Mandre then turned to face his target.

"You never did recognize me, did you?" Mandre questioned Mars. "I was one of the four in the room, along with Vilnius, during your eager and infamous consent to The Dictator Decree. *You* made Vilnius and me this way, Mars. You made all of this happen." He waved toward the chaos in the stadium.

Mars was again convicted but knew he had to make peace with himself. He'd never again ignore or dismiss people as he once had. He realized that the people in his life and all around him, whether he had dealings with them or not, were important. His fall from grace had taught him a thing or two about life at the bottom.

"Maybe I created your circumstances," answered Mars, "but you made your own choices. Choose now to surrender, Mandre, because *you*, by having turned against Olympus and the legacy of Cupid, *you* have made yourself

an arrant enemy, and you I'll show little mercy."

Mandre cocked his head in questioning defiance.

Mars wished he had a bite of ambrosia, but went on. "Pluto spreads fear and hate. That's his twisted, godly role. Cacciari misleads desperate beings into bad acts to escape starvation. You, however, had no motivation other than power. You chose to become the right hand of evil. You would destroy the world not to be fed but to win a princeship. Whatever part of you that was once noble enough to be a love angel has rotted during your stay in Hell. Your only hope now is to surrender and accept your punishment."

Wow, Mars thought. *That sounded pretty good. Maybe I do have Dad's flair for intimidation.*

But our Well-Spoken Wooer had no more time to congratulate himself, as an arrow zinged past his ear. Mars turned his head to watch its trajectory; it struck a Styx corpse, which disappeared in a sudden puff of smoke – another deadly arrow meant for him.

Bellowing his worst, Mars drew his own arrow, and Mandre followed suit. Their eyes burned for a fraction of a second before the two unleashed a barrage. Those arrows that collided mid-air tore apart with a resounding crack, but those that managed to hit other beings released dramatic effects, despite not being touched by blood.

A minotaur grazed by Mars' love arrow turned on the spot to snuggle Jarel. The latter, shocked, looked to

Mars, who in turn offered an encouraging nod. Jarel petted the beast gently and asked for help defending himself and his friends. And so the bullman became the newest soldier for Mars' army. Likewise, *Mandre's* arrows caused more than one of Mars' new soldiers to turn on each other or anything nearby.

Mars tried his best to watch where stray arrows hit and reverse their bad effects, but he couldn't take his eyes off Mandre for long. Surprisingly to Mars, Mandre was a fierce opponent. His arms blurred like the blades of a blender as he grabbed and shot arrows. His face was fierce with intense concentration.

Pluto has really trained this guy, Mars thought between shots. This reasoning was surely easier for the Laurel-Resting Lord to believe, as he'd never admit his own failure to train.

It was while following one of Mandre's ricocheting arrows that Mars saw one of the giant, grey crocodiles topple Jarel's minotaur. Mars couldn't even shout a warning; by the time he'd opened his mouth, the reptile had clamped upon Jarel's leg and yanked him to the ground.

Mars ran toward him, terrified that Jarel would lose the leg. He zigzagged to avoid Mandre's arrows. It seemed to take *forever* to get close. He'd almost reached him when he looked up just in time to see Cornelius dive out of the sky.

Corny landed on the croc's back and drove both

his thumbs into the behemoth's eye sockets. The beast roared and released Jarel, then thrashed wildly. Cornelius grasped the ridges of its back to stay on. Someone threw him a studded whip, and Corny swung it until it snagged across the creature's open mouth. Mars watched incredulously as Cornelius pulled the makeshift reins and drove the creature toward Mandre.

"Way to go, Corny!" shouted Mars, thankful for the few seconds free. He sprinted through the battling Fallen and allegiance-less monsters to reach Jarel's side; his friend was bleeding and panicking.

"Jarel! Hold on!" Mars shouted, placing a hand on Jarel's chest to steady him. It worked. Jarel stopped squirming. Mars peeled off his detested pink polo, grateful that he had it. He put a corner of the fabric in his mouth and ripped a strip with his teeth. Then another. He fumbled but managed to tie them together into a longer one.

"Good thing you taught me this, Jarel," said Mars with false calm, "because it's going to save your hide, general!"

Jarel watched as Mars tied his first really tight knot ever – and his first tourniquet – just above the gushing wound.

"Next time try to keep your eyes open for giant crocodiles from Hell, will ya?"

Jarel answered with a nod.

Mars ripped two more strips and tied them over

the wound itself, loosely, to keep out sand. The blood that had been gushing soaked the fabric but was slowing. Mars waved for one of his new soldiers to come over. It was the dark-haired doubter who'd apparently decided right was right after all.

"Stay with him. Keep him lying down but pass along his orders." Mars turned without waiting for a response. He intended to find Cornelius and Mandre but noticed that Tamara wasn't where she'd been before.

Terror wrapped itself around his heart. He looked around: Jarel. His nurse. Tommy sitting in an aisle. Cornelius riding the crocodile and Mandre shooting arrows into it – the croc's lower jaw had dozens of shafts sticking out, and the beast was growing more enraged by the second.

All around the Colosseum, angels and beasts battled. Serpents occasionally raised their coils and slapped them around small groups, drawing them in to their doom. Winged wraiths wrapped their wings around the inattentive; when they opened their wings, their victims would fall out, sucked dry. Pluto remained on the Colosseum floor clutching his chest. Cacciari bent at his side, but Mars couldn't spare them another moment. *Where's Tamara?* he begged.

And then he spotted her. Some of The Styx dead were carrying her and Tyrone toward the highest wall.

Tamara and Tyrone kicked and screamed and batted their wings, but the black-crusted corpses weren't

slowing. Several reached the wall and jumped over. Either they were crashing onto the ground or – Mars shuddered at the thought – they were hoping to reach The River below! The Dead no doubt smelled Styx on Tamara and Tyrone and wanted them back.

Mars leapt onto the benches and sprinted up. He shot arrows the entire way, his ever-full quiver barely able to replenish itself fast enough. With each arrowstrike, a body fell, and, unlike Pluto with his godly strength, these corpses *stayed* down. Only the river water itself would reanimate them, and Mars fleetingly knew they were better off hit by his arrow than kept in Hell's eternal suspended animation.

The two carcasses carrying Tyrone were almost to the top. Mars snagged a pair of arrows and set them together. He released faster than ever before. The double projectile separated to pierce the hand of each corpse. They lost their grip and tumbled back with Tyrone onto the benches.

Mars kept firing. Tamara was almost at the top. So was he.

"No!" Mars shouted.

Tamara screamed and struggled against the ghouls holding her arm and wings. She was seconds away from eternity in The Styx.

"Stop!" Mars commanded and fired. His unaimed arrow pierced the one holding her wings, but too late.

They tumbled over the ledge just as Mars reached it. He launched himself over the wall after her. As he grabbed her outstretched hand, he felt someone grab an ankle and pull. The jolt of the stop shook loose the grip of The Styx corpses pulling Tamara. They plunged toward the earth, tumbling head over heels, until they slipped through terra firma and presumably splashed into the river below.

In that moment, Mars registered three things: he couldn't face a future without this woman, that he'd have dived into The Styx with her to fight their way out, and that there were a whole lot of police lights gathering outside this Colosseum.

Someone shouted, "Jumper!" Of course, they couldn't see whoever was holding him nor Tamara hanging by her hand. Mars looked over his shoulder to see Tyrone struggling to keep him up. Mars looked back over toward the humans outside the arena. Yup, he realized. They'd just see him hanging upside down at the wall's edge.

He felt movement and looked back to Tamara. She opened her bent wings and flapped upward just enough to wrap one wing around Mars and shield him from the gawking eyes below. Beating her other wing, she hoisted him and herself up. With Tyrone's help, they managed to pull Mars' bulk back over the wall. All three fell gasping right in front of the top-floor museum dedicated to Eros – or *Cupid*, as he became known to Romans. *At least these people knew who to worship*, Mars thought shamelessly.

He turned his eyes back to the arena floor, where chaos continued. Animals gnawed on everything and everyone within reach. His army was attacked from all angles, but they seemed to be holding their own. Mars knew it was now or never.

He got to his knees, still struggling from exertion. "Tyrone," he said, gulping down air. "I'm going after Pluto. If I fail, run from this place. Keep Tamara safe." He turned on his knees toward her, took her hand, and kissed her palm. To her he said, "I wish I'd have met you sooner." He chuckled. "Maybe then I wouldn't have been such an arrogant braggart."

She frowned. He stroked her cheek with a finger, thinking, "I do love you," and then got to his feet and ran down the steps toward Pluto.

He had a job to do. His men were in danger. It was only when he'd nearly reached the wooden floor that he remembered her saying she could hear thoughts. *Ha,* he laughed to himself. *Way to declare yourself, oh, Master of Love. Ay.*

Mars reached Pluto just as the villain rose.

"My lord!" said a voice, weak and pleading. "How could you do this? Don't leave me!"

"Consider your contribution to my health a down payment on your debt." Pluto hissed.

The figure at his feet shifted, and Mars saw that it was Cacciari.

"I left you *some* life," Pluto continued. "You'll survive to surrender your soul another day."

"But your promise! Our deal! A thousand years of my soul for mortality with Rachel!"

The Sultan of Sin laughed mercilessly, and Cacciari lowered his head. He crawled toward the wall and cowered in its relative safety.

Mars suddenly understood their unlikely allegiance. Cacciari himself was trapped: he'd made a deal with the devil – for his men and for a girl. For love. The God of Love could not condone the means, but he could sympathize with the motivation.

Suddenly Mars saw out of the corner of his eye Cornelius charging his fantastic crocodile forward to pin Mandre at the wall. The crocodile had so many arrows sticking out of the underside of its jaw, Mars wondered how it remained standing. It looked fierce and angry, and, as if to squelch any question over its unfailing strength, the creature bucked and sent Cornelius hurtling back.

In an instant, it was just the crocodile and Mandre. Mars brought his hands together, gathered a ball of liquid water, and sent it storming toward the beast. The water splashed harmlessly on the croc's craggly face, but the reptile turned to see who'd wet it, and Mandre turned to jeer at the water's failure to harm.

"Surrender now," Mars warned him.

"Never," was the reply.

Mars looked deep into the beast's eyes and then turned away. Mandre lost his given chance to escape, and the crocodile snapped its jaws over Mandre's upper half. In a blink, Mandre's lower half separated and collapsed. The beast retreated, spitting out arrows and throwing back its head to swallow the torso treat. Mars couldn't quite reach sorrow, as this fiend had gleefully championed Pluto and fired a death arrow at his beloved. His demise was fate.

Mars next turned his attention to Pluto and found that he had been watching, too. Losing his right-hand man seemed to trigger a switch within The Dark Lord. He raised shaking arms.

What fresh hell is this? Mars asked himself.

"These are your last moments," Pluto told Mars. "With your death and the eradication of Love, I will be king of all!" He clapped his hands together, and the ground trembled violently.

Mars struggled to maintain his footing. The shaking ground knocked angels off their feet. Mars feared that the Colosseum's upper walls might fall onto the stands and his army. He feared the ground opening up, him falling in and unable to fly out. He feared for Tamara. He looked to where he'd left her and spotted her alone. Tyrone had left her!

Tamara hovered at the top of the wall. She had her hands cupped to her mouth and shouted, as if to the police below. Mars listened hard.

"Don't cook clown!"

What? Mars asked himself, *Who's cooking clowns? Why is she yelling to the police? They can't hear her – or see her.* Mars hoped they wouldn't come.

Mars knew he had to stop all this, even if he had to sacrifice himself – and he immediately recognized it as the ultimate act of love. So he dug the point of another arrow into his aching wound. Seeing the arrowhead thick with golden ichor and feeling himself grow progressively weaker, Mars steadied his breath, aimed his arrow, and fired it into Pluto. A direct hit to the heart.

Pluto fell again to his knees. Mars knew that, with one more hit, Pluto would be a goner, but Mars wasn't sure he had much blood left to give before he'd lose consciousness himself.

The opportunity never arrived. The floor's center fully opened. Mars fell to a knee just feet away from the yawning crevice and fumbled for a handful of arrows, preparing for what might appear.

What came forth, charging from the depths like ants pouring from an anthill, were hellish beings Mars had never imagined. There were skeletons of dragons that moved as if they still had flesh on their bones, octopi with fangs in place of suction cups, and tarantulas the size of cars. It appeared that Pluto had called up all of Hell for battle.

Strangely, the air around them turned suddenly cold and damp rather than hot and dry, as Mars would

have expected from the bowels of the earth. Mars returned the arrows to his quiver and began twirling his hands for a water attack.

But it never happened. A sudden flash of light, so bright it could only come from the sun, blinded the entire mass of beings – thousands of warriors, dozens of beasts, and two gods.

When the light subsided and Mars could see again, he spotted Apollo, who gave him a nod, and his father, looking furious and storming in.

Mars Senior held the chariot reins in one hand, masterly controlling his four immense black stallions. The horses frothed and snorted and looked angrier than Mars ever imagined horses could look. But it was Senior's move with his other hand that struck terror – even in his son. Senior wagged his index finger from side to side like a parent scolding a rebellious child. And Mars knew who that child was – Senior's Uncle Pluto.

"We'll have a fair fight, Pluto!" boomed Senior as he soared once around the Colosseum.

Mars looked at Pluto, who was both at death's door and furious – so he was pretty much in a normal state except for the suffering heart. But, unless Pluto was stupid, which isn't a word often used to describe The Destructor of Departed Souls, he'd be intimidated by history's best and most fearsome warrior.

"I do not yield to you, God of War, nor will I recall

my servants!"

So maybe he was stupid. Or just stubborn. Same thing sometimes.

Senior banked his chariot sharply to land, like a cop slamming his squad car's brakes to pursue kids throwing tomatoes. Senior's horses trampled several tarantulas with their furious touchdown. He released their reins with a single shake of his wrist, and the steeds immediately set to stampeding more monsters underhoof.

"Then I will destroy your army myself, Lord of Death! Son," Senior called, turning toward Mars, "carry on with the first wave. I'll dispense with this new riff-raff myself. Seems to me," – he glared at Pluto – "a god should fight at least some of his own battle." The message was clear: Senior didn't like Pluto's minions doing all his dirty work. Senior set immediately to hacking the dragons to pieces.

Pluto laughed bitterly – and weakly. "Dragons and tentacles may be no match for you, War Lord, but how would you fare against my fiercest pet?" And with that cryptic question asked, the arena floor obeyed The Sire of Suffering and spat out the largest animal yet.

Chapter 29

THE MASSIVE MUTANT

OR

THE MOMENT

Every beast and monster stepped back from the chasm when out of it stepped the giant, territorial, and crazed three-headed guardian of The Gates of Hell. For all Tamara loved that mutant mutt, Mars couldn't help but think it induced nearly as much horror as Pluto himself.

The canine's six eyes were entirely blood red in rage. Its snarls shook the air. Its meat-encrusted, plaque-coated teeth revealed the gruesome diet of a ruthless carnivore. Its muscular body, in its fierce and predatory stance, froze nearly everyone, such that they feared a mere blink of their eyes would induce his pounce. Only Mars Senior looked excited about the challenge of slaying *that* freak; he swung a table-sized ax in warning.

Pluto, still weak as he was, chuckled and smacked a hand on Cerberus' flank. He pointed at Senior with his other hand and whispered, "Sic 'em."

Cerberus growled, flattened his six ears, and shifted his weight to his haunches for the pounce.

"Dad!" Mars screeched. He reached his father's side at the same time Tamara landed in front of them, her hands and legs splayed. Mars was aghast.

"Tamara! No!"

He swung around ahead of her, facing her, and wrapped his tattered wings protectively around her, putting himself between the cur and her. Mars tensed for the strike that would mangle him and hoped Tamara could escape or his father would save her. But seconds passed and nothing happened. Mars lowered his wings just enough to look over his shoulder at the hound.

It hadn't moved. Its heads were tilted sideways in confusion. And then. Then. The eyes changed. They went from solid red to two colors: white rims with warm, golden brown centers.

The dog raised its stance. It wagged its tail. It stuck out its tongues, panted, and woofed appreciately.

Mars looked back at Tamara. She was inches away from him but not paying Mars one ounce of attention. Instead, she was smiling brightly at Cerberus. Behind her, Senior looked bitter; the girl had robbed him of a mighty duel.

Mars looked past his dad to see a completely still amphitheatre. Even the wildest creatures watched breathlessly.

A loud slap, skin on skin, broke the silence, and Mars turned back to see Cerberus cowering, tears in his sad eyes and his tail tucked between his legs. He rubbed a nose against the arena sand, trying to sooth the spot that Pluto had struck.

"Cerberus!" Pluto's deep voice boomed. "Obey! Attack!"

Cerberus whined and shuffled a few steps away. When he looked at Tamara, so did Mars.

Her beautiful smile had turned into a furious scowl. She glared at Pluto before returning a soft gaze to Cerberus. When their eyes connected, she smiled sweetly and clicked her tongue twice while patting her thighs. "Here, boy!" she called.

Cerberus' tail and heads rose simultaneous. His tongues flopped out, and the dog happily bound over to his new, *favorite* master, the far gentler and sweeter one. Mars couldn't sympathize with Cerberus more for being under her spell. Even Senior nodded, impressed.

Pluto roared and fell to one knee. Mars knew a decisive moment when he saw it. He turned and walked the distance between the two of them while drawing a final arrow across his wound, reopening it. The blood loss was getting serious. Mars struggled for a moment to focus but then set the arrow onto the bow and aimed.

It was then that he heard a trio of whimpers.

Mars didn't lower his weapon.

He heard his name and light footsteps approaching from behind. Mars felt Tamara's hand settle gently on his right bicep, which had begun to shake under the strain of the taut string. He said nothing. Held the position. Waited for her to speak.

"Mars," she repeated softly.

He didn't move a muscle. Kept his eye on Pluto. If Pluto so much as twitched, Mars would send him back to The Underworld as its new, most famous victim.

"Mars, Cerberus doesn't want him *dead.*"

Mars remained frozen. Only, this time, now he was frozen in indecision. From the moment he set the last arrow, he had questioned himself. Asked what he was doing. Maybe it was his newfound sympathy for those tread underfoot by the higher classes – and Pluto was certainly disrespected by his peers in Olympus, those literally higher up. Or maybe it was some whispering memory from Mars' youth, being taught that the gods were appointed for a reason, that their domains needed them, and that whomsoever killed a god was to take his or her place. Mars certainly didn't want to take over the job of Leader of the Lately Lifeless.

Whatever the reason for his actions, Mars knew in his heart that he could never kill anyone in cold blood. In the heat of battle, yes, he could kill, like he did to defend himself and others against Mandre's poisonous arrows. But The God of Love couldn't *mercilessly* kill and have that on his conscience. Mars remembered something his mother had taught him when he was very young, just a toddler, and people teased him for his little red arrows with red hearts on the end. She said, "He who loves, *forgives.*"

Cerberus whined again, and Tamara leaned in

close to not be heard by others. "Pluto is defeated, Mars. Everyone knows it: his pets, his army, everyone. He won't have enough love angels to complete his plan. And think of poor Cerberus," she added with a sigh. "*People* should be so loyal as *dogs*. Please, for his sake, don't hurt Pluto."

Mars didn't move. The blood on his arrow was drying. The wound at his wrist was closing again. He looked at the hand rested on his bicep and felt love for its owner. Tamara's word was now his command, just as surely as it had been for Cerberus.

And I'm no murderer, Mars said in his head. *I'm good.* And he knew most beings *were.* And for Tamara's sake, he had to be his best.

He lowered the bow with arrow still nocked – just in case Pluto got any last second ideas – and took a few steps backward, shielding Tamara with his body while forcing her to move back, too. When he reached a safer distance, he heard gasps and animal noises all around.

His took his eyes off Pluto to gauge the crowd. They weren't gasping at his mercy. Instead, they were looking up. When he did the same, he saw why.

Chapter 30

LIGHTNING

OR

GODS AND THEIR GAMES

Swooping from the sky was a small band of Heavenly Hosts led by a magnificent flyer. The entire group was backlit by the late-day sun, but Mars could see that the leader's dive was fearless, with wings pulled back and chin pointing the way. Mars squinted to see closer. It took a shift in the group's trajectory for Mars to finally see them clearly, and, when he did, he was shocked to see that the guide was … *Tyrone!*

The former flying flunkie was descending spectacularly. As he approached the ground, he spread his sleek, jet black wings for the final glide and stroke before touching down on his feet as gently as a moth.

Mars had been watching his driver so intently and with such awe that he didn't notice the others until they touched down behind him. There was Habandash, his chunky, balding self, now wearing a yellow jogging suit. Pip fluttered around his head like a nervous, living halo that Habandash looked quite ready to swat. And the final guest was – *oh, my!*

Mars couldn't believe he hadn't notice him at first, and it's quite a thing to say that you hadn't notice The

King of the Gods, especially when so few had seen him before, save the Olympic Council. But there Jupiter was, and Mars recognized him immediately, as did everyone else – but for differing reasons.

The King of the Gods could be objectively described as tall and compactly muscled. That much was visible even through his long, white robes, which twinkled like stars. His high cheekbones looked sculpted. His nose was long, straight, and regal. His lips thin. His white skin unblemished. But it was the eyes that struck the strongest emotion: shockingly blue and guarded by eyebrows that anyone could tell would be a gateway to happiness or a slamming weight of disapproval. In his right hand, he carried a long scepter. An eagle, his legendary companion, settled to his left.

Mars saw in Jupiter his father's angularity and general build. Tamara saw an intimidating and likely impossible-to-please authoritarian. Cornelius saw ancient wisdom swimming in the lord's ocean-wave eyes. And still others saw different attributes and flotsam, according to his or her fears or expectations. They all, however, recognized mighty power when they saw it, and so Mars and those whom he led knelt. Senior nodded. Pluto was still on one knee, so a few of his supporters bowed or lowered themselves as their anatomy allowed. Mars spotted fanged octopi struggle to squoosh themselves flat; it was the best they could do and ridiculous at the same time. He took it

as proof, though, that Pluto's forces believed him conquered.

"This battle is heard all the way to Olympus!" boomed Jupiter.

Senior raised his bloody ax and whooped a triumphant war cry. No one else moved.

Jupiter ignored his bloodthirsty son, not that he wasn't proud of him, to address Mars Junior. "Rise, son of Mars … my grandson."

Mars rose, feeling pretty important being pointed out like that, but he was also a little hacked that he'd never seen his grandpop before. Next he worried that he might be blamed for the whole thing. Police sirens blared. Mars remained silent.

"The great god Apollo circumnavigates Earth daily and sees all. Every day he reports on its well-being. Of late, he has reported ill tidings.

Pip fluttered to Jupiter's side (not unlike Mandre had done after Pluto's display of power) and added in an excited, high pitch, "That's right, Mars! Why, Jupiter, his high majesty, says-"

Jupiter tapped him with the scepter, and Pip's whole body froze mid-air. The little kibitzer fell to the ground like a discarded porcelain figurine.

Mars pressed his lips together to stop himself from laughing. Pip, that little fart, had his surprised and frozen face planted in the arena sand and his super-pointy wings jetting up like sails. *Serves him right,* thought Mars, *for*

interrupting a god – and for siding with Mandre in the first place!

It would be a long time before Mars would let *that* go.

Jupiter continued speaking as if nothing had happened. "Apollo's warnings were confirmed when this faithful and daring angel" – he swept his hand toward Tyrone – "flew into my castle to report a great battle of Good versus Evil – and how Good needed help."

"My son was defending Good, Father, showing nerves of steel in battle," answered Senior. "Junior had the fight won. I merely stepped in to keep it fair."

Mars had never heard such extravagant praise heaped upon him. Naturally, the acts his father praised had to do with fighting and would appeal to him the most. Mars wondered if he shouldn't have started picking fights years ago.

"If the fight is unfair," Jupiter reflected aloud, "and if it involves Good versus Evil, surely my brother Pluto is involved."

Jupiter's vision turned toward his wayward brother, the most despised of the three brothers Jupiter, Neptune, and Pluto. Pluto was the one charged – or punished, depending on your point of view – with presiding over The Underworld. Jupiter and Neptune were luckier and got the other two realms of the universe: Sky and Waters, respectively. It was always a tenuous truce.

Pluto sucked in air, which rattled his overworked lungs. He was severely wounded.

Jupiter stepped forward and waved a hand. Pluto's furrowed brow relaxed, its owner given temporary comfort. Then Jupiter rubbed his own brow and asked in a tone of muted exasperation, "The plot this time, Pluto?"

"An army of your exiled angels firing arrows of hate," Pluto explained simply through labored breath. "Hate consumes your subjects. I take over the world." He grabbed his chest to settle his newly searing lungs.

Jupiter pursed his royal lips in clear annoyance. Then he sighed loudly like a parent tired of repeating reprimands.

"Pluto, Pluto, Pluto. A novel try. Clever even. But you're lucky that this fierce warrior" – he pointed to Mars (and no one spoke out about Mars' diaper now) – "this champion in combat, didn't finish you off. Better luck next time."

Mars wasn't sure if the luck was wished upon Pluto or himself.

Pluto's eyes squeezed into slits.

"Out of courtesy," announced Jupiter, "which you continue to deny *me*, I'll add, we'll discuss this privately at another time."

Pluto opened his mouth to protest, but Jupiter pointed his scepter toward his disagreeable kin and commanded, "Go home."

A streak of lightning poised overhead. Pluto threw his hands over his head in defense but couldn't stop the blazing stream from swooping down on him and taking him away. The resultant crash of thunder resounded in the arena, emphasizing Pluto's speedy and unwilling departure.

Mars turned his face toward Tamara to see her equally shocked face. He leaned in and whispered, "Yeah, I really hoped Pluto would get more punishment than just being sent home – where he'll eventually regain his strength."

Tamara nodded the smallest nod ever.

Jupiter waved his scepter again, and a fresh swarm of lightning bolts hovered over the Colosseum. They plummeted toward the Earth and struck Pluto's beasts, which disappeared in a chorus of screams and thunderclaps, much more dramatically than their master, followed by the putrid Fog of The Underworld.

When the echo of those horrible sounds died, Mars heard not just the police sirens but a couple hundred car alarms blaring. He hoped he could sneak out of there without the mortal police arresting him.

Mars looked around and noticed that the entire angel army remained, even those who'd remained loyal to Pluto.

Jupiter shook his white robes and a few remaining sparks of electricity fled from him back to their wild blue yonder. Yee haw.

"And now back to you," Jupiter spoke, setting his gaze on the former Lord of Lovers and seeming oblivious to all the beings straining in bows and curtsies.

Mars gulped. *Jupiter will punish me,* he thought, *for nearly killing his brother – or for failing to.*

Every eye was on Mars. The Flab Master wished he had on a shirt and tie – or at least a shirt, even if it had to be the pink one he'd torn for a tourniquet. He sucked in his gut.

"Sir, I..." Mars wanted to say he was sorry for all the trouble he'd caused with The Decree and for being bad enough at his job that he had to be forcibly removed and for this little "disturbance" here in Rome, but there was so much to say, he didn't know where to start. He settled on the idea that he would pledge allegiance to Jupiter and beg to be allowed back into heaven, where both he and his followers could do the most Good at whichever entry-level job Jupiter had available.

But before Mars could speak, Jupiter did. "You have shown much growth, young Mars. You were ... *straying* before you lost your title. Since then, you've become a leader, a defender for Good, compassionate toward your enemies."

Mars was surprised at the praise but not so shocked that he'd accept it all.

"Sir, I had a great deal of help from a courageous few. As for compassion, it was this lovely angel who showed

it most." He reached down for Tamara's arm and helped her straighten from her prolonged, back-breaking curtsy. She stood but kept her eyes down. "Tamara showed love and compassion to this animal," – Mars gestured toward Cerberus, who was also bowing, his heads on his forepaws – "which provided a decisive turning point in battle. She showed compassion even to Pluto." Mars waved toward the spot where Pluto had been. What met his eyes, however, was Cacciari lying just beyond, curled in the sand near the wall to which he'd crawled earlier. He was barely breathing. Mars turned back to look at Jupiter.

"I considered jetting him with the beasts back to The Underworld, but he would not have survived the lightning ride. Perhaps he will survive here on Earth. Perhaps not." Jupiter said it in such a way that suggested Cacciari's survival depended upon someone giving the god a reason to save him.

Mars looked into the stands for Jarel. He spotted him sitting next to the dark-haired angel, who was bowed yet still managing to put pressure on the wound. Jarel nodded, and Mars had to acknowledge again: He who loves, forgives. *And really,* Mars reasoned, *Cacciari's been done wrong by me, Jupiter, AND Pluto. I don't want MY name showing up on that list twice.*

So he turned again to address the king. "Sir, this fallen angel led the army which delivered Pluto's arrows."

Some of The Fallen in the crowd rustled. A few

hissed in anger.

"But," Mars added with a dramatic pause, "I believe The Fallen were coerced through the threat of starvation, mutilation, or worse. The possibility of violence against them does not excuse their every act, but as enlightened gods," – he nodded to Jupiter and Senior – "and loving angels," – he gestured toward the stands – "we cannot watch this fellow angel die as the result of Pluto's latest double-cross. Pluto drained nearly all this angel's life to save his own, and that after promising him the only thing he ever wanted."

All eyes focused on Mars. It was clear that no one but Mars and Jarel knew Cacciari's secret. Mars would normally have felt wrong revealing it, but Cacciari's life depended on Mars' indiscretion.

"Cacciari exchanged his services for the promise of mortality."

Chapter 31

WASTING A PERFECTLY GOOD SNOWBALL

OR

LATE FOR THE PARTY

What?!" came a chorus of calls from the crowd.

"Mortality?!" asked others.

"Why'd da Boss want some'n as useless as dat?" asked the most acute voice of all.

The crowd didn't understand. A quick glance at Tamara told Mars that she remembered the conversation about love being a weakness. He hoped she wouldn't think he was exploiting that weakness now.

Jupiter's eagle fluffed its feathers and screeched. The crowd silenced at once. Jupiter nodded at Mars to continue.

"Cacciari wished for mortality so that he could be seen by and live alongside the love of his life, who is herself mortal. Pluto might eventually have granted Cacciari his mortality, but he would probably have taken it away that same day in his lust for souls and cruelty. With all due respect to *your* greatness, sir, your brother isn't known for square deals."

Senior cleared his throat in warning.

Tamara slowly raised her hand to her neck.

"But you," added Mars quickly, hoping to maintain

the goodwill on the floor, "*are* known for keeping your word and even that of others."

The hint made without any demand spoken, Jupiter nodded and walked across the sand to Cacciari. He then tapped his scepter on the shoulder of the unconscious angel.

Cacciari stirred. His cheeks became ruddy and his breathing deeper, more regular. After a few moments, he raised himself onto his hands.

"I grant you mortality, Vilnius Cacciari, you who ran afoul but was once a representative of Olympus. You may seek your life, love, and fortune on this earth, and the agents of Heaven and Hell shall grant you peace. However, you, like all humanity, will be judged according to how you lived. If you win the lady's heart and live in such a way that would displease Pluto, I shall see to it that your sunset comes together; neither will live a moment without the other. But see to it that you live well, new mortal, for my brother would welcome you into The Underworld with malice and revenge in his heart."

Cacciari stared disbelievingly at Jupiter. A minute ago, he was pleading for his life with Pluto. Now he lay before the king of the gods, who was granting his fondest wish.

Mars was suddenly struck – as violently as a storm – by the force of Cacciari's love for Rachel. *Wow!* Mars thought, forced by it for a moment to close his eyes. *That's potent stuff! Was that love, even as powerful as it is, somehow*

obscured by his contact with Pluto? Mars reopened his eyes, comprehending that, as stunning as Cacciari's love was, it still didn't match what he felt for Tamara. Then again, no one can feel love for another more than the one in love with that other.

Feeling suddenly upbeat from all those love vibes and seeing as how Jupiter seemed so keen on his work, Mars decided to make one more request of The Sky King. "Sir," said Mars. "You've shown such generosity to one who led forces against you. How much generosity might you show to the remaining Fallen?"

Senior took a discreet step sideways toward Mars, then whispered, "Time to shut up now, Junior." The rank and file held its collective breath.

Jupiter lifted his arm high. Then he twirled it a bit and squeezed it into a fist. When he opened his fist, everyone could see that he held a snowball.

"Was it not odd, Mars, that the air turned so suddenly cold and damp this far inland and at the heat of battle?"

Mars remembered thinking so himself. He understood Jupiter's hint mere seconds before The God King announced it. "Neptune, The God of the Sea, your great uncle, sent the salty sea air to help you fight and to better hear events unfold. Apollo watched from above. Both say you offered Pluto's soldiers a choice unlike they've had in many years."

Jupiter dropped the snowball onto the sand, where it flattened on impact. Only a bit of the top remained white, and Mars somehow saw it as a metaphor for what was coming.

Jupiter turned to The Fallen and raised his scepter. "Those who fought for Mars' cause, those who battled Pluto and his forces, will be welcome anew in Olympus. They will be reinstated as worthy Celestial Defenders and Angels in fine standing."

Cheers broke out. Exultant angels took to wing, flying loop-de-loops in delight. Cornelius was so moved, he covered his eyes with a hand and turned away; he wasn't the only one sobbing in rapture.

"And the rest?" asked Mars, seeing their heartbroken faces. He knew it was awful to interrupt the festive mood of the Reinstated, but he couldn't help being deeply concerned for the future of The Still Fallen, not only for their eternity but for the short term. Anyone who knew history knew that leaving an enemy beaten, bitter, and utterly hopeless was a sure pathway to renewed war. Mars had, after all, seen the bitter harvest of World War I ripen into World War II.

"No enemy may be allowed to live within the very walls of your kingdom, Son," said Senior, hoping to put his progeny in his place before Jupiter did so more forcefully.

"But they must have hope of redemption, sir," Mars answered as much to his father as to his grandfather. "If

they right their wrongs and prove their worth and eventual allegiance over time, sir, can't they be given another chance?" Mars thought for a second how glad he was to have helped Olympus and given The Fallen a second chance. "We all make mistakes, sir. I know I did," he added with a nod to Jupiter, "by not serving you with enough vigor and enthusiasm. It was a mistake I won't make again, I assure you. I'd like it if these angels could right themselves. They, like all of us, have potential for greatness."

Jupiter stood as still as if he were made of marble. Habandash shuffled over to him with his brisk, little steps. In his yellow track suit, he looked like an animated banana. Jupiter bent to hear his whispered advice, then straightened.

"Mr. Habandash remembers all his angels and chooses to vouch for their skills and previous mind-sets. He advises a probation period." Jupiter lifted his scepter once more – Mars guessed it made everything more official – and proclaimed, "The Fallen who failed Olympus in this matter have six months to prove new intent. Spread kindness and charity, love and compassion, tenderness and graciousness, until your hearts soften once more and you remember what it is to be an Angel of Love. The Heavens will be watching."

Those Fallen who intended to make the most of this opportunity straightened for the challenge. Others bowed their heads in shame. Some looked thoughtful. A few, offended. *Who knows what* they'll *do?* Mars wondered.

"And now back to you," repeated Jupiter for the second time, addressing Mars before the bleating sheep could interrupt him again. Mars remained silent and still. About time.

"Olympus finds itself in need of a God of Love. Your powers to rouse deep and lasting love have been desperately missed on Earth and above. Should you wish to return as its newly and rightfully redressed champion, Olympus would be most happy to welcome you. The throne and title are yours once more, *Cupid*."

Mars stammered at being called Cupid again.

As his mouth gaped, a fast-moving and pearly cloud cleared the wall of the Colosseum just beyond him. Everyone peeled their eyes off the stuttering deity to investigate this new distraction, and the mysterious cloud quickly settled at center stage.

The mob tensed in fear until the cloud opened like a flower, revealing a large clam shell balanced at the hinge. The front half of the shell opened down to a hiss of pink smoke, momentarily obscuring its contents, while the back shell remained upright to create an iridescent background. And then the smoke cleared to reveal Mars' mother, naked as a wood nymph but with her hair and hands, as usual, covering the strategic parts. She was smiling like a mermaid from the seas' depths.

The cloud below her feet, likely as enamored of her as everything and everyone else, formed itself into steps.

As Venus popped out of her shell and descended onto them, she grabbed bits of cloud to cover herself. Barely. She ended up with the world's smallest, gauziest bikini. The eager stared hard, hoping for gauze failure.

Whispers and sighs floated all around as if carried on a breeze. "That's Venus!" and "Mars' mother!" and "She's breathtaking." Even some of the female angels looked smitten.

Venus raised her arms to take in the bronzing Mediterranean sun before sighing contentedly. "Ah, Jupiter. 'Tis a fine day for a reinstatement. Heaven doth know the toil of mine young Mars to returneth the Fallen to Heaven's fold."

Mars flattened his arms at his side and waved his hands at the thighs, trying desperately and *silently* to get her to stop talking before Jupiter rescinded his offer.

"But let us not pretendeth that erst decision rests solely with thee."

Jupiter straighted, unswayed.

Senior smoothed a hand over his body armor to squeegee off the serpent scales and bloody bits. Then he sidled over to Venus' side, smiled wolfishly, and said, "Hi, Pookie. Where's my vacant brother Vulcan, who's foolish enough to let you out of his sight?"

Venus raised an eyebrow, turned up the corners of her mouth in the smallest of smiles, and offered a one-shouldered shrug. She didn't back away, rather took

a teasing step closer. Then she spoke for all to hear.

"Jupiter doth place the crown upon gods' heads, howbeit the angels wield the throne."

"Truly?" asked Cornelius, who was probably the only one in the whole stadium besides Jupiter who could understand *both* her language and her meaning.

"Yay," she answered at the same time Tommy asked, "Wha' da pretty lady say?" He was staring intently at her curves and only vaguely addressing Corny.

Venus turned to face her son, and the entire multitude shifted with her. Of course they would.

"Mom." Mars didn't know what else to say. There was so much to say. And nothing to say.

"Hale be thou, Son," she cooed in return.

Senior was already kissing her bare shoulder. Jupiter fixed his gaze on something well past her.

"Mom, in the nicest possible way I'm going to tell you, don't 'hale' me. Where have you been? I've been battling here and could have used more help."

"Mine son, anon a butterfly doth spread its wings, all the world doth stare."

"What?!" demanded Mars.

"E'er I doth show mineself afore battle, no battle doth ensue."

Mars again didn't know how to react. *So, if she'd have shown up, there wouldn't have been a battle?* He didn't know whether to be madder that it was true or that she

didn't see advantage in it.

Cornelius came to understand how Mars got his ego.

"To harness the hearts of angels and gods, thou hadst to fight agin the odds."

"Mom, please no poetry. And, Dad, you've got an audience. Please."

Senior had Venus' hand in his own and had kissed her from fingertip to clavicle – in front of thousands of equally enamored spectators.

Mars shook his head in fatigue. "Okay, Mom, you didn't show up here earlier because you wanted events to unfold. Okay. But what do you mean, 'the angels wield the throne?'"

"Advice you entreat'd, and advice I didst give. Listen to thy mother and longer thou shouldst live."

Clearly she's not going to give up on the poetry, Mars thought, resigned. *Fine. It's her shtick.*

"Dost thou not recall thy words, that I 'pull rank' against thy king?"

Jupiter's head snapped back to rain fury with those angry brows, but the God of Thunder allowed a glance at Venus and ... *decided* in his benevolence to let her speak.

"I saidst to thee, 'Tis the word of Jupiter and the labours of the angels that bestoweth the noble honor of Cupid'. The angels, Fallen and Honored alike, must wisheth for thee to lead. By *their* approval and also that

of Great Jupiter, thou reclaimest thy throne."

Jupiter cleared his throat, and the skies shook from it. Everyone seemed to break free of their enchantment, save Senior, who asked Venus if it wasn't time they got a room.

Police sirens still blared. Mars heard the booted footsteps of earthly soldiers approaching one of the stadium's far entrances.

"Enough of this fooling around!" stated Jupiter emphatically. "The gods can disagree about just where we get our powers, but that won't happen here. Mars, do you accept your crown or do you abdicate?"

Chapter 32

MOM RUBS IT IN

OR

SWAT TEAM TACTICS

Mars put his hand to his chest and stated loudly, "I do proudly accept the honor and privilege of Lead Lover." Mars looked at Tamara. She beamed in pride.

"Then return to Heaven, Cupid! Take your crew and accepted angels. The ceremony in Paradise Plaza begins in one hour's time!" With that, Jupiter tapped Pip with his scepter, and the little zit sputtered and kicked himself out of the sand. Jupiter stepped over to Cerberus, too, and also tapped him, saying, "Fly." Then Jupiter opened his own magnificent, huge, white and gold-tipped wings and launched into the sky. Habandash followed with his red-and-blue striped wings. Pip flapped his pointy, little, see-through, buggy wings furiously to catch up but couldn't cover nearly as much distance per stroke as the rest.

The reinstated angels didn't hesitate a second. They took off after Jupiter en masse as if fearing that Heaven's Gate would slam shut behind him. Mars noticed Jarel shoo away his male nurse; Tommy flew over and scooped Jarel out of the stands to join him at center arena.

The Still Fallen *also* took to the air. The one holding Mars' tray flew to him, but, before he could say anything,

Mars raised a hand for silence. He reached for the tray handle and called up another 50-some squares and passed them around. It took eight before he felt himself grow strong enough for the flight home. Then he handed the tray back with a nod and advised the angel, "The Fallen will need nourishment. Please be generous."

The angel nodded – it was almost a bow – and took flight. So many angels were taking off at once that the Colosseum looked like a wasps' nest under attack. Frenzied. And their differently colored wings, with so many varied shapes and sizes, made the mass of beings look like fluttering stained glass. In mere seconds, the only beings remaining in the ancient ruin were Mars, the now *un*-Fallen Four, Cerberus, Venus, Senior, his horses, and Cacciari.

"Come on, Darlin'," murmured Senior in Venus' ear. "We got an hour to ourselves. Let's catch up, uh, *alone* somewhere."

Venus' cell phone rang. She dug into her cleavage and pulled it out.

Now where was she hiding that? Mars asked himself because she didn't seem to have it when she popped out of that clam shell naked as a jay bird.

Senior snatched the phone from Venus' hand and crushed it in his bare fist.

"I'll get you another phone and anything else you might like. Just don't ask me to endure listening to a

conversation between you and any other male."

Venus didn't answer him or even flinch, almost as if she'd planned it. Ignoring the display of temper, Venus turned to her son again and asked, "Didst thou not see? Mine words rang true. 'A mere scratch of thine arrow changeth worlds. Love e'er conquereth, and with it thou hast banish'd Pluto and reclaim'd thine honorable name."

"Thanks, Mom."

She smiled sweetly at him and also at Tamara before disappearing in a shrinking ping of light.

Senior growled in frustration and whistled for his horses to reassemble. "We gotta find that gal within an hour's time!" he warned them, and, with a shake of the reins, he and his well-built horses stampeded after her. The wolves on the war chariot sniffed the air for her while prowling the baseboard. Trampled chunks of tarantula legs and burnt octopus arms fell from the sky, slipping off the horses' hooves as the steeds lifted off. Plop. Plop. Plop. Chunks dropped onto the sand and withered away.

Mars – *oops!* – rather, the newly-reinstated, again-reigning, he's-back-and-feeling-great-about-it, super-stoked *CUPID* – looked around.

We did it! he thought to himself. *I can't believe it.* He would have loved to bask in his triumph, but there were three maimed beings who needed rides – Cacciari, Jarel, and himself.

Cornelius stepped forward and said, "If you're

contemplating transportation, sir, you needn't concern yourself. I'll transport Mr. Cacciari to his lady friend's abode. We'll stop for flowers for a good first impression. As for Jarel, you could fly him up, sir, as a way of returning the favor."

Cupid looked at him screwy and thought, *This angel may be smart, but he's also lost his mind – or at least his memory.* "My wings," he replied, "can't offer enough lift to spin a helicopter seed, Cornelius, and I don't like being reminded of it."

Corny laughed. Whether it was about the helicopter seeds or something else, Cupid didn't know, but he didn't find much to laugh about when it came to his wings.

"Mr. Cupid, sir," Cornelius said with reverence once more. "Do you still not understand your mother's words?"

Cupid stilled and awaited further veiled insults about his stupidity.

"Venus said it takes the word of Jupiter *and* the labours of the angels to bestow the noble honor of Cupid. You have both, so you are Cupid once more."

"Yeah, I got that," Cupid answered curtly.

"Well, sir, Cupid is a *flying* god. *Will* your feathers to regrow."

Tamara chuckled, getting the concept faster than Cupid. Cerberus panted joyfully at her side.

Cupid understood, but he didn't move. He didn't dare hope his wings could regrow at his command, an act

that would prove he really *was*, truly, officially, Cupid once more. Still, Corny hadn't steered him wrong yet, so Cupid extended his mangled wings, closed his eyes, and thought hard about needing his wings for fresh Love Hunts.

Gasps told him that something was happening. When he snapped open his eyes to look at his wings, he saw that the feathers had not only regrown, they were now longer, stronger, and their pure whiteness gently tapered to a deep cerulean blue. *A gift from Jupiter,* he was sure. *A reminder of all that'd passed.*

Cupid bent his knees and leapt into the sky. He zigged and zagged and looped and swooped and rose and dived and generally acted like a newborn cherub who'd just discovered mastery over gravity. When The Loopy Lover got his exuberance a bit out of his system, he dropped next to Tamara, who laughed at his open delight.

"Come to think of it," added Cornelius, his fingers on his chin in deep reverie, "you may never have lost your title of Cupid at all. Jupiter certainly withdrew his consent, but if his love angels – in their hearts – still employed their skills for *you* rather than *Mandre*, then you remained Love's Reigning Monarch all along."

"Wwwwhut?" Cupid asked stiffly.

"And it sounds like your faithful mother tried to tell you."

Cupid closed his eyes and let out a slow, hissing, furious breath. He often couldn't understand his mother's

way of speaking. *And her riddles and poetry! Ay!*

And is that *why she froze me on stage when Habandash was taking away my whammy stick? To maintain my dignity until I reclaimed my throne*?

And does that mean, he asked himself, reaching the logical conclusion, *that my problem was with* Jupiter *rather than* Pluto*?!*

"Wait, wait, wait!" interjected Jarel, who Cupid noticed hadn't coughed once since The Fog was sucked into Oblivion. "If'n he wasn't banished and was still a god an' all dat, why, yuh, could he be seen by da humans?"

"There!" Cupid shouted, thrusting a pointing hand at Jarel and hoping the question would stump Cornelius because, if Cornelius was right, they'd all gone through a whole lot of trouble for nothing.

Cornelius looked upward, pondered a second, and came up with a perfectly reasonable and infuriating answer. "Cupid could probably be seen because he *believed* himself to be exiled. Our beliefs have strong influence on our lives. Beliefs often become our reality. Cupid limited himself as only *we* can do to *ourselves.* As a god, he has greater powers than us, so when he truly believed himself exiled and a resident of Earth, he unwittingly made himself visible to Earth's other residents as well."

Cupid closed his eyes again and thought back to his bender and the thin redhead with the blue eyes who called him 'sugar' and asked him not to cry. He gasped,

and his eyes shot opened. He remembered. It was when he'd been at his lowest and had wished for someone to notice his suffering. *She did!*

"Sir, you appear to agree with my theory," observed Cornelius.

Cupid hurriedly asked, "Sooooooo, when Habandash took my mojo–"

"Never happened, sir," Corny attested. "Well, Mr. Habandash *attempted* to consign your powers onto Madre, and might have transferred some of it, assuming the love angels desired Mandre as their leader. Then Mr. Habandash would have succeeded. But we don't know if Mandre had the love angels' full support, and we probably never will."

Cupid raised an eyebrow at him.

"Leaders often don't know how much support they enjoy – or lack – until the mutiny begins."

Cupid's head was starting to spin. Too much info. Too much intrigue. Too much doubt.

"Well, if we, yuh, gonna make dat party, we bes' get goin', prodded Jarel, and, for once, this was a *good* party.

Cupid bent down to scoop him up and turned to address everyone. "We meet back at Paradise Plaza. I'd like all of you to join me at center stage. Tamara?"

"Yes, Cupid," she answered, and Cupid liked the way she said it, not as his title but as his name. She smiled.

"I'd like you at my side if you're willing." *Forever*

more. Then he froze, remembering that she could hear some of his thoughts.

She didn't react in any way to the added thought. She simply said, "I'll be there."

So Cupid, Jarel, Tamara, and Cerberus took off toward Olympus. Cupid took it as a good sign that Tommy willingly left Tamara in his care; T-Bone instead joined Cornelius in escorting Cacciari to his new life.

As they cleared the stadium walls, Cupid heard a stampede of boots and a chorus of deep-voiced commands issued from below. He turned to see large teams of armed men dressed in black swarm every entryway. The SWAT forces shouted for anyone there to freeze. Two rather reckless officers leapt onto the wooden floor, which dematerialized as the immortals requiring its presence left. The human pair fell into the hypogeum below unharmed, but they'd question their sanity later. Cupid lingered a moment to watch their brethren search for the danger that initially brought them there. A few scratched their head at its absence.

Cupid laughed and kept ascending. He was happy as a clam – at least a clam that his mother hadn't *booted* for the use of its shell.

He just hadn't planned on another rendezvous with The Fates.

Chapter 33

THREE LOVES
OR
BOOGERS AND BABES

Dusk was setting in. Orange and purple light swam in The Mist. The scene might have been exquisite had the Fates not been floating at Heaven's Gate, guarding the entrance. They wore their usual muted red robes; Morta added an ill-tempered scowl to her look.

She's mad over the parade of Fallen love angels returning here – angels whose threads she can't cut. Cupid was happy to be her spoilsport. Still, knowing better than to dismiss The Fates again, Cupid stopped and bowed respectfully, still carrying the increasingly heavy Tyrone. Tamara and Cerberus followed suit. He hoped to get past the ancient matrons without any trouble, but no encounter with The Fates was ever that easy.

Decima, the Apportioner, measurer of lifespans and the only one to show Cupid pity, spoke first. She recited three lines lightly before Miss Scowl-and-Scissors took over in her bitter, cryptic, pointing-her-witchy-fingers sort of way:

"One challenge met,
One yet undone

To prove your worth as Mars' son."

"To face the fear
Of what you seek,
Destroy yourself! And become weak!"

Cupid stuck out his lower jaw in barely hidden frustration. *Why don't they* ever *say what they mean?!* He was a wee bit tired of people not expressing themselves clearly. But The Fates held a look of suffering no fools – nor their questions – and lowered themselves into The Mist. *So I guess they don't feel chatty,* Cupid decided. *Fine. I wouldn't understand them anyway.*

With just a sliver of the sun left above the horizon, Cupid considered waiting for Apollo. He wanted to thank him for watching over them and alerting Jupiter and Neptune, but he knew he was expected and running out of time, and he felt really awkward carrying his friend like a newborn baby, so he readjusted Tyrone and took off for Paradise Plaza. He was delighted to see the entire Olympic populace gathered there once more. They seemed festive under the brightening stars.

In his old life, Cupid would have sauntered jovially through them to garner as many kisses and tight lady-hugs as possible. Now he *flew* over them with Tamara at his side and Cerberus behind. The dog garnered all sorts of amazed and fearful looks. At one time, Cupid would have

been jealous over having to share the limelight. No longer. Instead, he concentrated his energy on The Fallen and spotted them way off to the left, gathered together and being given a wide berth by the rest of Heaven's Hosts. This troubled Cupid, but he continued to the stage, conjured a chair, and set Tyrone on it. Tamara settled between them. Tommy and Cornelius raced in and quickly dropped onto the stage. Cerberus landed behind it, followed his tail a few times, and then dropped onto his belly.

"My fellow Olympians," began Habandash, who'd popped out of nowhere to commence the ceremony. All eyes turned his way. All ears listened intently – except Cupid's. He knew all that had happened and knew the end result, too. What he didn't know yet was where he stood with Tamara, what tomorrow would bring. Here he was getting his castle again and all he could think about was how cold and empty it would be without her. He breathed deeply for courage and caught a faint hint of her strawberry scent.

"The Fallen were once our brothers and sisters – and are so again," Habbi continued.

Cupid looked *at* them – and *around* them – and saw little fraternal love. Heaven's beautiful angels openly stared. Some held their nose. In retaliation, a Fallen Angel picked his own nose with a leaden arrow and flicked a booger their way.

Cupid knew the arrow's evil power was nullified

here. He also knew The Fallen would need a lot of help in their transition back into Olympus; Earth had rubbed off on all of them, and Earth wasn't terribly respected here.

Just as Cupid considered what action he might take to smooth things over, his well-intentioned but scene-stealing mother materialized on stage – fully dressed for a change but still eliciting sighs of longing. Cupid noticed battle gore smudged on her belt. *So apparently Senior caught her after all.* Venus didn't acknowledge her son at first. Instead she engaged the assembly.

"Mine love and gratitude to ye Fallen Angels, still marked with battle brine. Thine honor is restored. Ye require naught more than a bath to cleanse thineselves, as do all creatures great and small. I honor thee."

At Venus' enchanting words, many of the angels who'd shown wariness or open hostility toward The Fallen relaxed their tension. How couldn't they? *Everyone* wanted to please Venus. Always. Cupid was satisfied that The Fallen would be welcome back.

Habandash spoke again. Something about Mars reinstated as Cupid. Applause. His bow and arrow presented. Bedazzled again with rubies and diamonds and mega-mojo. His sparkling, clean white suit popped onto him. Ladies' squeals. A lacy underthing was thrown his way.

But Cupid just couldn't get jazzed about fresh propositions. The two most important women in his life

were standing beside him, and they didn't even know each other. It was time for *everyone* to know them.

Habandash yielded the stage, presumably for Cupid's acceptance speech. Cupid stepped forward.

"My, things have certainly changed, haven't they?"

The crowd laughed nervously, perhaps reminded how some of them had *welcomed* the change.

"Over the course of the next weeks, you'll undoubtedly hear about the events leading to my return as Cupid. Whatever you hear about the fearlessness and tenacity of the angels standing beside me will likely understate their courage. These angels" – he stepped to the side to show The Fallen Four – "are Olympic Heroes."

During the ensuing applause, Cupid whispered to Habbi, "And I've got specific jobs I want for all of them."

Habandash sighed, accepting that even a humble Cupid would want his way.

Cupid stepped forward again to the front of the stage, suddenly so nervous he worried he'd break out in a rash. He was about to do something he'd never done before but knew needed to be done *really* publicly to be believed. The crowd silenced, and Cupid spoke. "Yes, things have changed, and I've changed, too. What's changed most for me *personally*," he said, pausing for effect, "is that I love."

There was no visible reaction from the crowd. Nothing. Not a cry nor a murmur nor a laugh. Cerberus' heads lolled as he fell asleep. *Curious,* Cupid thought. *I'll*

try again.

"I may have been Cupid, The God of Love, once before, but I didn't fully *understand* love until I met this angel." He stepped aside once more to sweep his arm toward her. "Tamara Rumavina has shown me what true love is." He plucked a circle of gold and a huge, green jewel from his newly bedazzled bow and pressed them together. Then he bent to one knee, took her hand, and offered her the ring he'd just made.

"Tamara," he said loudly enough for all to hear. "You are the love of my life, and I beg you to stay with me for a day or the rest of our lives. You are my heart, ma coeur. Be mine, mon angel. I love you."

Finally the crowd stirred, but Cupid couldn't spare them a glance; Tamara was looking down at him, her face unreadable.

"That's three times you've said you love me," she whispered.

Cupid tried to remember three whole, separate declarations; he thought he was doing pretty well with just this one.

She ticked them off with a finger. "One, when the gladiators arrived and you begged me to go, you just said it. Just like that. *I love you.*" The corners of her mouth curled ever so slightly. "Two, just now. And, three?" She left the question hanging.

"Three?"

"Right after you pulled me from The Styx Dead. You *thought* it. I heard."

Cupid suspected she'd heard that last one. He wasn't ashamed. He just wanted to hear it back.

"You called love a weakness," she reminded him, leaving him aching for her response. His knees weren't feeling too great kneeling, either.

"Love is a weakness only when you're too fearful to abandon yourself to its great power. Love is the strongest thing there is. It's stronger than Death – it defeated Pluto. It's stronger than War – Venus unseats Senior every time he looks at her. Love is everyone's deepest emotional need. We all want someone to hold, even if it leads to madness." Cupid ran his hand down his face searching for more eloquent words. He instead went with the simple ones. "I love you, Tamara. I hope you can love me back."

Tamara's face blossomed in a wide, sweet smile. "Now I believe you and can honestly say I love you, too, Cupid."

Cupid struggled to his feet and hauled her in for a kiss that was rather more passionate than public decorum allowed, but he *was* The God of Love and Passion, and he *was* seriously in love and passion.

He swore he felt those fireworks again, and he knew for sure that something happened because, when they broke apart, heart bubbles were dancing all around them. Cupid watched the little, purple things float and

bob for just a moment before he spotted Tommy's distorted expression through one. The bubble popped.

Tommy shook his head and sighed but said, "If you're what she wants…"

"He is," Tamara reassured him.

"And she is to me," promised Cupid.

Tommy nodded his acceptance.

"Mother?" Cupid called for an introduction. He was almost surprised she'd stayed – even during a time such as this. His mom never stayed anywhere long. It was part of her mystique: her absence, her rarity. Yet there she was – for him, he was sure. "Mom, this is Tamara. The One."

Venus air-kissed Tamara on both sides of her head and then hugged her son, whispering in his ear, "Of course thou art in love. 'Tis what we do."

"No, seriously, Mom," he whispered back. "I'm crazy about her."

Venus pulled away, nodded at Tamara, and then disappeared in a blink. The Goddess of Love. Mysterious. Go figure.

Habandash loudly cleared his throat, and everyone on stage was brought back to reality. "I'm very happy for you. Both. The God of Love should be in love, don't you think?" He offered a knowing grin. Cupid didn't know what to say.

Night had pressed fully down upon them. Habandash dismissed the crowd. Some came forward to

congratulate Cupid, and he was gracious and shook hands and smiled and chitchatted a bit, but he just wanted to take Tamara home to his place for the first time forever.

"Listen to what I'm thinking, Tamara," he quietly suggested to her during a break in the action. He paused, then added, "When we get to my place, I'll show you."

Tamara merely pursed her lips in answer, never one to wear her heart on her sleeve. In truth, she'd lost the ability to hear thoughts right after the battle. Hers was a short-lived power, fleeting, probably because she'd used it to warn everyone about Pluto's fast approach, which led to the battle in which he was ultimately defeated, and a power that comes from his domain isn't likely to linger long to assist in his defeat. Tyrone had used *his* power to fetch Jupiter, Tamara was sure. She'd guessed his power was dauntless fortitude. It would counteract his life-long cowardice when it came to flying – only he wouldn't notice the loss of Styx power if she never mentioned it to him. She, however, noticed her loss of power right away. *But no need to tell Cupid that,* she thought to herself. *A girl does need to keep a few secrets.*

"That's pretty good, Tyrone, but how about the old man at the bus shelter?" asked Cupid. "He's seriously lonely. I can smell it from here. The shelter's got him blocked on

three sides, though. What do you think?"

"It'd be easiest to wait until he moves out of there," answered his driver.

"Oh, let me give it a try!" challenged Tamara. Cupid chuckled. It was their first Love Hunt together, and of course she wanted to best them.

Cerberus sat on his haunches at her side, taking up a whole lawn. He'd become the first and largest animal to ever reside in Cupid Castle.

Tyrone, Cupid, and Tamara had returned to The Safe House neighborhood, as Cupid had promised himself he would. They *flew* there, as he'd also promised himself he'd do more, although sometimes they rode on Cerberus' back.

Tyrone preferred flying to riding the dog. He was now a far superior flyer than most angels but would still occasionally drive them places in the limo when foul weather required it. Tyrone was thrilled that he no longer had to stop to refuel; the limo's tank stayed forever full, fueled by The Fury of War, a gift from Mars Senior for faithfulness in battle.

And Tamara was now the only angelette to sit inside the limo. It took Jarel a few weeks, as Cupid's new butler, to graciously send away the other angelettes, the ones who would show up to be a part of Cupid's daily entourage. Jarel wanted to make friends with them himself, but Cupid made it clear: Cupid's Castle was Tamara's,

too – and hers alone. That was about the only command Cupid could force on Jarel; otherwise, it was the butler who ordered around the master. Kept him in check. Reminded him to *"stay humble an' work hard 'cuz I ain't gonna go back ta, yuh, livin' on da streets, and, if'n you mess up, Cupid, and, yuh, lose me ma place in Heaven, I'sa huntchoo down da res' of mah days, so, yuh, don' you go an' fergit it."*

Tamara faced the empty lot where The Safe House had stood before being torn down for pest infestation. She set her arrow and fired. The arrow banked off a fire hydrant to lance the calvous old gent in the gut.

"The way to a man's heart is through his stomach," she said smartly, but Cupid got the feeling she was just covering up for a low shot.

Still, it struck true, and the old man would live out the remainder of his days with the sassy number-caller at the bingo hall; she was always batting her eyes at him, even if the batting did nearly make her false eyelashes fall off. The two were made for each other.

Seeing Tamara back doing what she loved, being a love angel, made Cupid endlessly happy, and he dipped her for a kiss. Tyrone turned away as usual. Cupid vowed he'd find Tyrone his ideal mate, too, right after he got through this first Hit List.

Cupid pulled it out. The first thing he noticed, at the very top, was the name Rachel Kiskis. Cacciari's love. Cupid knew she already loved him in return, but,

as her mysterious suitor was formerly invisible to her for reasons she surely didn't understand, Rachel needed a little push to trust her heart. Cupid was happy to provide it. He pointed to the name for the others, and they smiled broadly upon seeing it.

The second thing Cupid noticed about The List was its beautiful new penmanship. The List was never prettier, never so well-planned, organized, and cross-referenced. Cornelius was much better suited for the job than Habandash, who was glad to be relieved of the duty so that he could concentrate on other things.

Tommy was Habandash's other new assistant, in charge of monitoring The Still Fallen and providing them *lots* of convenient opportunities to commit acts of kindness that'd earn them Heaven's Goodwill. Tommy was perfect for that job, too; The Fallen were never so *gratefully* taken care of.

It seemed all of Heaven had returned to the right path.

Chapter 34

BURDENS OF SUPREMACY

OR

THE PUPPET MASTER

And so you see, Mere Mortal, how my brilliant scheme rectified the far-reaching troubles of the day, how I regained a Love God worth talking about while getting Pluto back under control. One could blame Apollo or The Fates, if one were so inclined; they warned me of The Fallen's work with Pluto, but naturally it falls upon me, the King of the Gods, to set all to rights.

Before you judge me as cruel or capricious, Oh Wingless One, understand that he who is in charge of everything everywhere must sometimes soil his hands.

Pluto's plots command attention, but I will not destroy my own brother. And so it seemed to me to be Cupid's turn to pull his weight around here. I ordered the removal of that Happy Hustler from my kingdom, from his comfortable palace and his pampered lifestyle. In so doing, he was made to appreciate what he'd lost and so work hard to regain it – and then honor it when it was his once more. I forced the boy to grow up, Human, just as your kind must.

My Agent Amor now fully understands why love is not to be trifled with or risked on reckless shots. Love may often seem arbitrary, Mortal, but it is the strongest force. All

of humanity seeks it. They devote songs to it, dress themselves to attract it, dream of it. Venus was right: Love conquers worlds.

And I am not without kindness. Cupid would not have willingly bowed to love had he seen his or Tamara's names on the Hit List. He did not realize how strong love could be nor how ready he was to settle down. But I *was ready for him to settle down, and when the Lord of the Skies demands it, so it will be. It was Fate.*

Just don't tell Cupid. Then again, you'll never get that chance. Mortals don't see Love's arrow flying their way. No one knows when love will strike. No one except Cornelius, Cupid, and me. Only we know when your turn will come.

Heh, heh.

Who's Who in Order of Appearance

Cupid - Roman god of love, affection, and desire. Son of Venus and Mars.

Tyrone - Love angel, chauffeur, and personal assistant to Cupid.

Pip - Jupiter's cherubic messenger.

Habandash - Jupiter's personal assistant charged with overseeing Olympic and Earthly affairs.

Mandre - Love angel best known for challenging Cupid to his throne.

Jarel Wright - Fallen love angel, one of The Fabulous Fallen Four, and gopher to Cacciari.

Vilnius Cacciari - Also known as The Boss. Witness to The Deadly Dictator Decree and Earthly leader of The Fallen Angels. Secret admirer of Ms. Kiskis.

Venus - Roman goddess of love, beauty, and fertility. Older than Jupiter, the king of the gods. Married to Vulcan, the god of the fire, volcanoes, and metalworking, yet is a frequent paramour of Vulcan's brother, Mars, with whom she bore Cupid.

Tamara Rumavina - Fallen love angel, one of The Fabulous Fallen Four, and Cupid's lead spy.

Cornelius Brewster - Fallen love angel and The Fabulous Fallen Four's lead thinker.

Tommy Redding - Fallen love angel, one of The Fabulous Fallen Four, and Tamara's strongest protector.

Mars (Senior) - Roman god of war and father of Cupid (Mars Junior).

The Fates - Goddesses of destiny, measurers of lifespans, and guardians of Heaven's Gate. Older and likely stronger than the reigning monarchs. Frequently speak in riddles. Nona spins the thread of life, Decima measures its lifespan, and Morta ends life in the thread's cutting.

Charon - Pluto's ferryman and carrier of souls across The River Styx to The Underworld.

Cerberus - Three-headed hellhound and guardian of the entrance to The Underworld.

Pluto - Roman god of The Underworld and ruler of the dead. Brother of Jupiter and Neptune.

Rachel Kiskis - Mortal dancer intrigued by a secret admirer.

Apollo - Roman god of the sun and truth. Son and watchman of Jupiter.

Neptune - Roman god of water, the seas, and earthquakes. Brother of Jupiter and Pluto.

Jupiter - Roman god of sky and thunder. King of the gods. Brother of Neptune and Pluto.

When did you start writing?
I've been writing my entire adult life as a reporter and anchor for TV, radio, and newspapers. I've had thousands of reports published or broadcast, but I didn't start writing fiction until about ten years ago. Creative writing was a way for me to let my mind run free. Looking back, I realize that I was always a voracious reader who held great respect for authors, those mysterious strangers from another place and time who could somehow touch my heart, soul, and funny bone.

What made you want to write a story based on Roman mythology?
I have always loved, loved, loved mythology. Mythological stories are the ancient tales of how things came to pass and the eminent beings involved in their creation. Many of these supremely powerful beings have deep character flaws that trigger far-reaching, long-lasting trouble. That's like ambrosia to me: multi-layered characters with their own agendas, each causing trouble in his or her own way.

So who's your favorite Roman god?
That's such an unfair question. They're all interesting in their own way, with their own powers and quirks, behaving in the way befitting their calling. But fine. If you're going to pin me down, I might say Venus. As the beauty of every woman, Venus may arouse desperate longing in the gods and men around her, but she isn't cruel. In fact, the men who have seen her may desire her, but they're also simply left glad to have glimpsed her in their lifetime. Her presence enough is a gift, and much more so if she chooses to reciprocate their attentions. Unlike her, Cupid's behavior does involve cruelty at first, through his arrogance, which is why we don't like him so

very much at the start of the story. But Venus is more than her outward beauty, which is just a mask. Venus is smart. She had the answer for Cupid way before anyone else. And she was fun to write. Her "thees" and "thous" so offend her son.

Which scene was your favorite to write?

The duel. I was terrified to write it at first, honestly, because I knew so much was riding on that scene. Cupid didn't just have to lose to Mandre. He had to lose spectacularly, be humiliated by his performance, end unquestionably defeated, yet be entertaining. Whew! That's a lot! Thinking it through a bit, however, I realized the shellacking had to happen in Paris, Cupid's Paris, the city of love. And once I'd settled on that, I realized how much fun it would be to write about the sites there. And Pip made it aggravatingly awesome. Another favorite scene was Mars' entrance. He is an overpowering presence.

The first scene starts and ends with emphasis that mortals couldn't see the gods. What's the significance?

Making immortals invisible not only conceals their comings and goings, but it later becomes a metaphor for how Cupid perceives greatness. To his mind, his shame is more glaring than his former glory. He can be seen. His eventual mastery of his visibility reminds him — and the reader — that fame, honor, wealth, all those trappings of success, may have made him feel worthy of the spotlight, but it was only when he was willing to sacrifice himself did he learn that the spotlight wasn't the goal.

Did you plan your story's every turn or do you let your characters drive the chariot?

Ha! I was much better at outlining as a child than I am now. I would love to say that I sweat over every twist of plot well in advance and thus all I'm left with is to write from one bullet point to the next,

but that would be a big, fat lie. When I sit to write, I'm familiar with the general direction of the plot. I have an understanding of what character types I need to get me there, but once the characters have popped themselves into existence, they generally take over and send me in directions that I hadn't planned. They do that because they become sentient beings with their own free will. I can change their circumstances and frequently do so to create the outcome I wish, but, if they're to remain true to their characters, they will react in a manner predictable to their inner selves. Interestingly, that can create some reactions that I wouldn't have planned — *had* I planned — which I don't.

Do you see yourself in any of the characters or the situations they find themselves in?

Oh, sure. Every author draws from his or her experience to write scenes and characters that feel genuine. Is any one character really me? No. All of the characters have a bit of me and a bit of people I know and a bit of people that I don't know and quite a bit of pure imaginings. The inspiration for my characters and their situations come from years of intermittent sitting on my chair typing away and wondering, "What if this?" and "Who might think that?"

What happens next in the story?

Poor Cupid. Although he faced big challenges in *God Awful Loser*, he still has a lot to learn and much more trouble to get into. A rather epic challenge looms ahead of him, and so I'm happily in the throes of the second installment of Cupid's adventures, called *God Awful Thief.* I'm having fun with new characters and molding Cupid into a god worth talking about.

Acknowledgments

This book would not have been possible without my husband, Jeff Miracola, who is a creative force in the universe, who deeply inspires me, and who unfailingly believes in me. He brings his own and others' characters to life — and brings life to my life, for that matter. I thank him so much for showing me that whimsy is worthy.

I thank my children, Corina, Antonia, and Armando, who root for me tirelessly. It means so much.

It's not possible to give enough thanks to Keith Pitsch, Valerie Johnson, and Christine Esser, who perfected this story and form the best writers' group imaginable.

Many thanks go to the Wisconsin chapter of the Society of Children's Book Writers and Illustrators for guiding wanna-be's into are's.

And finally I thank the Roman gods themselves for cluttering my brain the past few years with thoughts of how they might handle modern situations. The resultant bursts of laughter at the most inappropriate times have others convinced I'm mad. Thanks, gods. Thanks a lot.